Deadlands

Horrors of the Weird West

The Weird West™

Horrors of the Weird West

Compiled and Edited By: Christopher L. McGlothlin, M.Ed. & Shane Lacy Hensley
Written By: Tim Beach (Animal Men, Headless Horseman, Mexican Dragon, Tarnished Phantasy, Texas Skeeter, Walkin' Fossil), Scott Beattie (Canker), Cyrille Bordeaux (Hand), Tom Cashman (Dread Wolf), Lawrence Champion (Chupakabara), Jim Crocker (Braincrawler, Duster, Weeping Widow), Christopher Dolunt (Humbug, Poison Woman, Stone Man, Will o' the Wisp), Mark Drotos (Scarecrow), Jacques DuRand (Pox Walker), Lee Garvin (Black Regiment, Bloodwire, Bogie Man), Shannon Glasgow (Two-Faces), John Goff (everything else; too many to list!), Francis Hamer (River Leviathan), Tom Harrison (Horned Serpent, Skinshifter), Shane Hensley (Terrormentals), H.B. Huntley (Bone Fiend), Philip Kelley (Tunnel Critter), Erik Kjerland (Flesh Jacket), Tony Lee (Kangee), Steve Long (Barranca Prowler, Appalachian Giants, Appalachian Witches), Jim Lowder (Mourning Mist), Christopher McGlothlin (Succubus), Mike McLaren (Saddle Burr), James McPherson (Chinook), Chris Nelson (Pit Wasp), Guillaume Nonain (Dark Beast), Michael Platt (Union Pride Ghost Train), Dave Radzik (Dread Wolf, Night Raven), John Richard (Braincrawler, Wave Shadow), Patrick Wallen (Sin Eater) and Joseph Wolf (Nagual, Scarecrow).
Layout By: Shane Lacy Hensley
Interior Illustrations: *Cheyenne Wright, Richard Pollard, Kevin Sharpe, & Steve Bryant*
Cover: Pete Venters
Deadlands Logo by: Ron Spencer
Weird West Logo and interior graphics by: *Charles Ryan*
Special Thanks to: John Goff for his invaluable assistance and advice, the New Gamers Order (nGo 4-Life!), Shane Hensley, Hal Mangold, Lee Bansen, John Hopler, the Deadlands Listserver Posse, Mick Foley, and most of all, Jesus Christ and my Beloved Wife, Tanith McGlothlin, whose love and understanding know no bounds.

Author's Dedication: To the incomparable Christopher Lee, in sincere appreciation of his many great performances in the best horror films yet made.
Editor's Dedication: To Ryan Dancey, for last minute advice and for crusading for the OGL in the first place.

Table o' Contents

Pinnacle Entertainment Group, Inc.
P.O. Box 10908
Blacksburg, VA 24062

Visit Pinnacle's **Weird Website**

WWW.PEGINC.COM

PINNACLE ENTERTAINMENT GROUP, INC.

Things That Go Bump in the Night

In *Deadlands: The Weird West D20 Rulebook* we gave you a handful of nasties to start you off in your adventures. This book is chock full of all manner of creepy crawlies for you Marshal types to throw at your posse. Most of these monsters are unique to the Weird West, but there are also a number variations on common critters that are sure to keep your heroes on their toes.

Well, let's not waste any more time jawin' about what's in here, let's dig in!

Special Abilities

You can find the details on common special abilities, like Fearless and Undead in the *Deadlands: The Weird West D20 Rulebook*. Most other Special Abilities are described under the individual abomination profiles.

However, before we get down to the brass tacks of the monsters, we've got a new special ability—Swarm—that needs a little explaining

Swarm

Certain animals (and abominations) have the special ability to attack en masse. They rely on numbers to make up for what they lack in strength and size. Creatures with the special ability Swarm deal damage based on the number of the critters that make up the horde.

Make one attack roll for each person being attacked by the swarm, and the targets may not take any active defense against the swarm. Standard tactics are of no use against a mass of tiny opponents!

The description tells the number of creatures required to Swarm an opponent and the

amount of damage done by the critters on a successful attack. Less than that amount does no Swarm damage to a victim. For every multiple of the required number, add another die of damage. Also, the more attackers, the more likely they are to actually hit their sorry victim, so add a +1 to the swarm's To-Hit roll for every multiple of the swarm number after the first. For example, nibblers do 1d4 damage for every 10 in the horde, so 50 nibblers get a +4 to their To-Hit roll and do 5d4 damage.

Remember, the numbers are animals per unlucky cowpoke, not total animals.

As you've probably guessed, this makes critter hordes nothing to sneeze at! Although a hero can probably knock out one or two of the swarm on every action, he's usually got to take out 10 or more to drop the swarm a notch. Your posse is probably going to show rats and the like a little more respect from now on, Marshal!

Animal Men

Medium-Size Humanoid (Animal Men)
Hit Dice: 3d8 (13 hp)
Initiative: +0
Speed: 30 ft.
AC: 10
Attacks: By subtype
Damage: By subtype
Face/Reach: 5 ft. by 5 ft./5 ft.
Special Qualities: Subtypes
Saves: Fort +1, Ref +3, Will +1
Abilities: Str 9, Dex 11, Con 11, Int 9, Wis 11, Cha 10
Skills: By subtype
Feats: By subtype
Climate/Terrain: Any Temperate or Warm
Challenge Rating: 1
Alignment: Always lawful neutral
Advancement: By character class

All animal men are basically human in shape (bipedal, manipulative appendages, etc.), but each type retains obvious characteristics from their previous, purely animal, forms. They are clad in simple (often ragged) clothes, and usually carry weapons or tools. Thus far, only bears, dogs, pigs, pumas, rabbits, and raccoons have been transformed into animal men, but additional species–including birds and reptiles—are under consideration.

Their genesis occurred about eight years ago, when a young English woman, one Lady Pamela Danvers, visited the Weird West with her husband. She was an amateur scientist, and when the happy couple visited the Great Maze, she became very interested in ghost rock and its properties. Her experimentation with it quickly became obsessive, until her husband, rather disgusted with the directions of her experiments, returned to Britain.

She didn't even notice his absence.

Being enamored of Charles Darwin's theories on the development of the species, Lady Pamela was anxious to learn if various animals could be evolved toward human stature and intelligence. She started by making solutions of ghost rock and various chemicals, force-feeding it to animals. When the results of this proved unremarkable, she hired a couple of thugs to find some human "volunteers."

Eventually the manitous' whispers led Lady Pamela to construct a sort of ray projector, which she dubbed the Evolver. With this device, her solutions and no little surgery skill, she began combining humans and animals, creating a batch of anthropomorphic servants.

At present, Lady Pamela claims an entire island in the Maze, and she occupies a small house and large laboratory built near its center. The island is also populated by nearly 100 of her unholy creations, only some of which turned out as she expected. Those judged as successes are treated as favored pets and live near her in handmade huts, while the failures are regarded as wild animals and fodder for future experimentation. They live in caves or in rough-hewn hovels scattered about the island.

Lady Pamela has been careful to inculcate a healthy dose of awe in all her creations, and they see her as a capricious, godlike figure to be worshiped and feared. She in turn uses them to collect needed supplies from nearby islands. This includes any unfortunate trespassers they happen to encounter, who are put to use in her experiments.

Combat

Though capable of employing guns and other weapons, animal men (especially the larger types like bear and puma) are prone to savaging their opponents with their claws and teeth.

Subtypes (Ex): *Bear:* +3 Str, +2 Con, +1 Wis, +2 Cha; Intimidate +5, Wilderness Lore +5; Power Attack; 2 claw attacks 2d6+1 damage

Dog: +2 Con, +2 Int, +1 Wis; Spot +5, Wilderness Lore +5; Track; Bite 1d6 damage

Pig: +2 Con, +2 Int, +1 Wis, +1 Cha; Ridicule +4, Wilderness Lore +5; Track; Bite 1d4 damage

Puma: +1 Dex, +1 Wis, +2 Cha; Hide +5, Move Silently +5; Brave; 2 Claws 1d6 damage

Rabbit: +1 Dex, +1 Int, +1 Wis; Hide +5, Sense Motive +5; Run

Raccoon: +4 Dex, +1 Int; Disable Device +4, Open Lock +4, Pick Pocket +4, Ambidexterity

Automatons

Medium-Size Construct
Hit Dice: 3d10 (16 hp)
Initiative: -1 (Dex)
Speed: 15 ft.
AC: 19 (-1 Dex, +10 natural)
Attacks: Gatling gun +1 ranged; or pincer claw +5 melee
Damage: Gatling gun 2d8+1, pincer claw 1d4+3
Face/Reach: 5 ft. by 5 ft./5 ft.
Special Attacks: Self-destruct
Special Qualities: Fearless, spell immunity
Saves: Fort +1, Ref +0, Will +0
Abilities: Str 16, Dex 8, Con –, Int 6, Wis 7, Cha 7
Skills: None
Feats: None
Climate/Terrain: Any land
Challenge Rating: 3
Alignment: Always lawful neutral
Advancement: 4-9 HD (Medium-Size)

Automatons are roughly humanoid in shape, consisting of a large torso (housing the ghost-rock boiler), piston-driven limbs and a brassy, cylindrical head. One arm ends in a pincer-like claw while the other terminates in a Gatling gun attached at the elbow.

Automatons are one of the most fearsome constructs to lumber from the laboratories of Dr. Darius Hellstromme. These enormous, iron-plated, mechanical men have seen much action battling gangs of other rail barons or guarding Hellstromme's facilities. They are usually encountered in small groups of three to five, although lone automatons have been encountered (on some sinister mission for their amoral master, no doubt).

Currently, most automatons are crafted individually, giving each of the metal monsters a unique appearance. All conform to roughly the same design specifications, but there is sometimes variation in their operation capabilities. Gear or piston-driven limbs are

attached to a well-armored torso section, housing ghost-rock boiler. Atop the body, a metallic cylinder rests, housing the real secret of the automatons' design.

Many theories have been offered for the automatons' intelligence, ranging from complex clockwork to midgets in metal suits. The truth is far more sinister. Using a concoction stolen from Baron LaCroix, Hellstromme has found a way to reanimate and implant undead brains into his steam-powered monstrosities. The undead mind provides the automaton with the ability to react to changing conditions that would completely befuddle a simple clockwork mechanism.

For obvious reasons, Hellstromme has no desire to see the inner workings of his creations exposed. To that end, each automaton is wired with a powerful explosive that destroys the brain and most of the device's internal parts should the automaton be disabled in combat. As an added bonus, the explosion is powerful enough to injure —or even kill—any opponents nearby.

Combat

These metal monsters never surrender, but for them this is rarely even an issue. Automatons have a grasping claw in one hand and a full-sized Gatling gun in the other. (If fully loaded, the automaton has 60 rounds for the Gatling.) Like land ironclads, automatons mow down their opponents with Gatling fire and if necessary, crush them with their powerful pincer claws.

Self-destruct (Ex): If an automaton is reduced to 0 hit points, the thing immediately explodes with the force of a single stick of dynamite (4d10 damage, Burst Radius 10). The only way to stop the detonation is to render the zombie brain "unconscious." This is nearly impossible, but certain magical or mad science effects might short-circuit the brain.

Spell immunity (Ex): Only spells, hexes, miracles and the like that affect inanimate objects can target the automaton's frame. Arcana like Soul Blast which only works on animate objects, has no effect.

Barranca Prowler

Medium-Size Beast
Hit Dice: 3d10+1 (19 hp)
Initiative: +1 (Dex)
Speed: 35 ft., 20 ft. climb
AC: 16 (+1 Dex, +5 natural)
Attacks: 2 claws +3 melee, bite -2 melee
Damage: Claw 1d6+1, bite 1d6
Face/Reach: 5 ft. by 5 ft./5 ft.
Saves: Fort +4, Ref +4, Will +0
Abilities: Str 12, Dex 12, Con 12, Int 7, Wis 7, Cha 7
Skills: Balance +6, Climb +9, Hide +6*, Intimidate +5, Listen +5, Move Silently +6, Spot +5, Tumble +6, Wilderness Lore +5
Feats: None

Climate/Terrain: Warm Mountains and Underground
Challenge Rating: 1
Alignment: Always neutral
Advancement: 4-6 HD (Medium-Size), 7-9 HD (Large)

A barranca prowler looks like an emaciated sabertooth tiger made out of scabrous red rock. It closely resembles the walls of the canyons it inhabits.

This abomination, found in the Copper Canyon area (and elsewhere throughout northern Mexico), is known as the barranca prowler (or, to some peasants, *el gato del diablo*—the Devil's cat). It lairs in caves and abandoned mines, and feeds off of whatever it can catch. It seems to find the taste of human flesh particularly succulent. Barranca prowlers have adapted well to their environment. They are extremely stealthy, using their natural grace and appearance to blend into the rocks. If necessary, they can climb like a mountain goat; sometimes it almost seems as if they can run right up a bare rock face!

Combat

The creature's favorite tactic is to ambush a group of people, snatch one of them, and carry him up a cliff-side to a position where the victim's friends can't rescue him. Then it enjoys a leisurely meal.

Skills: Barranca prowlers receive a +4 bonus to all Balance, Listen, Move Silently, Spot, Tumble, and Wilderness Lore skill checks. They enjoy a similar bonus to Hide skill checks in their native environment.

The Black Regiment

Medium-Size Undead
Hit Dice: 2d12 (13 hp)
Initiative: +0
Speed: 30 ft.
AC: 10
Attacks: Enfield Musket +1 ranged; or rifle bayonet +2 melee
Damage: Enfield Musket 2d10, bayonet 1d6+1
Face/Reach: 5 ft. by 5 ft./5 ft.
Special Attacks: Fear
Special Qualities: Undead, fearless, officers, coup
Saves: Fort +0, Ref +0, Will +3
Abilities: Str 12, Dex 11, Con –, Int 7, Wis 9, Cha 6
Skills: Climb +5, Hide +5, Listen +4, Move Silently +5, Spot +5
Feats: Exotic Weapon Proficiency (rifle bayonet)
Climate/Terrain: Any land
Challenge Rating: 2
Alignment: Always lawful evil
Advancement: As gunslinger character class

The Black Regiment consists of reanimated soldiers slain on both sides of the War Between the States, whose uniforms have turned black by their own shed blood. The men of the Regiment still carry most of the accoutrements they carried in life, and in most respects, they look like walkin' dead (detailed in the *Deadlands: The Weird West D20 Rulebook*). The only members of the unit who seem to have any individuality are the Lt. Colonel, who wears an elaborate uniform befitting his rank., and the Bugler, whose horn sounds a bloodcurdling charge.

Whenever a critical battle between the Gray and the Blue occurs (such as the Second Battle of Bowling Green in 1876), there 's a possibility of the Black Regiment appearing. It arrives through a gate from the Hunting Grounds, siding with the underdog and bringing sufficient numbers to even the odds. This is all done at the Reckoners' behest, with the aim of producing greater bloodshed and terrifying as many soldiers as possible.

Although the individual members can be killed (again) easily enough, the Regiment itself cannot be destroyed. At the end of a battle, the Black Regiment returns to the Hunting Grounds, replacing any lost members from amongst soldiers recently killed in action. The troopers then "rest" until called upon again by their unholy masters.

Combat

The men of the Black Regiment prefer to fight viciously rather than effectively, favoring charges with their rusty bayonets. They attack their chosen enemy mercilessly, but do not act in any way to protect their "allies." In fact, if an ally gets in the way or questions their actions, they quite happily turn their fury on them.

Fear (Su): The bugler can sound his horn once during each battle for every twenty men on the opposing side. Each time it is sounded, everyone on the opposing side must make a Will saving throw against DC 17.

Undead (Su): Immune to mind-influencing effects, poison, sleep, paralysis, stunning, and disease. Not subject to critical hits, subdual damage, ability damage, energy drain, or death from massive damage.

Officers (Ex): In addition to the statistics listed above, the Lieutenant Colonel has a base 6 HD and the Intimidate +6 skill, as well as the Dead Eye and Exotic Weapons Proficiency (cavalry saber) Feats.

Coup: A Harrowed who kills the bugler can thereafter use his horrific horn.

Blob

Medium-Size Ooze
Hit Dice: 2d10+11 (33 hp)
Initiative: +0
Speed: 5 ft., 20 ft. swim
AC: 10
Attacks: Pseudopod +1 melee
Damage: Pseudopod 1d3 (s) and acid
Face/Reach: 5 ft. by 5 ft./5 ft.
Special Attacks: Acid, improved grab, swallow whole
Special Qualities: Damage reduction 25/fire, blindsight, fire weakness
Saves: Fort +1, Ref +0, Will -2
Abilities: Str 9, Dex 10 Con 12, Int –, Wis 6, Cha 6
Skills: None
Feats: None
Climate/Terrain: Aquatic
Challenge Rating: 6
Alignment: Always neutral
Advancement: 3-4 HD (Large), 5-6 HD (Huge)

The blob consists of a virtually shapeless mass of acidic protoplasm, although it often assumes a large pancake shape, about 20' across and 2' thick. It is virtually invisible in water, somewhat resembling a mass of fish eggs floating just below the water's surface. Occasionally, the gory remains of its victims may be seen within its form.

Blobs live in both fresh and saltwater. Because of their relatively fragile bodies, blobs favor marshes, ponds, lagoons, and other calm waters.

They are virtually invisible, making them very difficult to detect beneath the surface of the water. Their acidic bodies quickly eat through just about anything, up to and including thick boat timbers.

Combat

Hunting for a blob consists of floating around its pool hoping to drift into a meal. Only rarely do these creatures actively seek out prey. However, if prey contacts them—"prey" being anything organic, even a wooden boat hull—the monster contracts quickly around it.

Acid (Ex): The blob's only attack is to smack at an opponent with an acid-covered pseudopod. If the blob hits, the acid continues to burn at the beginning of subsequent rounds unless washed off with alcohol. It reduces its damage by a die type each round until no further damage is caused.

Improved grab (Ex): Blobs can grab any target equal in Size or smaller.

Swallow whole (Ex): A blob can envelop its prey, and the victim then takes 6d6 damage at the beginning of every round thereafter. The only way to escape is to kill the blob.

Fire weakness (Ex): Fire does 2d6 damage to a blob. The creature recoils from flame, but isn't really smart enough to run away; instead it tries to find a way around the fire.

Bloodwire

Small Beast
Hit Dice: 1d10-2 (3 hp)
Initiative: +1 (Dex)
Speed: 35 ft., 15 ft. climb
AC: 12 (+1 size, +1 Dex)
Attacks: Thorns +0 melee
Damage: Thorns 1d3-1 plus blood drain
Face/Reach: 5 ft. by 5 ft./5 ft.
Special Attacks: Blood drain, improved grab
Special Qualities: Blindsight
Saves: Fort +0, Ref +3, Will -2
Abilities: Str 7, Dex 12, Con 5, Int 5, Wis 6, Cha 5
Skills: Balance +4, Climb +7, Hide +4, Jump +4, Move Silently +4, Tumble +4, Wilderness Lore +4
Feats: None
Climate/Terrain: Warm or Temperate Plains
Challenge Rating: 1
Alignment: Always neutral
Advancement: 2-3 HD (Small)

Related to tumblebleeds (detailed in the *Deadlands: The Weird West D20 Rulebook*), this thorny, vine-like abomination is indistinguishable from barbed wire until it feeds. Afterwards, the engorged bloodwire looks like fat, red milkweed.

Bloodwires have done much to escalate the already violent hostilities between many sheepherders and cattle ranchers in the Weird West. To the casual observer, the puncture wounds left by the bloodwire's vicious thorns resembles small-caliber gunshot wounds (except, of course, that bullets cannot be found in the wounds). However, such details are usually overlooked in the cattlemen's rush to blame sheepherders, and a murderous exchange of retributions and reprisals between the two is the inevitable result.

Combat

Bloodwire wraps itself around fences with barbed-wire on them, and waits for prey to come close. Then, the bloodwire lashes out, wrapping itself around a victim and draining blood through its thorny tendrils. Once fed, the bloodwire slowly slithers along the fence to find a fresh spot where it can lurk safely.

Improved grab (Ex): Bloodwires are able to grab Medium-Size targets or smaller.

Blood drain (Ex): Once a bloodwire has its thorns in a victim, it holds on and drains blood at the rate of 1d6 hit points per round. Bloodwire saliva contains an anti-clotting agent, so hit points lost in this way return at the rate of 1 per day. A Heal skill DC (10) made to examine wounds made by a bloodwire reveals that the wounds are not, in fact, from any gun.

Skills: Bloodwires receive a +2 bonus on all Balance, Jump, Move Silently, Tumble and Wilderness Lore skill rolls.

Bogie Man

Medium-Size Monstrous Humanoid
Hit Dice: 5d8 (22 hp)
Initiative: +4 (Dex)
Speed: 30 ft.
AC: 14 (+4 Dex)
Attacks: 2 claws +6 melee
Damage: Claw 1d4+1
Face/Reach: 5 ft. by 5 ft./5 ft.
Special Attacks: Fear, hush
Special Qualities: Vulnerability, coup
Saves: Fort +1, Ref +8, Will +5
Abilities: Str 12, Dex 19, Con 11, Int 9, Wis 13, Cha 18
Skills: Climb +5, Disable Device +5, Hide +6, Intimidate +6, Listen +5, Move Silently +6, Open Lock +5, Pick Pocket +5, Spot +5, Use Rope +5
Feats: Dodge, Mobility
Climate/Terrain: Any land
Challenge Rating: 2
Alignment: Always chaotic evil
Advancement: 6-15 HD (Medium-Size)

The bogie man is a gangly and spindly abomination, made out of dried twigs and sticks, with a dry tumbleweed for a head. No one has ever heard him speak, and it is unknown whether he can.

This creature—whose name parents invoke to frighten unruly children into good behavior—and its fearsome reputation has been made very real by the Reckoners. Once spawned in the Hunting Grounds, the bogie man uses his stealth abilities to sneak from place to place in an effort to produce as much terror as inhumanly possible. It aims specifically at frightening children, and its special powers prevent them from reporting his cruel and deadly mischiefs.

Combat

The bogie man is careful not to let adults see him, and he goes out of his way to make sure children witness his shenanigans. He likes to pull nasty pranks that hurt or kill adults. If he can frame some poor innocent child for the deed, all the better. He loves nothing better than to see a hapless child punished for something that he has done.

Fear (Su): This creature is the stuff of nightmares. Anyone unfortunate enough to catch sight of this abomination must make a Will saving throw against DC 19. For children (under 16), the DC is 20.

Hush (Su): Any child (under 16) who sees the bogie man and fails a Will saving throw against DC 19 is unable to tell any adult about the critter. Children can tell indirectly, by telling another child or writing it down (if this skill is known to them), but the young 'un is not likely to be believed, especially since they'll be compelled to deny it if confronted on the matter by a skeptical adult.

Vulnerability (Su): A child with a melee weapon can kill the bogie man with one blow if he succeeds at a Will saving throw against DC 17 and can manage to hit the horrifying beast in combat.

Coup: A Harrowed killing a bogie man gains a permanent +4 bonus to Move Silently skill rolls.

Bone Fiend

Small Undead
Hit Dice: 6d12 (39 hp)
Initiative: +2 (Dex)
Speed: 35 ft.
AC: 14 (+2 size, +2 Dex)
Attacks: Up to 10 claws +5 melee, bite +3 melee
Damage: Claw 1d4+2, bite 1d3+1
Face/Reach: 2 1/2 ft. by 2 1/2 ft./0 ft.
Special Attacks: Bone explosion
Special Qualities: Fearless, blindsight, undead, variable size, fast healing 25
Saves: Fort +2, Ref +4, Will +8
Abilities: Str 14, Dex 15, Con –, Int 11, Wis 16, Cha 15
Skills: Climb +7, Hide +10, Intimidation +9, Jump +9, Listen +9, Move Silently +9, Spot +9, Swim +7
Feats: Multiattack, Power Attack
Climate/Terrain: Any land
Challenge Rating: 7
Alignment: Always chaotic evil
Advancement: 7-8 HD (Small), 9-10 HD (Medium-Size), 11-12 HD (Large)

The "heart" (so to speak) of a bone fiend is a human skull, colored as black as pitch. Beyond that, the creature varies in size and appearance due to its ability to add additional bones to its mass, giving itself up to six legs and as many as four arms, provided enough bones are nearby. The bone fiend is the skeletal kin of the 'glom.

Bone fiends are created when a manitou finds a human skull with at least a little bit of brain matter left and sets up shop. It starts in whatever bits of gray matter are still left, then the creature spreads its essence throughout the skull itself. (This is what turns the skull black.) It then sets about assembling a bony body for itself and waits for its first hapless victims to arrive.

Due to the nature of their powers, bone fiends are usually found in places where sudden great losses of life have occurred, such as at Fort Negley. The entire Union garrison there was killed in an explosion during the Battle of Nashville back in 1864. Today, its corpse-filled ruins house a large bone fiend which preys upon unwary travelers to the Tennessee capital.

Combat

The lair of any bone fiend is always knee-deep in spare parts, which enables it to use its ability to quickly reshape its form and repair any damage inflicted on it to the fullest. It goes to great lengths to protect its black skull, always focusing its senses through another bony noggin which serves as its "head". The black skull is then hidden elsewhere (like inside its chest or—if it doesn't plan on going anywhere—in a suitable location somewhere nearby).

Bone explosion (Su): If the fiend is desperate or has a large surplus of bones, it might choose to use this attack, hurling its body's component bones outward with the same effect as a stick of dynamite, causing 4d10 damage (BR 20). It takes two full rounds for the bone fiend to take shape again.

Variable size (Su): While the bone fiend usually assumes the size and general shape of a person, it can increase to Large Size (about 10 feet tall) provided it has enough bones at its disposal, or shrink down to Tiny Size. A change in size requires a round.

Undead (Su): Focus-black skull; The ebony cranium must remain within 50 feet of the animated bones, or they collapse. In addition, the bone fiend can place the skull inside a cage of bones, giving the vital piece AC 19.

Immune to mind-influencing effects, poison, sleep, paralysis, stunning, and disease. Not subject to critical hits, subdual damage, ability damage, energy drain, or death from massive damage.

Fast healing (Su): As long as there are bones to be had, the bone fiend's body can't be killed, only temporarily disrupted. Missing pieces can be replaced easily next round so long as intact—or relatively intact—bones remain nearby. It takes one action for the bone fiend to use this fast healing ability.

Braincrawler

Diminutive Beast
Hit Dice: 4d10-2 (14 hp)
Initiative: +0
Speed: 30 ft., 15 ft. climb
AC: 14 (+4 size)
Attacks: Bite +5 melee
Damage: Bite 1d3-2
Face/Reach: 1 ft. by 1 ft./0 ft.
Special Attacks: Compulsion
Special Qualities: Weaknesses
Saves: Fort +2, Ref +4, Will +4
Abilities: Str 5, Dex 10, Con 5, Int 9, Wis 17, Cha 15
Skills: Climb +7, Hide +12, Knowledge (local) +7, Listen +6, Move Silently +7, Spot +6
Feats: None
Climate/Terrain: Any land
Challenge Rating: 1
Alignment: Always chaotic evil
Advancement: 5-12 HD (Diminutive)

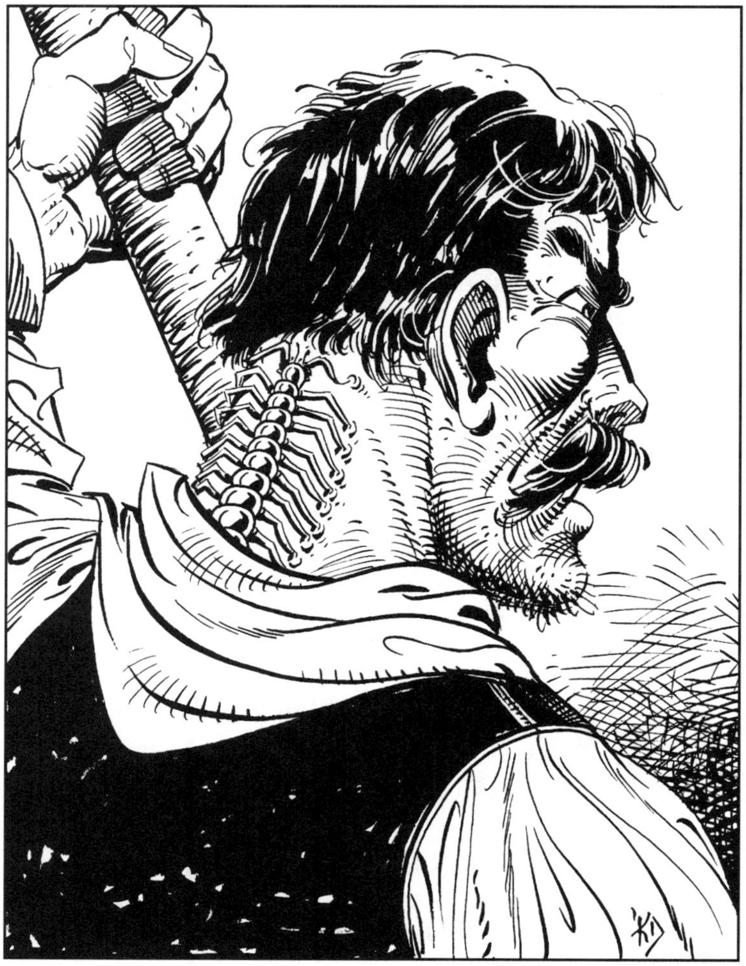

A braincrawler is a dark-colored, multi-legged, wormlike abomination about six inches in length. They are more commonly recognized by the open but painless wound on their victims made when the braincrawler burrows into the back of the neck and the base of the brain, through which it can be seen writhing around.

Once attached, the 'crawler whispers dark tales to the victim, and lives off its host's terror. This has an interesting side effect: the 'crawler eats the fear before the host can feel it, making the victim completely unafraid. This artificial bravery removes any inhibitions the unfortunate victim may have had and, combined with the braincrawler's dismal whisperings, causes madness to grow in the host's mind. Eventually, the victim's psyche gives in, and the parasite takes over completely.

The critter isn't very smart, and its host doesn't talk except for the occasional one-syllable word. It does however "remember" a few facts from the victim's life (like where they lived) and the faces of a few friends—now potential hosts for the critter's offspring.

When the braincrawler (often referred to as "the voices" by a victim) takes control, the host changes physically as well. First, the victim's eyes become a solid black, reflecting the spiritual evil of the braincrawler. Second, because the critter sits in the victim's brain running the show, it increases the host's resistance to pain. Finally, since the parasite has different tastes, the victim isn't very picky about what he eats, and insects, worms, carrion, and human flesh are all considered good snacks. Alcohol is avoided, because of braincrawler's vulnerability to it.

A few braincrawlers have made it into populated areas, and in an area with several inhabitants, braincrawlers can reproduce very quickly. Each critter can produce offspring if well-fed on fear, and after the young leave through the host's ears or nose to find other likely victims, madness can spread quickly through a town. Entire settlements have fallen prey to these insidious creatures.

Combat

Braincrawlers always strike while the potential victim sleeps. They are attracted to people who live in fear, especially those whose sanity has suffered, making them easier to control. These critters also prefer victims who live far from other people, since they have no one to help them find the 'crawler.

Compulsion (Su): From the moment the braincrawler attaches itself to a victim's brain, the victim gains the Fearless special ability. A victim must make a Will saving throw against DC 7 plus the area's Fear Level to remain in control of their own actions as long as a 'crawler nests in his noggin. The DC increases in difficulty by 2 for every day the braincrawler remains attached. The first time the victim fails their saving throw, they gain a dementia (use the mad scientist's Dementia Table in the *Deadlands: The Weird West D20 Rulebook*).

The Int, Wis and Cha ability scores are for a "typical" braincrawler victim. If a posse member or prominent extra is infected, use their ability scores instead.

Weaknesses (Ex): If the back of a victim's neck can be doused in alcohol greater than 100 proof (in combat this requires a hit against the victim's normal AC +10), the 'crawler must make a Will saving throw against DC 5 or be forced to head for greener pastures. The braincrawler can also be removed by setting it on fire, but the victim takes damage from the flames. No matter which method is used, the victim suffers 1d6 damage for each week or portion thereof that the critter was attached.

Canker

Diminutive Aberration
Hit Dice: 3d8+3 (22 hp)
Initiative: +1 (Dex)
Speed: 30 ft.
AC: 15 (+4 size, +1 Dex)
Attacks: 2 claws +10 melee
Damage: Claw 1d4+6
Face/Reach: 1 ft. by 1 ft./0 ft.
Special Attacks: Gaze attack, filament spray, implantation
Special Qualities: Puppetry
Saves: Fort +4, Ref +2, Will +3
Abilities: Str 18, Dex 12, Con 16, Int 5, Wis 9, Cha 11
Skills: Climb +5, Hide +13, Jump +5, Move Silently +6, Perform (acting) +1, Spot +6
Feats: None
Climate/Terrain: Any land
Challenge Rating: 4
Alignment: Always chaotic evil
Advancement: 4-9 HD (Diminutive)

Cankers looks like an insect or similar beast, and might be mistaken at first for a prairie tick, though the canker is much more insidious, as these critters live like hermit crabs in the bodies of their hosts. The canker's hard-shelled body starts out small, about the size of a chicken's egg, but grows over time, reaching feelers and legs into the recesses of the body to gain nourishment.

The canker is depression and worry given form, a cancerous expression of the distress of the mind. Prior to the Reckoning, a person under such stress might simply have taken ill with ulcers or even consumption. However, since that dark day, the Reckoners have taken to placing seeds of their energy into people consumed by despair, bringing those feelings to life, complete with a hard shell and a malevolent consciousness.

After the canker has lived in its host for about a month, it begins consuming the internal organs and taking over their function, extruding weird appendages wherever it needs to reach. After about six months, it even reaches its feeding tube up into the victim's head to consume the eyes, which it then replaces with its own, on long, jointed eye-stalks.

The canker eventually achieves complete control over the host's body, at which time it starves the victim's brain until it loses all higher function, leaving just enough of the host's original mind to know the horror it suffers. The body is just a shell controlled by the canker.

After this, it can no longer safely leave the host body completely. (When it exits to implant an egg in another host, it leaves various limbs and tubes extending down its deranged host's throat.)

The parasite is adept at mimicking behavior, too. It takes years for a canker to take complete control of its host, and by this time it can do a passable impression of that person. Still, it is but an impression, and the creature is nothing more than a sophisticated (and disgusting) parrot. It cannot learn anything new and does not respond well to new situations.

Cankers can reproduce by implanting eggs inside a victim. They do this by prying open the victim's mouth and forcing a new egg down their throat. Once in the poor sod's belly, the egg is hatched by exposure to stomach acids. Soon after, the chitinous thing starts to grow.

The new canker is an exact duplicate of its parent, including its knowledge to the time of reproduction. Thus, it is possible for an infant canker to know many lives' worth of knowledge and behavior. However, the implantation process often turns violent, and the canker sometimes has to kill the host before the egg is implanted.

Combat

Cankers are formidable foes but not very dangerous in a toe-to-toe fight, especially if forced out of the host body, even partially. They are possessed of a sinister cunning and usually use the innocent appearance of their host to lure a victim away from their compadres and then do him in. They may appear as seductive as a pale debutante or in other innocent guises such as a physician or priest.

These abominations choose new hosts carefully. They prefer loners, folks that aren't going to be missed by anybody. Alternatively, they tend to pick the distraught or insane, since if the host suddenly decides to disappear from society (as he's bound to), chances are good that no one is going to suspect the real reason for this.

Gaze attack (Sp): If a canker is far enough advanced to have replaced the eyes of the host with its own beady peepers, it can use these to hypnotize a victim. A person must make a Will saving throw against DC 13 to resist the canker's weird influence. A dominated person performs simple functions within the experience of the canker, usually something like "protect me" or "kill them all." The domination ability is most often used to get a victim to hold still for the implantation of an egg.

Filament spray (Ex): The canker can spray out a sticky, weblike stuff from a little tube near its mouth. It can also stick the tube out from its host's mouth to do the same. The stuff isn't strong enough to use as a weapon (equivalent to an average gauge of rope), but it's pretty useful for confining victims while the canker's offspring grows inside.

Implantation (Ex): The canker must first grapple and Pin the intended victim. It can do this either while using a host body or when scuttling about. After a successful grab, it extends a nasty-looking organ and sticks it down the victim's gullet to implant an egg. To succeed, the canker must keep the victim pinned for three straight rounds.

Puppetry (Ex): By the time the canker takes over the host body, it can mimic the host fairy well, using its Perform skill, which gains +1 for every month it has been in its host. In addition, it can mimic the host's Int, Wis and Cha with scores up to 11 in each.

Carcajou

Small Beast
Hit Dice: 5d10+3 (42 hp)
Initiative: +6 (Dex)
Speed: 50 ft.
AC: 19 (+1 size, +6 Dex, +2 natural)
Attacks: 2 claws +7 melee, bite +2 melee
Damage: Claw 1d6+3, bite 1d4+1
Face/Reach: 5 ft. by 5 ft./5 ft.
Special Attacks: Armor-piercing claws
Special Qualities: Fearless
Saves: Fort +7, Ref +10, Will +2
Abilities: Str 16, Dex 23, Con 17, Int 9, Wis 13, Cha 14
Skills: Balance +6, Climb +6, Hide +10, Intimidate +6, Listen +6, Move Silently +6, Spot +6, Tumble +7, Wilderness Lore +5
Feats: None
Climate/Terrain: Any Temperate land
Challenge Rating: 5
Alignment: Always neutral
Advancement: 6-10 HD (Small), 11-15 HD (Medium-Size)

A carcajou is a 3' tall, nightmarish version of a wolverine. Its mouth has two rows of triangular, serrated teeth and its paws are tipped by 3" claws capable of scoring stone. The monster's fur is a dark brown, with lighter coloring around its muzzle. Its eyes are large and have oddly human-like irises.

The beast has the same ferocity as a wolverine, but with a great deal more strength—and razor-sharp claws and teeth to back it up. However, all this fury comes at a price—the carcajou is constantly hungry. As a result, carcajous prey on almost any animal, even wiping out small herds of cattle that wander near their lairs. They also strip trap lines (and trappers, if they're unlucky). On the rare occasion the creature bags more food than it can consume, it regurgitates what has already eaten and gorges again.

Combat

In order to conserve its energy, carcajous hide under rocky overhangs or fallen logs near game trails and water holes. It lunges at its prey in a whirlwind of fang and fur, making short work of any animal up to—and including—a full-grown bear.

Armor-piercing claws (Ex): The carcajou's target receives no AC bonus due to armor.

Catamount

Large Beast
Hit Dice: 9d10+1 (58 hp)
Initiative: +3 (Dex)
Speed: 40 ft., 20 ft. climb
AC: 12 (-1 size, +3 Dex)
Attacks: 2 claws +9 melee, bite +4 melee
Damage: Claw 1d6+4, bite 1d4+2
Face/Reach: 5 ft. by 10 ft./5 ft.
Special Attacks: Fear
Special Qualities: Chameleon coat, mimicry, manipulative paws, night vision
Saves: Fort +7, Ref +9, Will +4
Abilities: Str 18, Dex 16, Con 13, Int 9, Wis 13, Cha 12
Skills: Balance +6, Bluff +5, Climb +12, Hide +8*, Intimidate +5, Jump +4, Listen +6, Move Silently +6, Spot +6, Swim +4, Wilderness Lore +5
Feats: None
Climate/Terrain: Any land
Challenge Rating: 6
Alignment: Always neutral
Advancement: 10-27 HD (Large)

The catamount is a 10' long great cat—a good deal larger than a mountain lion. Its coat is usually a mottled brown and tan, but this changes according to its background. Although its paws are markedly more hand—like than those of other cats, the true indicator that the creature is more than a mere animal is in the malicious intelligence that shines in its eyes.

These abominations are as intelligent as the average cowpoke and a fair amount more cunning. It's well within their abilities to locate a trap, move it to a different location, and use it to capture the original trapper.

Combat

Catamounts are solitary predators who use their uncanny voice to mimic human cries for help or screams. Its favorite method of ambush is to hide on an overhanging branch and lure a victim underneath. Once in position, the catamount digs its rear claws into the limb and swings down with its body to snatch the victim back up into the tree, where it quickly guts him and feasts. Often the catamount leaves the remains in the branches, further confusing any hunters.

Fear (Ex): After dark, the abomination's yowl has a spine-chilling effect on folks up to a mile away. Anyone within earshot must make a Will saving throw against DC 14. It takes the catamount one round to yowl this way.

Chameleon coat (Ex): The catamount can subtly change the patterns and color of its fur to match its background, giving the monster a +8 on Hide skill rolls.

Mimicry (Ex): The catamount can change its yowl to sound like a woman's cry for help or even a frightened scream.

Manipulative paws (Ex): A catamount's paws are very flexible, allowing it to carry objects a short distance. Its rear paws are also very dexterous and it can hang from a branch using only its hind legs. If it attacks at the end of this leap, it can attack with two claws and a bite at a +2 to its to-hit roll.

Night vision (Ex): Catamounts have low-light vision, but not nightvision.

Cemetery Wolves

Medium-Size Beast
Hit Dice: 2d10 (11 hp)
Initiative: +1 (Dex)
Speed: 30 ft.
AC: 11 (+1 Dex)
Attacks: 2 claws +2 melee, bite -3 melee
Damage: Claw 1d6+1, bite 1d4
Face/Reach: 5 ft. by 5 ft./5 ft.
Special Qualities: Manipulative paws, scent
Saves: Fort +3, Ref +4, Will +0
Abilities: Str 12, Dex 12, Con 9, Int 7, Wis 10, Cha 7
Skills: Climb +5, Hide +5, Intimidate +4, Listen +5, Move Silently +4, Spot +5, Wilderness Lore +5
Feats: None
Climate/Terrain: Any land
Challenge Rating: 1
Alignment: Always neutral
Advancement: 3-6 HD (Medium-Size)

This monster looks something like an overgrown coyote with a hairless nose, protruding teeth, and odd but highly dexterous forepaws. The front legs are more heavily muscled than the back, giving the creature a strange hump to its spine. Its fur is dark brown with a black stripe along its back and a random spotted pattern on its sides. The monsters communicate through a series of yips and barks that sound almost like maniacal laughter or screaming.

The creature is adapted to its carrion-eater role, much like a vulture. Its muzzle is bare of fur, so that gore doesn't get trapped there as it burrows into a corpse to snatch at prize bits. Its paws have long, hardened claws to allow it to dig up shallow graves quickly. Finally, its mouth is filled with several canine teeth that jut outward from its nearly lipless mouth for ripping dead flesh quickly.

Cemetery wolves are found across the Weird West. However, they're most concentrated along areas of frequent battles between the Confederacy and the Union or shallow mass graves. Although it feasts on corpses, the cemetery wolf also preys on those too wounded to defend against it. Many screams that echo through the night after a battle are due to packs of these monsters moving among the still-living casualties left on the field. Occasionally, it may dig in established cemeteries, which invariably leads to suggestions of ghouls among those who know of such things.

Combat

These monsters usually hunt in packs of 10-20. They are *extremely* cunning, exhibiting near-human intelligence, and able to communicate with each other through their high pitched barks and howls. This allows them to make effective use of the numerical advantage they usually enjoy.

Manipulative paws (Ex): The monster's forepaws can perform simple hand-like actions. For example, it can open coffins, turn doorknobs, or even undo clothing. It cannot, however, manipulate hand weapons or deal a good poker hand.

Skills: Cemetery wolves receive a +2 bonus to all Climb, Hide, Intimidate, Listen, Move Silently, Spot and Wilderness Lore skill rolls.

Chinook

Large Magical Beast
Hit Dice: 10d10+4 (95 hp)
Initiative: +0
Speed: 30 ft.
AC: 9 (-1 size)
Attacks: 2 claws +13 melee, bite +11 melee
Damage: Claw 1d6+4, bite 1d4+2
Face/Reach: 5 ft. by 10 ft./5 ft.
Special Attacks: Blizzard, heat wave
Special Qualities: Hibernation
Saves: Fort +11, Ref +7, Will +4
Abilities: Str 18, Dex 11, Con 19, Int 6, Wis 12, Cha 14
Skills: Climb +8, Intimidate +6, Intuit Direction +8, Listen +8, Move Silently +8, Spot +8, Wilderness Lore +8
Feats: Cleave, Multiattack, Power Attack
Climate/Terrain: Any Cold or Temperate land
Challenge Rating: 8
Alignment: Always neutral
Advancement: 11-20 HD (Large), 21-30 HD (Huge)

The chinook is a massive beast (as large as a Kodiak bear) that looks like a giant wolverine with gray and brown markings. It has oversized paws with large claws to move easily over snow or through mud. Even more vicious than the animal it resembles, the chinook is extremely dangerous to any and all that stray into its path.

Its rather colorful name comes from the warm wind that causes early thaws in the Northwest Territory. Like the warm wind, the chinook creature represents a dangerous alteration in prevailing conditions.

The chinook hibernates in summer, but emerges from its slumber in the late fall. The beast is a dedicated carnivore, and its massive size and appetite enable it to hunt any and all creatures found in the Pacific Northwest, even humans.

Combat

Chinooks, though unintelligent by conventional definitions, have the arcane ability to manipulate local weather conditions, altering them to suit its needs. It can cause a localized "heat wave" capable of melting snow almost instantly, and even transforming soft earth to a tarry consistency. It uses this to trap prey or harm pursuers and can also create blizzard-like conditions to cover its retreat.

Blizzard (Su): The chinook can start a miniature blizzard that typically manages to spawn a true storm. The chinook uses the blizzard as cover to return to its lair. The little storm (about 600 feet in diameter) usually only blinds people, but if they fail a Wilderness Lore skill check against DC 10, they wander in circles in the blizzard, losing all sense of direction. If a real storm starts, a lost victim can freeze to death.

Heat wave (Su): Once per day, the chinook can cause the air temperature within 300 feet to soar to about 60° in one round, even from -20°, and stay at that temperature for 10 minutes. This causes snow and ice to instantly begin melting. In the mountains, this can make the area ripe for an avalanche or mudslide. After this ability is used, any loud noise (like a gunshot or the roar of a chinook) has a 1 in 20 chance of causing an avalanche or mudslide, whichever is more appropriate. Victims caught downhill from the event suffer damage as if they'd been caught in an explosion of dynamite (4d10 to 9d10, depending on how much stuff lands on them, with BR 20).

Hibernation (Ex): If found and attacked during the warmest months of the year, it receives a -4 penalty to all its rolls. It does not suffer this modifier in spring or fall when it is partially active.

Skills: Chinooks receive a +4 bonus on all Climb, Intuit Direction, Listen, Move Silently, Spot and Wilderness Lore skill rolls.

Chupakabara

Medium-Size Monstrous Humanoid
Hit Dice: 4d8+2 (26 hp)
Initiative: +1 (Dex)
Speed: 35 ft.
AC: 11 (+1 Dex)
Attacks: 2 claws +5 melee, bite +3 melee
Damage: Claw 1d6+1, bite 1d8
Face/Reach: 5 ft. by 5 ft./5 ft.
Special Qualities: Move unseen, resurrection, coup
Saves: Fort +3, Ref +5, Will +4
Abilities: Str 12, Dex 13, Con 14, Int 8, Wis 9, Cha 9
Skills: Climb +5, Hide +7, Listen +7, Move Silently +7, Spot +7, Wilderness Lore +7
Feats: Multiattack
Climate/Terrain: Any land
Challenge Rating: 2
Alignment: Always chaotic evil
Advancement: 5-12 HD (Medium-Size)

This abomination is a small gray or brown creature with a vaguely monkey-like appearance, a large head, long arms, and short legs. Each of the creature's hands and feet has three digits, each of which ends in a vicious claw, and it has a rounded mouth filled with jagged teeth. They are nocturnal and have large round eyes.

A chupakabara (Spanish for "goat-sucker") is produced when the Reckoners take note of a person who willingly betrays a family member. They send a spark of their energy to alter the betrayer. A person who becomes a chupakabara in this manner is always gray in color, and can only be killed by the person it betrayed.

If the betrayed person has the chance to kill the betrayer and doesn't, then he also becomes a chupakabara, and both beasts turn a greasy brown. Brown chupakabaras can be killed normally.

Combat

Chupakabaras feed on the blood of animals (usually domesticated beasts like goats), and like to sneak-attack their prey. Besides drinking blood, the chupakabara also likes eating the soft, tasty bits of critters, like eyes and lips, and can also reach its long arms down a critter's throat to pick out other "delicacies."

Move Unseen (Su): By expending 1 hit point each round the chupakabara can move without leaving a trail. When moving this way, it appears as a fast-moving blur and all attacks made against it suffer a -4 penalty.

Resurrection (Su): Slain gray chupakabaras always return to life the next night unless the person it betrayed delivers the killing blow.

Coup: Harrowed who feast on the essence of a gray chupakabara gain its ability to move without leaving a trail (at the same cost of 1 hit point per round).

Skills: Chupakabaras receive a hefty +3 bonus on all Hide, Listen, Move Silently, Spot, and Wilderness Lore skill rolls.

Clockwork Tarantulas

Medium-Size Construct
Hit Dice: 2d10 (11 hp)
Initiative: +1 (Dex)
Speed: 30 ft., 30 ft. climb
AC: 16 (+1 Dex, +5 natural)
Attacks: Bite +2 melee; or acid spray +2 ranged
Damage: Bite 1d3+1 and acid, acid spray 3d6
Face/Reach: 5 ft. by 5 ft./5 ft.
Special Attacks: Acid spray, acid bite, self-destruct
Special Qualities: Spell immunity, wall-crawling, fearless
Saves: Fort +0, Ref +1, Will -1
Abilities: Str 12, Dex 12, Con —, Int 5, Wis 7, Cha 5
Skills: None
Feats: None
Climate/Terrain: Any land
Challenge Rating: 3
Alignment: Always lawful neutral
Advancement: 3-6 HD (Medium-Size)

Clockwork tarantulas stand about 3' high and resemble enormous, mechanical versions of their namesakes. Eight gear-driven legs, each over a yard long, emerge from the bulbous, armor-plated body housing the clockwork gears that drive the machine. The head contains a set of sharpened, hollow tubes that function as the mechanism's primary weapons, or "fangs."

These are another of Hellstromme's devices designed to give his rail gangs an edge in a fight. Driven by a complex clockwork mechanism, the tarantulas are larger than the average dog and scuttle about on 8 gear-driven legs. The sight of these mechanical spiders scurrying around is bone-chilling.

Like automatons, the duplication of these machines is beyond the ken of most inventors, because Hellstromme has combined black necromancy with mad science. However, clockwork tarantulas don't rate human brains; instead, they're guided by reanimated animal brains.

Hellstromme guards the secret of the tarantulas' control just a closely as that of the automatons. However, instead of implanting an explosive, he uses the mechanism's own acid to dissolve its brain case should it ever be incapacitated.

Combat

The mechanical arachnids are terrifying opponents, made more so by the potent acid that they inject or spray at targets. Their metal plating makes them somewhat resistant to normal firearms and, just like automatons, these devices are absolutely fearless and fight accordingly.

Acid bite (Ex): If the tarantula bites its opponent in melee, it has punctured his body with a pair of metal "fangs" and injects acid. The acid does 3d6 damage on the round the hit took place. The acid continues to do damage at the beginning of subsequent rounds as it spreads through the victim's system. Reduce the number of dice done by one each round after the initial hit (i.e., 2d6 on the first round, 1d6 on the second, etc.).

Acid spray (Ex): The tarantula can use its "fangs" to spray acid a short distance. When sprayed, the acid has a Range Increment of 5 ft. and does 3d6 damage. Acid fired in this fashion does *not* continue to cause damage. A tarantula has enough acid for 12 sprays or bites in its reservoir.

Self-destruct (Ex): If a tarantula's mechanism ever stops, it vents acid from its reservoir into its brain case, destroying the secret of its construction. The reservoir actually holds 13 shots, so that there's always enough of a reserve left for this act. Anyone within 6 feet of the gizmo when this happens is splashed for 1d6 damage per remaining shot.

Wall-crawling (Ex): Tarantulas can move at their normal Speed up any surface soft enough for them to sink their barbed legs into, i.e. most wood, trees, people, etc. They can even hang upside down from a ceiling.

Spell immunity (Ex): Only spells, hexes, miracles and the like that affect inanimate objects can target the tarantula's frame. Arcana like Soul Blast, which only works on animate objects, has no effect.

Dark Beasts

Large Magical Beast
Hit Dice: 11d10+3 (93 hp)
Initiative: +1 (Dex)
Speed: 30 ft.
AC: 10 (-1 size, +1 Dex)
Attacks: Bite +12 melee, 8 claws +10 melee; or ice dart +11 ranged
Damage: Bite 1d6+2 and blood drain, claw 1d8+1, ice dart 1d6+2
Face/Reach: 5 ft. by 10 ft./5 ft.
Special Attacks: Improved grab, blood drain, ice dart
Special Qualities: Damage reduction 10/-, light sensitivity, focus
Saves: Fort +10, Ref +8, Will +4
Abilities: Str 14, Dex 13, Con 16, Int 9, Wis 13, Cha 13
Skills: Climb +7, Listen +6, Move Silently +7, Spot +6, Wilderness Lore +7
Feats: Dodge, Multiattack, Power Attack
Climate/Terrain: Underground
Challenge Rating: 10
Alignment: Always lawful evil
Advancement: 12-33 HD (Large)

Because dark beasts are always hidden in shadows or twilight and their corpses turn into oily smoke when struck by bright light, no precise description of them can be given. From what can be gathered, they have a vaguely humanoid form with about a dozen clawed arms and legs, which give them a spider-like appearance.

According to a century-old Wichita legend, these creatures are spider spirits that gain nourishment from darkness and human blood. Regardless of whether they are ancient beings or new abominations created by the Reckoners, dark beasts are every bit the fearsome monsters described in the legend.

Dark beasts are gifted with limited intelligence which enables them to speak simple sentences and imagine devilish schemes to capture the human beings from whom they drain blood for nourishment. They live only in deep caves with hidden entrances. The typical "clan" is composed of a mated couple and their hideous spawn.

The greatest strength of the dark beast rests in their dark hearts, for a dark beast cannot be slain unless its heart is pierced. Unfortunately for anyone who might want to do so, the creatures can remove their hearts and leave them in the lair while they go into the night to hunt. The bulbous red masses of the dark beast's hearts hang from the ceiling of the lair, waiting for their owners to return.

Destroying the heart of a dark beast instantly kills the beast that owns it. Of course, dark beasts never leave their lairs totally unguarded. Usually, one or two stay behind as guards for the hearts, as well as for any prisoners. In addition, the hearts are usually protected by traps (pits and falling rocks are favored).

Combat

Dark beasts usually try to ambush humans, setting traps in wilderness areas near their lairs. They grab their victims, then bite and drain blood. Many victims are drained until they die, while others are severely weakened. These are taken back to the lair of the dark beasts and thrown in nightmarish pits, so they might provide grisly meals for several days.

Young dark beasts can also spit deadly darts of black ice, useful for driving victims into ambushes. These darts are said to be generated in their cold, dark hearts.

Blood drain (Ex): Once a dark beast has bitten a victim, it holds on and drains blood at the rate of 1d6 hit points per round.

Ice dart (Ex): Only young dark beasts can use this. The dart does 1d6+2 damage with a Range Increment of 10 ft.

Light sensitivity (Ex): Dark beasts cannot bear strong light. They never go out in daytime, and torches keep them away until they find a way to get the torchbearer to drop his torch.

Focus (Su): A dark beast without its heart does not die when it reaches 0 hit points. Instead, it immediately retreats, able to do little but run away. The wounded dark beast returns to its lair, where it slips its slimy heart back into its body and rests, unconscious and helpless, for a full day. When it awakens, it is completely healed. The only way to kill a dark beast is to destroy its heart. A single point of damage is enough to destroy it.

Demon

Large Outsider (Chaotic Evil)
Hit Dice: 11d8+3 (82 hp)
Initiative: +1 (Dex)
Speed: 30 ft.
AC: 15 (-1 size, +1 Dex, +5 natural)
Attacks: 2 claws +14 melee, bite +12 melee
Damage: Claw 1d6+4, bite 1d3+2 and poison
Face/Reach: 5 ft. by 10 ft./5 ft.
Special Attacks: Poison
Special Qualities: Fearless, fire immunity, weaknesses, coup, damage reduction 5/-
Saves: Fort +10, Ref +8, Will +7
Abilities: Str 19, Dex 13, Con 16, Int 10, Wis 10, Cha 12
Skills: Climb +14, Intimidate +12, Knowledge (arcana) +11, Listen +11, Move Silently +12, Ridicule, +12, Sense Motive +11, Spot +11
Feats: Dodge, Multiattack, Power Attack
Climate/Terrain: Any land
Challenge Rating: 9
Alignment: Always chaotic evil
Advancement: 12-22 HD (Large), 23-33 HD (Huge)

These abominations stand about 9 1/2' tall and are very broad-shouldered. Their skin is usually a deep—almost blackish—red, and their eyes are orange pools of flame. They have gaping maws filled with shark-like teeth that drip an acidic venom. Their arms reach to their knees and end in three-fingered claws, each the size of a child's forearm. Their legs may have a scaly or coarse-haired covering, while their feet may end in three-toed feet or bird-like claws.

Fire-and-brimstone spouting circuit preachers have regaled their congregations with tales of terrible demons waiting to torment their immortal souls for decades now. With the rise of cults practicing real black magic, it's not really a surprise that some of these "devil-worshipers" actually succeeded in summoning up a demon or two.

What most folks don't know, of course, is that these so-called demons are really just another type of servant for the Reckoners. Not wanting to let a prime source of fear go to waste, they've incarnated some of the stereotypical ideas of Hell's denizens into corporeal form.

There are more ways to "summon" one of these abominations than there to skin a cat. The real thing that matters is that the cultists or magician involved truly desire to call forth a being of Hell and be willing to perform some terrible deed to do so. Often this takes the form of blood or even human sacrifice, but it varies from cult to cult. These rituals nearly always leave some evidence, and anyone examining a summoning site can determine the magician's intent with a successful Knowledge (arcana) check against DC 13.

Seldom do the cultists have an inkling that they are nothing but cogs in the Reckoners plans. Once summoned, the arch-demon is bound to the corporeal world, but not to the whims of the magician or cult. It may pretend to be, but the creature places ever-increasing demands on the cult, hoping to elevate the local area's Fear Level. When the chips are down, the monster cares nothing for its human allies.

Demons draw much of their form from the concepts of the summoning cult or magician. As a result, they vary greatly in appearance, size, and power. Most conform very closely to the standard depictions of demonic beings common to the more lurid religious illustrations of the time.

Virtually any sort of power is available to these monsters. However, due to the influence of common beliefs, they tend to stick close to those abilities most often associated with Hellish inhabitants: strength, toughness, flame, poison, and the like. Fortunately, they also possess a number of weaknesses as a result of their quasi-religious nature.

For obvious reasons, these abominations are most frightening when tied to an blatantly "Satanic" or otherwise religiously-oriented cult. Often the greater terror comes from realizing the depths of corruption to which other humans have sunk through dealing with these abominations. Otherwise, they're just big, tough monsters.

Combat

These beings are never released to roam the land at will. That's totally out of character for a demon. Instead, these monsters answer the calls of unwitting cultists for power, and egg them on to greater and more horrific deeds in the name of the "Dark Master."

On those rare occasions demons are forced into direct physical confrontations, they take full advantage of their immunity to most attacks and rend their foes to shreds with their claws and teeth.

Poison (Ex): Anyone bitten by a demon is injected with a corrosive toxin and must make a Fortitude saving throw against DC 17. Success means the victim suffers 1d6 damage, and failure inflicts an additional 4d6 damage on the beginning of the next round as the acidic poison moves through the victim's system.

Fire immunity (Su): Fire and heat-based attacks do *no* damage to demons. Dynamite and similar explosions do half damage.

Weaknesses (Su): Silver weapons do normal damage to demons. Holy water splashed on them does 1d6 damage. Contact with any Consecrated item does 1d6 damage per round. Demons suffer -4 to all rolls on holy (Sanctified) ground. Exorcism destroys them.

Coup: Harrowed suffer only half damage from flame and heat-based attacks after slaying a demon.

Devil Rays

Large Beast
Hit Dice: 5d10 (27 hp)
Initiative: +0
Speed: 85 ft. swim, 75 ft. fly (clumsy)
AC: 9 (-1 size)
Attacks: Bite +4 melee; tail spike -1 melee (can only be used against opponents to its rear)
Damage: Bite 1d6+2, tail spike 1d4+1
Face/Reach: 5 ft. by 10 ft./5 ft.
Special Attacks: Swoop, improved grab
Special Qualities: Glide
Saves: Fort +4, Ref +4, Will +0
Abilities: Str 14, Dex 11, Con 10, Int 6 Wis 7, Cha 7
Skills: Listen +7, Move Silently +8, Spot +8, Swim +10, Wilderness Lore +8
Feats: None
Climate/Terrain: Aquatic
Challenge Rating: 4
Alignment: Always neutral
Advancement: 6-10 HD (Large), 11-15 HD (Huge)

Devil rays are 15' wide manta rays with a bony tail spike. The creatures have pitch-black skin, small black eyes on their leading edge, and a mouth on their underside. Two small, knobby projections jut from above their eyes, giving the impression of horns.

These beasts are the subject of many tall tales among sea-faring-folk, and unfortunately the stories are true—these large rays can fly for short distances. They also have a predilection for human flesh (what doesn't, anymore?).

Devil rays can leave the water and soar for up to 75' at heights of nearly 20'. This is more than enough to let them swoop across the decks of smaller vessels and snatch unsuspecting crew from the deck. Devil rays are nocturnal, and their dark coloration makes them nearly invisible after nightfall.

These abominations are found only in saltwater (such as is found in the Great Maze) and travel in schools of 10-20. A large group of them are capable of stripping a small vessel's crew without a trace, leaving a ghost ship.

Combat

A devil ray envelops its prey in its large wing like fins and gnaws away at exposed flesh and easily accessible organs. This technique prevents a devil ray from flying once it's snatched a meal. The creature lacks the jaw strength to effectively gnaw through bone, so the brain, eyes, lungs, and heart are left with the skeleton for more determined scavengers.

Swoop (Ex): If the devil ray makes a gliding attack on its victim, it does 1d3+2 damage in addition to its bite.

Glide (Ex): The devil ray must move its full swimming Speed in a fairly straight line for one round in order to fly The devil ray can only glide for a single round at a time.

Skills: Devil rays receive a +4 bonus to all Move Silently, Spot, and Wilderness Lore skill rolls.

Doom Cloud

Large Aberration
Hit Dice: 6d8 (27 hp)
Initiative: +4 (Improved Initiative)
Speed: 35 ft. fly (perfect)
AC: 9 (-1 size)
Attacks: None
Damage: None
Face/Reach: 5 ft. by 10 ft./5 ft.
Special Attacks: Asphyxiation
Special Qualities: Gaseous form, fearless, weaknesses
Saves: Fort +2, Ref +2, Will +5
Abilities: Str 5, Dex 9, Con 9, Int 9, Wis 11, Cha 9
Skills: Hide +5, Move Silently +6, Search +6, Spot +5
Feats: Improved Initiative
Climate/Terrain: Any land
Challenge Rating: 4
Alignment: Always chaotic evil
Advancement: 7-12 HD (Large), 13-18 HD (Huge)

In its natural form, a doom cloud is a 10' diameter sphere of blood-red mist. However, it may alter its form into nearly any other shape of equal or lesser volume by compacting itself. A faint set of menacing, putrid green eyes can be spotted high in the cloud with a successful Spot check against DC 7. These eyes are nearly 1' across each.

These strange abominations are only formed when a large number of folks die due to mad science's latest weapon of mass destruction, chlorine gas. Even then (fortunately for the inhabitants of the Weird West) it's a rare occurrence. These sentient, poison clouds are truly one of the most efficient killing machines created by the Reckoners. To date, only a few have been spawned, and most of those on the battlefields of northern Virginia.

Combat

Their gaseous nature makes doom clouds nearly impervious to attacks. It also makes their own asphyxiating attack insidiously effective—and deadly. Strong winds can be devastating to these creatures if they're caught in the open. To avoid being dissipated by weather phenomena, doom clouds stick to low ground, valleys, caves, and even buildings.

Asphyxiation (Ex): A doom cloud attacks simply by moving itself on top of a victim; since it can alter its shape, it can cover a good-sized area. Any creature or hero caught inside must make a Fortitude saving throw against DC 17 each round they remain inside it. Success means the hero has managed to hold their breath and not catch a lung-full of the monster. Failure means their Constitution is reduced by 2. As soon as their Constitution drops to 0, the victim buys the farm. Lost Con returns at the rate of 1 point per minute after they escape the monster. An airtight gas mask completely negates this attack.

Weaknesses (Su): Weapons made of pure iron (not steel) do normal damage. Strong winds, natural or created with magic, do 3d6 damage to a doom cloud each round. Electrical-based attacks do double damage. Non-area effect magical attacks (like Soul Blast or Consecrated weapons) only do half damage. As these monsters are more products of science than legend, Knowledge (arcana) skill reveals nothing about doom clouds. However, since the cloud is based on chlorine gas, succeeding at a Knowledge (chemistry) skill check against DC 13 exposes one of the doom cloud's weaknesses.

Doppelganger

A doppelganger is a malevolent supernatural being that studies and then impersonates a particular human being. After a period of observation, lasting up to a month or more, the doppelganger is able to nearly perfectly duplicate the person's actions and mannerisms.

However, the doppelganger seeks to spread discord and distrust, and to that end, it twists its victim's normal traits into cruel and evil actions. The abomination has an uncanny sense of its victim's location at all times. It either precedes or follows its target and performs foul deeds that are likely to get the unsuspecting cowpoke strung up when he arrives.

A doppelganger exactly duplicate's its victim's game statistics, including Ability Scores, Character Class, Level, Feats and Skills. If the human target has arcane abilities, the abomination uses black magic to replicate (in its own twisted way) the effects the hero might produce. For example, a blessed's doppelganger may call down burning holy light (Fireball) to consume a minor criminal—or even an unsuspecting innocent!

After committing its crime, the monster usually flees the scene, leaving the unsuspecting hero to take the blame. Only the doppelganger's target can wound the creature; it may feign injuries from other attacks, but no one else can truly harm it—not even with magical means.

These abominations always choose well-known or even famous people, because those individuals provide the greatest impact on society.

Note the doppelganger that replaced Confederate President Jefferson Davis is a rare and *very* powerful servant of the Reckoners. The abominations we're talking about here are far weaker and less concerned with the "big picture."

Dracula

Medium-Size Undead
Hit Dice: 12d12 (78 hp)
Initiative: +4 (Dex)
Speed: 50 ft.
AC: 14 (+4 Dex)
Attacks: 2 claws +12 melee, bite +10 melee
Damage: Claw 1d6+6, bite 1d4+3 and energy drain
Face/Reach: 5 ft. by 5 ft./5 ft.
Special Attacks: Gaze attack, improved grab, energy drain, fog, summon swarms
Special Qualities: Gaseous form, shapechange, maverick, undead, vampiric weaknesses, coup
Saves: Fort +9, Ref +13, Will +18
Abilities: Str 23, Dex 18, Con –, Int 15, Wis 20, Cha 21
Skills: Appraise +7, Climb +7, Diplomacy +8, Disguise +8, Hide +9, Intimidate +9, Knowledge (Europe, arcana, European history) +7, Listen +8, Move Silently +9, Profession (military, politics) +8, Ride +7, Search +7, Sense Motive +8, Speak Language (English, Magyar, Romanian), Spot +8
Feats: Cleave, Dodge, Multiattack, Power Attack, Run
Climate/Terrain: Any land
Challenge Rating: 12
Alignment: Chaotic evil
Advancement: As maverick character class

Dracula normally appears as a tall, dark-haired man with strong facial features, a high forehead, and thick eyebrows. His hands are broad, with thick fingers. The nails are cut to a sharp point and he has hair on his palms. His skin is always pale and he prefers refined, black clothing. Like many vampires, he casts no reflection in mirrors and despises garlic.

The Count's history is pretty much the stuff of legend nowadays—a Translyvanian nobleman cursed to feed on the blood of the living. However, in the Weird West, Bram Stoker's famous novel won't be written for another couple of decades. Only a few outside his home territory suspect he might be more than he seems—a rich, eccentric noble. The name Count Dracula *doesn't* strike fear into the hearts of all mortals in *Deadlands*. At least not yet.

Dracula, the most powerful vampire in existence, was once known as Vlad Drakul, ruler of a small country in what is now Romania. Vlad, while a military genius, had a few unsavory practices—among them a habit for sticking folks on huge sharpened posts, which gained him the nickname "the Impaler." So brutal was he that his actions resulted in his curse of vampirism back in the 15th century—when the manitous were still chained in the Hunting Grounds. That's a powerful lot of evil!

Now the Reckoning has begun, Dracula is far more powerful than ever. Although his home is in the Carpathian Mountains of eastern Europe, he does travel from time to time. On such journeys, he takes several coffins, as many as three "wives" (treat these as cinematic vampires, described on page 102) and a loyal retainer or two who knows his true nature. Dracula is old-blood nobility and usually surrounds himself with accoutrements of his wealth. While encountering him on the high plains isn't all that likely, his nibs could easily show up in any of the larger cities of the Weird West, or Back East if your posse has headed there.

Dracula is not tied in any way to the Reckoners (although his actions certainly fit well with their machinations). The Count has his own agenda and plans.

Combat

It's important to remember that Dracula has been around for over four centuries. In life, he was a plotter and schemer to do Machiavelli proud; in undeath, he's much, much worse. He has wealth and social connections in addition to his vampiric abilities. He's likely to *always* be a step-or three-ahead of any hunters. Dracula is a powerful foe for any Posse and should be nearly invincible-in or out of combat.

Improved grab (Ex): The Count can grab any target equal in Size or smaller.

Gaze attack (Sp): Dracula can command a victim to do his bidding if they fail a Will saving throw against DC 17. If the target is another vampire, their DC is 21. This takes a round, and Dracula must maintain concentration to exert his will on the victim.

Energy drain (Su): Anyone who has taken at least one hit point of damage from Dracula's bite can sense his general location, no matter the distance between them. The DC for a victim to regain a lost level is 21.

He has full control of the lesser vampires victims slain by his bite become. Every hit point Dracula drains heals one point of damage to himself.

Maverick (Ex): The Count has Evasion, Uncanny Dodge, Sneak Attack and Extraordinary Luck, as per the maverick character class.

Summon swarms (Su): Dracula can summon an enormous horde of lesser creatures (bats, rats, etc.) to fight on his behalf by spending 2 rounds mystically calling to them. Afterwards, the creatures attack his opponents as long as he concentrates.

Gaseous form (Su): Dracula can change himself to or from a mist in a single round. While in mist form, only area-effect attacks (explosions, large fires, sunlight) can harm him. He cannot fly in this form, but can creep into anything not airtight.

Fog (Su): Dracula can create a thick fog over an area roughly three miles in diameter. He, and anyone he chooses, can see normally within it. All others can only see only 15 feet and suffer a -4 to ranged attack rolls. The fog takes about 5 minutes to rise and lasts for an hour and a half.

Shapechange (Su): Dracula can assume the form of a massive bat or wolf. Use the appropriate animal profile, but increase Str and Dex by 4 each, while Dracula maintains his own Int, Wis and Cha. Either change requires 1 round to perform.

Undead (Su): Focus—heart (special). The only way to truly kill Dracula is to drive a stake through his heart, behead him, stuff his mouth full of garlic, and expose his remains to the noonday sun. Anything less temporarily defeats him.

Vampiric weaknesses (Su): Wood, garlic, holy water, roses, sunlight. Garlic and roses repel Dracula—he must make a Will saving throw against DC 10 to bypass them. Driving a stake through his heart (melee attack with a -20 modifier) paralyzes Dracula until it's removed. Holy water does 1d6 damage when splashed on him. Sunlight does 2d6 damage every round the Count's directly exposed to it.

Coup: Harrowed gain Dracula's ability to hypnotize living humans with his gaze. A victim may attempt to break control by making another Will saving throw, but they can only do so at the beginning of each subsequent round. The hero may maintain the power and still take simple actions that don't cause him to break eye contact with the victim.

Dread Wolves

Medium-Size Beast
Hit Dice: 3d10+1 (19 hp)
Initiative: +2 (Dex)
Speed: 35 ft.
AC: 12 (+2 Dex)
Attacks: Bite +3 melee
Damage: Bite 1d8+1 and disease
Face/Reach: 5 ft. by 5 ft./5 ft.
Special Attacks: Howl, wolf pack, disease
Saves: Fort +4, Ref +5, Will +1
Abilities: Str 12, Dex 15, Con 13, Int 8, Wis 11, Cha 11
Skills: Climb +6, Hide +5, Intimidate +6, Listen +5, Move Silently +5, Spot +5, Wilderness Lore +5
Feats: None
Climate/Terrain: Any Temperate land
Challenge Rating: 3
Alignment: Always neutral
Advancement: 4-9 HD (Medium-Size)

Dread wolves have blood-red eyes, and their mouths drip a bloody saliva that coats their fur with gore. Their mangy and ferocious appearance is intensified by a strong carrion stench. The smell and sight of a dread wolf causes normal animals to flee recklessly, and it doesn't do much good for people either

Dread wolves, sometimes called blood wolves or banshee wolves, are created whenever a pack of normal wolves consumes the flesh of an abomination or of one of the Harrowed. The corrupt essence of the flesh transforms the wolves into servants of the Reckoners and infects them with an unnatural form of rabies known as "bad blood."

Combat

Despite their appearance, dread wolves act much like normal wolves, traveling in packs of 4d4, looking for lone stragglers and other easy prey. However, these abominations are stronger, faster, and tougher than normal wolves and also have some special abilities. These creatures like to chase down lone victims until they drop from exhaustion, and then move in for the kill.

Howl (Su): Anyone who hears a dread wolf howl must make a Wisdom ability check against DC 18. If failed, the victim must flee the scene in terror.

Disease (Su): Anyone wounded by dread wolves may become infected with the disease known as bad blood. Its statistics are as follows: **Infection:** Injury, **DC:** 13 (+2 for each additional bite suffered), **Incubation:** 1 day, **Damage:** Psychosis.

The DC for any medical treatment received is equal to that of the initial Infection. Curing the disease with the Heal skill takes a number of days equal to the treatment DC. However, few people know how to treat the infection, and infected individuals are often simply put down.

The symptoms are similar to rabies, but much worse. Afflicted animals become crazed and bloodthirsty. Infected people become homicidal psychopaths, as well as cannibals. Early symptoms include headaches, stomachaches, and dizziness. Advanced symptoms include bloodshot eyes and bloody frothing at the mouth. Bad blood has no effect on the Harrowed.

Wolf pack (Ex): Every round that a target is attacked by two or more dread wolves at the same time, they must make a Fortitude saving throw against DC 17 or lose 1 hit point due to exhaustion.

Skills: Dread wolves receive a +2 bonus to all Climb, Hide, Intimidate, Listen, Move Silently Spot and Wilderness Lore skill rolls.

Duster

Tiny Magical Beast
Hit Dice: 2d10+1 (13 hp)
Initiative: +2 (Dex)
Speed: 35 ft.
AC: 14 (+2 size, +2 Dex)
Attacks: Touch +3 melee
Damage: Water drain
Face/Reach: 2 1/2 ft. by 2 1/2 ft./0 ft.
Special Attacks: Water drain
Special Qualities: Dowsing, camouflage, water vulnerability
Saves: Fort +5, Ref +5, Will +0
Abilities: Str 7, Dex 15, Con 12, Int 10, Wis 11, Cha 12
Skills: Climb +6, Hide +8, Listen +5, Move Silently +6, Spot +5
Feats: Dodge
Climate/Terrain: Warm Desert
Challenge Rating: 2
Alignment: Always chaotic evil
Advancement: 3-6 HD (Tiny)

Dusters appear as scrawny, emaciated, little rabbits, or some other critter that blends in extremely well with their surroundings. In the Weird West, looks can be deceiving, and the duster is no exception. Per ounce, they're the cutest little killers in the Weird West.

These critters live only in the most inhospitable and arid of places, waiting for unwitting travelers to see their sad little eyes and invite them into their hearts and other organs. They live by sucking the water out of other living beings. Those who have lived to tell of encounters with them believe the desert looks the way it does because of these malevolent little fur-balls.

Combat

Once among humans, they use their supernatural ability to absorb moisture and slowly empty all available water. Once they've done that, they move in closer and absorb the water from the bodies of the people they travel with, enjoying their gasps and slow death. Once their victims are dead, the duster drains any remaining water, leaving behind dried husks that look decades old lying in the burning sun. The thing is lightning fast and can easily dodge most attacks due to its small size and extreme nimbleness.

Water drain (Sp): In combat, the duster can use its water drain to devastating effect. If it manages to touch attack a living creature, it instantly drains some of the water from the victim's body. This attack inflicts 1d8 damage and lowers Str, Dex and Con by 2 each (until the victim can drink a quart of water per 6 points lost). Any victim who has all his water drained (has all three Abilities reduced to 0) dies, leaving behind a mummified, shriveled corpse. The attack has no effect on the Harrowed (whom the duster leaves alone because they have no useful water in their bodies anyway).

The duster can absorb up to five quarts of water per hour through the air. This includes water in closed containers within one foot. The critter doesn't get any bigger; the water just seems to be evaporating at a phenomenal rate.

Dowsing (Su): The duster can detect any water within 1 mile and quickly attempts to make contact with any detected source.

Camouflage (Ex): Dusters match exactly the dune-colored sand they inhabit. When still, they have a +8 to Hide skill checks, but this drops to +2 if they are in motion. The thing seems to kick up a little bit of dust wherever it goes, even in seemingly spotless places.

Water vulnerability (Su): Strangely, these critters are extremely vulnerable to the actual touch of water and avoid contact at all costs. More than one duster has been killed by being caught in a freak storm or by the attempts of a new human "friend" trying to give the "dirty little bunny" a bath.

If water touches any part of a duster except its cute little nose, it burns the critter and raises a horrible stink. Any water splashed on it inflicts 1d4 damage per ounce of water. Total immersion, though unlikely, kills a duster in two rounds, though it raises a tremendous cloud of stinking steam as the duster tries to absorb the water before it fries. Anyone breathing this foul steam must make a Fortitude save DC (15) or become stunned for one full round.

El Diablo Negro

Large Magical Beast
Hit Dice: 11d10+4 (104 hp)
Initiative: +3 (Dex)
Speed: 100 ft.
AC: 17 (-1 size, +3 Dex, +5 natural)
Attacks: 2 hooves +18 melee, bite +16 melee
Damage: Hoof 2d6+8, bite 1d4+4
Face/Reach: 5 ft. by 10 ft./5 ft.
Special Attacks: Fear, armor-piercing hooves
Special Qualities: Damage reduction 5/-, keen senses, coup
Saves: Fort +11, Ref +10, Will +4
Abilities: Str 26, Dex 17, Con 18, Int 10, Wis 12, Cha 12
Skills: Intimidate +7, Intuit Direction +6, Listen +8*, Move Silently +6, Spot +8*, Swim +8, Wilderness Lore +6
Feats: Dodge, Multiattack, Track
Climate/Terrain: Any land
Challenge Rating: 10
Alignment: Always neutral evil
Advancement: 12-33 HD (Large)

El Diablo Negro appears as a large, black horse the size of the largest Clydesdale. His eyes gleam with a faint red light in twilight or darker. His mouth is more like that of a wolf, stretching the length of his jaw and filled with large canine fangs. His hooves are as hard as iron and as sharp as axe blades.

According to legend, El Diablo Negro is a huge, coal-black, carnivorous horse. His territory is said to run from the Sioux Nations deep into Mexico, but he's usually reported in the western Confederacy or northern Mexico.

The legends are true about one thing—El Diablo Negro is a carnivore. Anything that moves is fair game for this abomination, but he favors horse meat and human flesh to all others.

El Diablo Negro isn't truly a horse, any more than los diablos are Texas longhorns. He's one of the more powerful servants of the Reckoners, a monster wearing the shape of a horse. Like los diablos, El Diablo Negro occasionally hunts down heroes who've been too successful in battling the minions of the Reckoners. When he does so, he is *always* accompanied by El Diablo Rojo.

Combat

This fearmonger often attacks outlying homes or small ranches, killing and devouring everything he can sink his teeth into. Though he lacks subtlety, El Diablo Negro more than makes up for that in raw supernatural power.

Fear (Sp): When El Diablo Negro lets loose his shrieking whinny, all normal animals automatically fail their saving throws (Humans roll their saving throws as normal, against DC 19). For most, this means the creatures flee at maximum pace in the opposite direction. However, he can paralyze horses with fright. El Diablo Negro can only do this once per round

Armor-piercing hooves (Su): EL Diablo Negro receive a +5 on to-hit rolls against targets with armor (natural or otherwise) when attacking with his hooves.

Keen senses (Su): El Diablo Negro's Spot and Listen skill checks to avoid surprise are always DC 10 or less. He gains a +2 to all Spot and Listen skill check rolls to find humans.

Coup: Any horse ridden by the Harrowed gains a Speed of 100. However, it also picks up a taste for meat—fresh or otherwise!

El Diablo Rojo

Medium-Size Fey
Hit Dice: 9d6+1 (40 hp)
Initiative: +1 (Dex)
Speed: 30 ft.
AC: 13 (+1 Dex, +2 worn armor)
Attacks: Winchester '76 +7 ranged; or stone tomahawk +6 melee; or knife +6 melee
Damage: Winchester '76 2d8+1, stone tomahawk 1d6, knife 1d4+1
Face/Reach: 5 ft. by 5 ft./5 ft.
Special Attacks: Spells
Special Qualities: Pact
Saves: Fort +7, Ref +4, Will +5
Abilities: Str 10, Dex 13, Con 12, Int 12, Wis 12, Cha 12
Skills: Black Magic +6, Concentration +6, Craft +6, Hide +6, Intimidate +6, Knowledge (arcana, Indian lore) +6, Listen +6, Move Silently +6, Ride +6, Spot +6, Wilderness Lore +6
Feats: Armor Proficiency (light), Maximize Spell, Quicken Spell, Track
Climate/Terrain: Any land
Challenge Rating: 4
Alignment: Always neutral evil
Advancement: None

El Diablo Rojo is a darkly-tanned and aging Apache with long white hair. His contempt for all humanity is obvious in the permanent scowl on his wrinkled face. He wears only knee-high moccasins, a tan loincloth, headband and a set of laced-bone chest armor. He is always armed with a number of weapons and often keeps a string of scalps on his belt.

The man now known as El Diablo Rojo was once a powerful Apache shaman in northern Mexico. After his entire tribe was hunted down and killed by Mexican soldiers, he forswore his humanity and sought the power for vengeance. The Reckoners were all too glad to oblige.

He is now a powerful black magician who stalks the mountains of northern Mexico and the western Confederacy. Recently, he somehow forged a bond with the monster El Diablo Negro and the two are now among the favorite "troubleshooters" of the Reckoners. Heroes that have survived an encounter with los diablos may be paid a visit by this pair if they continue in their do-gooding ways.

Although El Diablo Rojo despises Mexicans and kills them on sight, no human is safe from attack. Worse yet, he's picked up some of his monstrous companion's bad habits, taking up cannibalism in addition to his other practices. Fortunately for normal folks in the area, the two are so tied to the Reckoners' whim that they have little time anymore for simple slaughter and depredation.

Time and circumstances permitting, El Diablo Rojo likes to have some fun terrorizing his victims. He often goes after a target's friends, family and business before getting down to actually killing him.

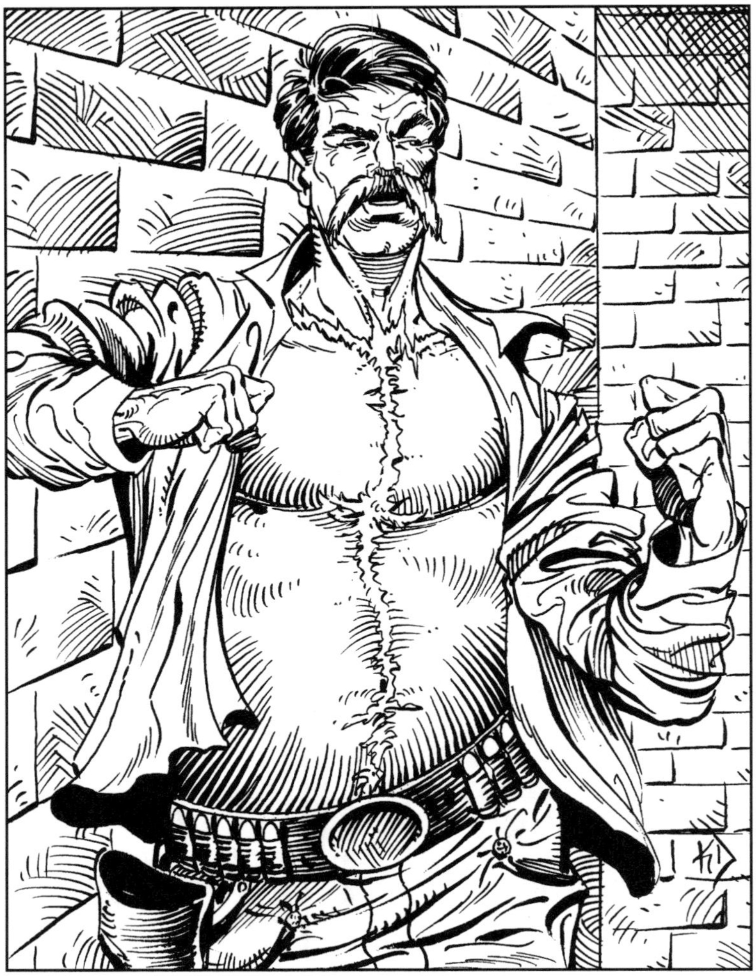

Combat

When he has a clear advantage over his opponents, El Diablo Rojo presses it ruthlessly, striking down helpless foes without mercy. Through his sorceries, El Diablo Rojo is able to communicate with the devil horse. The abomination even allows the Apache to ride him when necessary. This comes in handy when the two are overmatched. Both are more than willing to flee and strike again later from ambush.

Spells (Sp): Commensurate with his Hit Dice level, El Diablo Rojo has access to a wide range of black magic.

Pact (Su): El Diablo Rojo can communicate with El Diablo Negro on a telepathic level. Each of them *always* knows what the other is doing.

Flesh Jacket

Small Undead
Hit Dice: 3d12 (19 hp)
Initiative: +0
Speed: 5 ft., 5 ft. climb
AC: 11 (+1 size)
Attacks: Grapple -1 melee
Damage: 1d3-2 (s) plus compulsion
Face/Reach: 5 ft. by 5 ft./5 ft.
Special Attacks: Improved grab, compulsion
Special Qualities: Damage allocation, wall-crawling, blindsight, undead, fearless
Saves: Fort +1, Ref +1, Will +3
Abilities: Str 5, Dex 10, Con –, Int 9, Wis 9, Cha 5
Skills: Same as the host's; Climb +6, Escape Artist +6, Hide +6, Listen +6, Move Silently +6, Spot +6, Tumble +5 without host
Feats: Blind-Sight
Climate/Terrain: Any land
Challenge Rating: 5
Alignment: Always chaotic evil
Advancement: 4-9 HD (Small)

Without a host, the flesh jacket is a slithering mass of human skin. The skin appears largely intact, save for the slit up the middle of the back and the absence of all flesh above the neckline. When attached to a victim, others have a hard time noticing the thing's presence as long as the host wears heavy clothing and conceals the obvious existence of the flesh jacket (notably at the neck and chest). However, shaking hands with a controlled body might reveal the very loose skin.

Flesh jackets are fashioned by certain very powerful, very evil cults around the world. To create one, a black magician with the proper knowledge removes the skin from a willing cultist, and imbues the shorn hide with a weird sort of life. The spell also gives the flesh jacket limited mobility, and it can attempt to assume control of any victim it can envelop.

Once in control, the flesh jacket gains sustenance by invading the host's digestive organs with gory tendrils that allow it to consume the nourishment therein. Thereafter, for the host body to stay alive, it must consume enough to sate the flesh jacket while still supporting itself. This means the host of a flesh jacket becomes a voracious eater, consuming surprising amounts of food. If a host does not eat enough, the flesh jacket begins to devour the body.

While the flesh jacket can keep a corpse moving as long as the jacket is still healthy, the creature attempts to find a new host as soon as possible. Hauling around a carcass is no easy task, after all.

It is possible, but difficult to kill just the flesh jacket and free the host. It's recommended to subdue the host first before this is attempted. Otherwise the consequences can be unfortunate.

Combat

While without a host, a flesh jacket is quite vulnerable and very sluggish, with limited abilities. It waits until a victim is asleep, unconscious, or too injured to attack. They prefer to drop onto victims from above, using their wall-crawling ability.

Improved grab (Ex): Flesh jackets can grab Medium-Size targets or smaller, and without the use of a weapon.

Compulsion (Su): A flesh jacket who successfully grapples a host body forces the victim to make a Will saving throw against DC 17. If the victim fails, the flesh jacket gains complete control of the host, who can still comprehend what is going on with their body. The flesh jacket has access to all the host's memories and skills. For Int, Wis and Cha, the abomination can use its own score or the host's, whichever is higher. The Str, Dex and Con of the victim are increased by +2 each, as the flesh jacket lends the host strength for their mutual survival.

Wall-crawling (Su): Host-less flesh jackets can crawl along ceilings and walls at its full normal Speed.

Damage allocation (Ex): When a hit is scored on a flesh jacket with a host, roll 1d6. If the result is odd, all damage goes to the host. Otherwise, damage is divided between the host and the flesh jacket. Only one quarter of the damage (round down) from Piercing damage (such as stabs and bullets) applies to the flesh jacket, with the rest going to the host. Against Slashing and Bludgeoning attacks, as well as arcane assaults, the flesh jacket sustains one half damage (round down), with the rest going to the host. Fire damage is divided as well, with one quarter (round down) going to the host, and the rest to the flesh jacket.

Undead (Su): For a flesh jacket to be slain, it must be completely destroyed, such as by fire or acid.

Dr. Victor Frankenstein

Medium-Size Humanoid
Hit Dice: 10d6 (35 hp)
Initiative: +0
Speed: 20 ft.
AC: 10
Attacks: Punch +5 melee; or by weapon type +5
Damage: Punch 1d3 (s), by weapon type
Face/Reach: 5 ft. by 5 ft./5 ft.
Special Qualities: Mad scientist
Saves: Fort +3, Ref +3, Will +8
Abilities: Str 10, Dex 10, Con 11, Int 15, Wis 13, Cha 12
Skills: Alchemy +8, Appraise +8, Climb +6, Diplomacy +7, Heal +10, Hide +6, Knowledge (arcana) +8, Knowledge (chemistry, anthropology, biology) +11, Listen 7, Mad Science +11, Move Silently +6, Ride +6, Speak Language (French, German, English, Latin), Spot +7, Swim +6
Feats: Skill Focus (Heal, Mad Science, chemistry, anthropology, biology)
Climate/Terrain: Any land
Challenge Rating: 3
Alignment: Chaotic neutral
Advancement: As mad scientist character class

Doctor Frankenstein is a brown-haired man in early middle age. He is handsome, but not extraordinarily so, and he dresses in the most current fashions. However, when consumed by his quest (which is nearly always), his hair may be unkempt and his eyes show an almost irrational and fanatical gleam.

Victor is a Swiss-born mad scientist specializing in the study of life and death. He's one of the few researchers to successfully bring a corpse back to life, although, as most everyone nowadays knows, not with the results he'd hoped for. Using parts purloined from local graveyards, Victor fulfilled his scientific dream. He created a man and gave his creation life.

But something went wrong. Rather than the perfect specimen he had aimed for, his creation was twisted and freakish, a parody of humanity. When Victor refused to create a companion for the monster to share its existence with, it killed his bride, Elizabeth, on their wedding night. Since that time, the two—man and monster—have hunted each other across several continents—including North America.

Combat

Although Victor is a mad scientist, his creations are limited to experiment on the nature of life and death. Victor's desire to destroy the monster overrides any other consideration for him, and other people are merely tools in this pursuit. Therefore, he uses any means at his disposal to achieve his ends.

Frankenstein's Monster

Medium-Size Undead
Hit Dice: 11d12 (71 hp)
Initiative: +0
Speed: 20 ft.
AC: 10
Attacks: Punch +13 melee; or by melee weapon type +13
Damage: Punch 1d3+8 (s), or by melee weapon type +8
Face/Reach: 5 ft. by 5 ft./5 ft.
Special Attacks: Improved grab, constrict 1d3+8, berserk
Special Qualities: Rowdy, bond, pyrophobia, undead, coup
Saves: Fort +7, Ref +3, Will +5
Abilities: Str 27 Dex 9, Con —, Int 9, Wis 11, Cha 10
Skills: Climb +8, Hide +8, Intimidate +8, Listen +8, Move Silently +7, Spot +8, Swim +8, Wilderness Lore +8
Feats: Cleave, Endurance, Power Attack, Track
Climate/Terrain: Any land
Challenge Rating: 9
Alignment: Chaotic neutral
Advancement: As rowdy character class

Frankenstein chose the "best" parts for his creation, hoping to build a beautiful artificial specimen. Unfortunately, the sum of the parts turned out to be greater than the whole. Stitching scars mar much of the creature's body. Its eyes are glazed and yellowish, while its skin has a pasty pallor. Once beautiful features are contorted into a rictus of death by faulty facial muscles.

The monster itself is an odd amalgam of mad science and undeath. Although Victor's experiments brought the creature to life, it is sustained by an unholy tie to its maker.

Victor's monster has suffered the prejudices of all humans because of its horrific appearance. Because of that, it holds humanity in general in contempt. However, the creature holds an all-consuming hatred for its creator—the one who saddled its unwanted second life upon it.

The creature is not an unthinking evil brute contrary to some depictions, and can both read and write. After reading Milton's *Paradise Lost*, the monster has begun to liken itself to a modern-day Adam with Frankenstein as its unloving creator.

Combat

Adam uses his tremendous strength foremost in a fight, and can quickly strangle most foes into submission. If he is in control of himself, he chokes opponents unconscious, but his foes are much more likely to have their necks snapped if the Monster has gone berserk.

Improved grab (Ex): Adam can grab any target equal in Size or smaller., and employ this ability to strangle (constrict) victims without the use of a weapon.

Berserk (Ex): If Adam is wounded in a fight he automatically goes berserk. He gets two melee attacks each round, and gains a bonus of +1d3 to his damage rolls for every 16 hit points of damage he has suffered.

Bond (Su): Adam has a supernatural homing sense for Victor, no matter how great a distance separates the two.

Rowdy (Ex): Adam has the Thick Skin and Tough as Nails 2 abilities, as per the rowdy character class.

Pyrophobia (Ex): Fire does no extra damage to him, but Adam is terrified of it and seeks to escape open flame at any cost. If there is no route open for him, he goes berserk as above.

Undead (Su): Focus—Victor Frankenstein; In a doubly ironic twist of fate, as long as Frankenstein lives,

Adam *will* return to hunt him. Should Adam succeed in killing Victor, he dies as well.

Coup: Ending the Monster's existence raises the Harrowed's Str by two. However, it lowers his Int by one.

Gabriel Hound

Medium-Size Magical Beast
Hit Dice: 5d10+3 (42 hp)
Initiative: +1 (Dex)
Speed: 35 ft.
AC: 11 (+1 Dex)
Attacks: Bite +6 melee, 2 claws +1 melee
Damage: Bite 1d6+1, claw 1d3
Face/Reach: 5 ft. by 5 ft./5 ft.
Special Attacks: Curse, fear
Special Qualities: Damage reduction 5/see weaknesses, scent, weaknesses
Saves: Fort +7, Ref +5, Will +3
Abilities: Str 12, Dex 13, Con 16, Int 10, Wis 14, Cha 14
Skills: Climb +5, Hide +5, Intimidate +5, Listen +5, Move Silently +5 Spot +5, Wilderness Lore +5
Feats: Dodge, Track
Climate/Terrain: Any land
Challenge Rating: 6
Alignment: Always neutral evil
Advancement: 6-15 HD (Medium-Size)

Gabriel hounds are large (4' at the shoulder) black dogs, resembling either mastiffs or wolfhounds. Their hair is coal-black and unkempt. A red spark glimmers behind their pupils and a low growl constantly rolls from their throats.

Gabriel hounds (also called gabbe brecht or barghests) are sometimes associated with witches, werewolves, or other shape-changing humans. However, these large, black dogs are most often encountered as the forerunner of a more powerful evil.

The appearance of a Gabriel hound bodes ill for the person to whom it appears. Although others may see it, the first person to catch a glimpse of it is cursed by its power.

Combat

Gabriel hounds seldom attack outright—although it's not unheard of, by any means. Instead, the abominations make a brief, foreshadowing appearance, usually after dark and in a lonely area.

When they do attack, they first use their howl to frighten their victims into helplessness. Then, the hound's vicious bite is put to lethal use.

Curse (Sp): The hound has the ability to curse the first person to catch sight of it. The hero picks up a case of double bad luck—anytime they roll a natural 1, the result is always somehow life threatening. The curse lasts until the hero defeats a fearmonger; even killing the hound does not remove this curse.

Fear (Su): A hound forces any human within 75 feet who can hear its howl to make a Will saving throw against DC 7 to avoid being affected by this Ability

Weaknesses (Su): The hound takes full damage from silver weapons. Holy water does the beast 1d6 damage.

Gaki

Medium-Size Shapechanger
Hit Dice: 6d8+3 (45 hp)
Initiative: +0
Speed: 30 ft.
AC: 10
Attacks: 2 claws +5 melee, bite +3 melee
Damage: Claw 1d4+1, bite 1d3
Face/Reach: 5 ft. by 5 ft./5 ft.
Special Qualities: Fearless, damage reduction 5/see weaknesses, rapid healing, shapechange, weaknesses
Saves: Fort +8, Ref +5, Will +6
Abilities: Str 12, Dex 10, Con 16 Int 9 Wis 13, Cha 11
Skills: Bluff +8, Climb +8, Hide +8, Intimidate +8, Listen +.8, Move Silently +8, Perform (acting) +8, Spot +8, Wilderness Lore +8
Feats: Multiattack, Track
Climate/Terrain: Any land
Challenge Rating: 6
Alignment: Always chaotic evil
Advancement: 7-18 HD (Medium-Size)

In its normal form, a gaki appears like a decaying, emaciated corpse. However, it uses this form only to startle its victims before attacking; due to its shapechange abilities, it usually chooses a normal human appearance. The cat-form resembles a large, black-furred tiger.

A gaki is a powerful abomination, not a form of undead as popular legend suggests. It does, however, have the ability to turn itself into a tiger-like monster or impersonate others. These monsters are sometimes found near isolated graveyards, as they aren't above robbing fresh graves to sate their hunger.

A gaki is most likely to be found either in the Great Maze—especially near Shan Fan or Kwan Province—or plaguing Kang's Iron Dragon rail workers. While most Westerners would no doubt be terrified by a shape-changing flesh-eater, legends of this creature are well-known only among immigrants from the other side of the Pacific.

Combat

The creature may hunt in animal form or use its disguise ability to lure in unsuspecting victims by appearing as an attractive member of the opposite sex. After it has feasted on a victim, it may use their appearance as a lure to capture others, but it has no knowledge of the person's memories or personality. It can only mimic the physical form.

Rapid healing (Su): A gaki heals 3 hit points every 5 minutes.

Shapechange (Su): The gaki can mimic another human's appearance perfectly. It can also become a monstrous cat, as detailed below. The transformations take an entire round to perform.

Weaknesses (Su): A gaki takes full damage from a sword blessed by a Shinto or Buddhist priest. They cannot enter Sanctified ground, regardless of the religion.

Skills: Gakis receive a +4 bonus to all Bluff, Climb, Hide, Intimidate, Listen, Move Silently, Perform (acting), Spot, and Wilderness Lore skill rolls.

Gaki (Cat-Form)

Large Shapechanger
Hit Dice: 12d8+3 (90 hp)
Initiative: +2 (Dex.)
Speed: 65 ft., 30 ft. climb
AC: 11 (-1 size, +2 Dex.)
Attacks: 2 claws +11 melee; bite +9 melee
Damage: Claw 1d8+3, bite 1d6+1
Face/Reach: 5 ft. by 10 ft./5 ft.
Special Qualities: Fearless, damage reduction 25/see weaknesses, rapid healing, shapechange, scent, weaknesses
Saves: Fort +11, Ref +10, Will +9
Abilities: Str 16, Dex 14 Con 16, Int 9 Wis 13, Cha 11
Skills: Climb +15, Intimidate +10, Listen +11, Move Silently +10, Spot +11, Wilderness Lore +11
Feats: Multiattack, Power Attack, Track
Climate/Terrain: Any land
Challenge Rating: 10
Alignment: Always chaotic evil
Advancement: 13-24 HD (Medium-Size)

In this form, the gaki appears as a large, black-furred tiger with long, evil claws, wicked fangs, and a malevolent expression.

Combat

Rapid healing (Su): A gaki heals 3 hit points every 5 minutes.

Shapechange (Su): The gaki can mimic another human's appearance perfectly. The transformation takes an entire round to perform.

Weaknesses (Su): A gaki takes full damage from a sword blessed by a Shinto or Buddhist priest. They cannot enter Sanctified ground, regardless of the religion. Also, gaki in cat-form are vulnerable to sunlight, taking 2d8 damage each round. They can avoid this by shapechanging to humanoid form.

Skills: Gakis receive a +4 bonus to all Climb, Intimidate, Listen, Move Silently, Spot and Wilderness Lore skill rolls.

Ghosts

Haunts, spectres, phantasms, poltergeists—all of these are disembodied souls that haven't moved on to the afterlife and remain to plague the folks of the Weird West. All of these restless spirits fall under the heading of ghosts.

Below, we've listed several types of spirits to populate the old cemeteries and lonely roads of your campaign. These are by no means the only kinds of wraiths out there, but they should get your evil mind turning on haunts of your own.

Some of the more powerful ghosts may grant Coup to a Harrowed when defeated. If so, the character gains the Ghost power.

Common Weaknesses

Ghosts can usually be driven away or destroyed by means of the blessed miracle Exorcize. Consecrate Armament allows a weapon to affect ghosts, and Protection and Sanctify also affect them. Ghosts are considered "evil" for the purposes of these miracles, even if they are not malign.

Most miracles hexes and favors which require a Will Saving Throw work normally on apparitions as well, subject to specific exceptions chosen by the Marshal. On the other hand, Marshal, you may not want some big-britches hex-slinger gunning down your favorite ghost with his hopped-up six-guns. That's absolutely fine—it does kind of spoil the effect of a good haunting if the heroes can just walk up and blast the spirits!

If you choose to make them immune to normal magical damage methods, we've got you covered. There's another way for heroes to cleanse a place of an unwanted haunting, one that requires them to do a little leg—and mind—work. It's called an anchor.

Anchors

All ghosts have an anchor to the world of the living. This may take the form of an item, a place, or even a person. Some ghosts are even anchored to a particular action, such as avenging an act of violence or treachery. Regardless of its nature, the anchor is something that was of great importance to the apparition during life; a bit of diligent research should point a posse of ghost hunters toward a spirit's anchor.

While the anchor keeps the ghost on Earth, it is also the spirit's Achilles heel. A clever group of heroes can use the anchor to draw the ghost to them, or even, in some cases, vanquish the spirit from the Earth.

Each type of spirit is anchored in a different way; some, like haunts, vary from individual spirit to individual spirit. In the descriptions for each sort of ghost on the following pages, we've detailed what sorts of things anchor them and how the posse might use that to their benefit. Regardless of the type of apparition or what it's tied to, no spirit may ever travel or manifest more than 1 mile from its anchor.

Manifestation

In each ghost's description, we've detailed how the spirit appears when it allows itself to be seen by the living (or un-living). This is called its manifestation.

However, this description is for when the spirit makes itself fully visible. Ghosts have a great deal of freedom in how much of themselves they reveal. A wraith may choose to appear as a faint, diffuse light, a wispy outline, or even just the sensation of a presence. A good idea is to save the full manifestation for a high point in the session, or maybe even the climax.

The only limitation on a spirit's appearance is that it cannot appear as someone (or something) else. Ghosts are *not* masters of disguise!

Banshee

Medium-Size Undead (Incorporeal)
Hit Dice: 5d12 (32 hp)
Initiative: +4 (Improved Initiative)
Speed: 20 ft.
AC: 11 (+1 deflection)
Attacks: None
Damage: None
Face/Reach: 5 ft. by 5 ft./5 ft.
Special Attacks: Fear, shriek, death attack
Special Qualities: Incorporeality, sunlight vulnerability
Saves: Fort +1, Ref +1, Will +5
Abilities: Str –, Dex 10, Con –, Int 9, Wis 12, Cha 13
Skills: Hide +7, Intimidate +8, Listen +8, Move Silently +7, Spot +8
Feats: Blind-Fight, Improved Initiative
Climate/Terrain: Any land
Challenge Rating: 5
Alignment: Always chaotic evil
Advancement: 6-15 HD (Medium-Size)

Banshees appear as spectral forms that float a foot or so above the ground. Their lower extremities are nothing but tatters of fabric and most banshees are clothed in a gray or greenish-gray robe. A banshee's decayed face is contorted as if in horrible agony.

Banshees are the restless spirits of folks who died as a result of non-requited love. Often, they committed suicide after realizing their heart's desire was denied them. Occasionally, the banshee was actually murdered by the object of its affection. In either case, the banshee's death occurred in a remote spot and the body was unburied.

Legend depicts banshees as exclusively female, but there's nothing to prevent the ghost of a jilted man from becoming a banshee in the Weird West.

As a result of their failed love lives, banshees have a very distorted view on the world of the living. Banshees perceive beings of the opposite sex as their former—and now hated—love, while those of the same sex are rivals for affection. These spirits pretty much despise anybody!

A banshee's anchor is its former body. Providing the body with a proper burial, according to its religious beliefs, severs the link and destroys the banshee. On a subconscious level, the ghost is aware of the importance of its body and takes steps to prevent its discovery. Although the body remains near the site of its death, the body is usually hidden or camouflaged in some way. A banshee *always* manifests to protect its body from those who disturb it—even in daylight.

Combat

Banshees use their shriek and wail abilities to drive away interlopers, and will pronounce doom on an unfortunate victim as they flee.

Fear (Su): Anyone catching sight of a materialized banshee must make a Will saving throw against DC 19.

Shriek (Sp): A banshee can inflict damage by the bloodcurdling sound of its voice. All cowpokes within 30 feet of the banshee must make a Will saving throw against DC 19 when it shrieks, and those who fail suffer 1d6 damage. This takes two rounds to perform, and the banshee can shriek as often as it desires.

Death attack (Sp): Once per night, a banshee can cut loose with an truly unearthly wail that chills most folks to the bone. Any cowpokes unlucky enough to be within 30 feet of her when she does must make a Fortitude saving throw against DC 19, adding their Level. Success means they shake off the effects of the wail. If any unlucky stiff fails this roll, they suffer a heart attack and die.

Incorporeality (Su): Only hexes and enchanted (or Consecrated) weapons can hurt them. Exorcism is effective when cast on either the banshee itself or its body.

Sunlight vulnerability (Su): A banshee suffers 2d6 damage each round if it, or its anchor (i.e. its corpse) is exposed to direct sunlight.

Haunt

Medium-Size Undead (Incorporeal)
Hit Dice: 5d12 (32 hp)
Initiative: +4 (Improved Initiative)
Speed: 20 ft.
AC: 11 (+1 deflection)
Attacks: Touch +2 melee
Damage: Touch 1d8
Face/Reach: 5 ft. by 5 ft./5 ft.
Special Attacks: Fear, chill touch
Special Qualities: Incorporeality
Saves: Fort +1, Ref +1, Will +4
Abilities: Str –, Dex 10, Con –, Int 9, Wis 11, Cha 11
Skills: Hide +7, Intimidate +7, Listen +7, Move Silently +7, Spot +7
Feats: Blind-Fight, Improved Initiative
Climate/Terrain: Any land
Challenge Rating: 5
Alignment: Often chaotic neutral
Advancement: 6-15 HD (Medium-Size)

The appearances of individual haunts varies. Some are clearly ephemeral beings—you can see right through their ghostly forms. Others appear to be made of true flesh and blood, but bear horrible wounds or ghastly pale skin that reveals their true state. A chill always accompanies a haunt.

Haunts are the most common form of ghost. They are created when a person died while experiencing an extreme—usually unpleasant—emotion and is doomed to relive it or inflict it on others. The most common motivator for a haunt is revenge for a violent or treacherous death.

Unfortunately, although many haunts are not evil in intent, their undead state skews their perceptions, causing them to terrorize or even attack otherwise innocent folks.

Usually, a haunt is anchored to a specific place (most often that of its untimely demise). In a few rare instances, a haunt may be anchored to a vehicle, like a train or ship, where its death occurred; these "mobile" haunts can be cleansed in the same fashion as noted above for their more stationary brethren.

Combat

A haunt attacks anyone intruding in the place to which it is anchored, using its chill touch and fear attack to terrify its victims as much as possible before it can beat a hasty retreat.

Chill touch (Sp): Haunts can "touch" corporeal beings and inflict damage by chilling them. A successful melee attack does 1d8 hit points to the target.

Fear (Su): A haunt can inflict fear upon any human within 10 feet, which the victim must make a Will saving throw against DC 19 to resist.

Incorporeality (Su): Haunts are intangible, able to pass through walls, sink into the ground, and move their ghostly hands through an hombre's chest. Haunts cannot be harmed by physical weapons, unless the weapons are made of silver. Hexes and enchanted/Consecrated weapons can also hurt them, and exorcizing the area cleanses such spirits

Phantom

These are the least powerful (and therefore, the least dangerous) of all the ghosts haunting the lonely places of the Weird West. Phantoms—also called spooks, wraiths and phantasms—are merely spirits who've yet to realize their time has come. They remain tied to the site of their death until someone releases them from the limbo of undeath they are trapped in.

Phantoms are little more than supernatural "recordings" of the last moments of their former lives. The apparitions nearly always appear as virtually transparent images of their former selves prior to death. They often react to other unseen people or things as they play out their death scenes again and again.

A phantom's anchor is the site of its death. Exorcize cast successfully on the location dispels the spirit. Another method is for a hero to convince the phantom it's dead and should move on. That's no easy task—he must make a Diplomacy skill check against DC 21. Other forms of attack, magical or physical, do not affect phantoms.

These apparitions do not pose a threat to living beings other than a good scare. Anyone seeing a phantom "reliving" its death must make a Will saving throw against DC 17 or be affected by the Fear Special Ability. Other than that, phantoms do not interact with the corporeal world.

Phantoms are more an event than an abomination, an afterimage of a person's life rather than a free-willed undead. For that reason, we haven't provided any game statistics for them.

They are usually found in areas with a Fear Level of 4 or higher, and may be connected (often by death) with another, far more dangerous, abomination.

Poltergeist

Medium-Size Undead (Incorporeal)
Hit Dice: 3d12 (19 hp)
Initiative: +4 (Improved Initiative)
Speed: 20 ft.
AC: 11 (+1 deflection)
Attacks: Physical manipulation +1, melee or ranged
Damage: Physical manipulation 1d3, or by weapon type
Face/Reach: 5 ft. by 5 ft./5 ft.
Special Attacks: Physical manipulation, fear
Special Qualities: Incorporeality, spiritual anchor
Saves: Fort +1, Ref +1, Will +3
Abilities: Str –, Dex 11, Con –, Int 10, Wis 10, Cha 11
Skills: As in life, plus Hide +4, Intimidate +5, Listen +5, Move Silently +5, Open Lock +5, Pick Pocket +5, Spot +5
Feats: Improved Initiative
Climate/Terrain: Any land
Challenge Rating: 4
Alignment: Always chaotic evil
Advancement: 4-9 HD (Medium-Size)

Poltergeists seldom manifest visually, even when interacting with the physical world. When they do appear, they usually choose forms that are only vaguely humanoid in appearance—the more ridiculously monstrous the form, the better. They often choose to chill the air noticeably when present.

Poltergeists are often thought of as pesky, if somewhat spooky, pranksters. Like simple phantasms, poltergeists result from a soul's refusal to accept the death of its corporeal body. However, poltergeists are fully aware they're undead—they're just mean-spirited about it!

A poltergeist invariably chooses a victim for its supernatural temper tantrums, usually a child or adolescent. These apparitions are apparently jealous of the young one's life and vitality, and seek to make the target as miserable as possible.

The poltergeist's chosen victim is the spirit's anchor. There's seldom any readily apparent rhyme or reason as to the apparition's choice of target, but a little investigation usually reveals a tenuous link of some sort.

Combat

These spirits are able to interact with physical objects and use this ability to confound their victim. They may perform acts of vandalism or theft so that their target takes the blame, or they may rely on more straightforward scare tactics. Usually, the apparitions employ a mix of these, escalating from simple pranks to outright ghostly terrorism.

Physical Manipulation (Su): Poltergeists are fond of moving furniture, stealing valuables, locking/unlocking doors, and the like, often making their victim appear responsible. More malicious poltergeists even make subtle attacks this way, "knocking" poisons into foods, tripping victims on stairs or even smothering them with pillows.

A poltergeist can also fling small loose objects—books, glasses, rocks, etc.—with relative ease. It can hurl one of these objects per round for 1d3 damage with a Range Increment of 5 ft. Some truly powerful poltergeists can even manipulate weapons well enough to attack normally with them.

Once per day, a poltergeist can cause a storm of small objects or weapons to fly about, injuring and terrifying its targets. For three rounds, the poltergeist can make up to five projectile attacks per round.

Fear (Ex): Anyone taking damage from a poltergeist's attacks must make a Will save DC (10) or be affected by this ability. A poltergeist can also employ this ability if it manifests itself, and in that situation the DC is 19.

Incorporeality (Su): Poltergeists are intangible, able to move freely through corporeal objects. Poltergeists are immune to physical weapons, including those made of silver. Hexes and enchanted or Consecrated weapons can hurt them.

Spiritual anchor (Su): Exorcism has no effect on the poltergeist if cast on its anchor, but does work if used against the spirit itself. A hero who makes a Bluff, Intimidate, Diplomacy or Ridicule skill check against DC 25 forces the poltergeist to abandon its anchor (thus destroying it). A hero can make only one such attempt—ever.

Shade

Medium-Size Undead (Incorporeal)
Hit Dice: 5d12 (32 hp)
Initiative: +4 (Improved Initiative)
Speed: 20 ft.
AC: 11 (+1 deflection)
Attacks: 2 touches +2 melee
Damage: Touch 1d8
Face/Reach: 5 ft. by 5 ft./5 ft.
Special Attacks: Fear, freezing touch
Special Qualities: Incorporeality, spiritual anchor
Saves: Fort +1, Ref +1, Will +5
Abilities: Str –, Dex 10, Con –, Int 9, Wis 13, Cha 13
Skills: As in life, plus Hide +7, Intimidate +8, Listen +8, Move Silently +7, Spot +8
Feats: Blind-Fight, Improved Initiative
Climate/Terrain: Any land
Challenge Rating: 5
Alignment: Often chaotic neutral
Advancement: 6-15 HD (Medium-Size)

A shade's visual manifestation appears much like its murdered corporeal body, complete with wounds. The shade's appearance shows the effect of gradual decay, appearing to slowly rot as time advances. A noticeable cold accompanies any manifestation, and some spirits of this sort are accompanied by a faint odor of decay.

A shades is an apparition that maintains some tie to a living person—or group of people—responsible for the shade's death. Of all the types of apparitions, a shade is the most able to interact with the physical world, yet the spirit is prevented from acting on the one thing it most desires: revenge.

The apparition's anchor is the person or group to whom the shade is linked. The shade always manifests within one mile of the anchor (or one of the anchors, in the case of a group), no matter how far or fast the person has traveled since the spirit's last visit.

Combat

As a part of the spirit's curse, it is unable to directly affect the person responsible for its condition; it can manifest to its target—and even attack other humans—but it can *never* take direct action for or against its target. Shades can manipulate inanimate objects to hinder or even harm their targets or influence others to do so for them. They can even aid those opposed to there target (if the spirit is benevolent).

Fear (Su): Anyone catching sight of a manifested shade must make a Will saving throw against DC 19.

Freezing touch (Sp): Similar to some ghosts, shades can "touch" corporeal beings and inflict damage. However, the shade's touch is much more potent. Treat the attack as a normal melee attack, except the target gets no benefit from normal armor. A successful attack does 1d8 damage to the target. Magical protections are effective against this attack.

Incorporeality (Su): Shades, like all apparitions are intangible, and interact with the physical world only when they choose to do so. They cannot be harmed by physical weapons, even silver ones. Hexes and enchanted/ Consecrated weapons can hurt them. The same curse that prevents the shade from harming its anchor also prevents that person (or persons) from affecting it in any way. Even hexes, miracles, and the like are ineffective when wielded by the target of the spirit's wrath.

Bad Dreams (Su): Although it can't directly affect its anchor, a shade does plague the person, turning her life into a living Hell. A shade inflicts bad luck on its anchor until it is dispelled or satisfied, and anytime the target rolls a natural 1, the result is somehow life threatening.

Spiritual anchor (Su): Unlike most apparitions, bringing the guilty party (or parties) to justice is the only way to release a malevolent shade from its revenge. This isn't necessarily as easy as it sounds; the villain must be publicly proven guilty of the shade's death, not merely gunned down like a back-shooting bushwhacker!

Spectre

Medium-Size Undead (Incorporeal)
Hit Dice: 5d12 (32 hp)
Initiative: +5 (Dex, Improved Initiative)
Speed: 30 ft.
AC: 12 (+1 Dex, +1 deflection)
Attacks: 2 claws +3 melee
Damage: Claw 1d6+1
Face/Reach: 5 ft. by 5 ft./5 ft.
Special Attacks: Fear, incorporeal claws
Special Qualities: Spiritual anchor, incorporeality
Saves: Fort +1, Ref +2, Will +4
Abilities: Str –, Dex 12, Con –, Int 9, Wis 11, Cha 11
Skills: As in life, plus Hide +8, Intimidate +7, Listen +7, Move Silently +8, Spot +7
Feats: Blind-Fight, Improved Initiative
Climate/Terrain: Any land
Challenge Rating: 5
Alignment: Always chaotic evil
Advancement: 6-15 HD (Medium-Size)

These apparitions nearly always choose a frightening form in which to manifest. A black-hooded figure with skeletal hands or a pale-skinned corpse with glowing red eyes, long claws and pointed teeth are good examples of spectres' forms.

Most apparitions are linked to the material world by the nature or cause of their death—not so spectres. These abominations are the black hats of the ghostly dimension. Spectres are the spirits of particularly evil people who've been cursed to continue their existence in a state of undeath. The Reckoners aren't about to let a little thing like death cut short a good (if unwitting) servant's service.

Combat

Unlike most ghosts, spectres are driven by their hatred of all living humans and actively seek to cause harm to them. To that end, spectres have a limited ability to inflict physical damage on their victims—while remaining untouchable themselves! This is, of course, is their preferred battle tactic.

Incorporeal claws (Sp): A spectre can lash a victim with its claws, inflicting physical damage by damaging the victim's spirit! Once per round, the spectre can target a victim, forcing them to make a Will saving throw against DC 15. If the victim fails, the spectre's claws inflict 1d6+1 damage. Regular armor does *not* protect against this, although magical protections work normally.

Fear (Sp): A spectre can inflict fear on any human within 10 feet, and any such victim must make a Will saving throw against DC 19 to resist it.

Incorporeality (Su): Spectres are immune to physical weapons or attacks, unless the weapons are enchanted, Consecrated or silver. Damaging hexes, spells, favors, and miracles can hurt them (the spell caster must be able to see the spirit to target it, however).

Spiritual anchor (Su): Spectres are anchored to their former bodies. In addition to the weaknesses shared by all apparitions, spectres can also be defeated by exhuming their original bodies and burning them to ashes. Using the miracle Exorcize on the corpse has the same effect.

Living House

Colossal Aberration
Hit Dice: 37d8+9 (499 hp)
Initiative: +1 (Dex)
Speed: 0 ft.
AC: 8 (-8 size, +1 Dex, +5 natural)
Attacks: 5 thrown items +20 ranged
Damage: Thrown items 1d3+3 or 1d4+3
Face/Reach: 40 ft. by 40 ft./25 ft.
Special Attacks: Memory fog, climate control, thrown items
Special Qualities: Dominion, damage reduction 20
Saves: Fort +20, Ref +12, Will +24
Abilities: Str 16, Dex 12, Con 28, Int 13, Wis 15, Cha 16
Skills: Holdout +7, Intimidate +9, Listen +8, Perform (haunting) +9, Sense Motive +8, Spot +8
Feats: Point Blank Shot, Precise Shot
Climate/Terrain: Any land
Challenge Rating: 34
Alignment: Always chaotic evil
Advancement: 38-74 HD (Colossal)

Living houses appear to be large, three-story American Gothic houses. A large turret occupies the right corner of the front of the house, and a covered porch runs from the turret around the left. The paint is always a dreary gray and the shingles match it nearly exactly. A sense of brooding malevolence oozes from the edifice, and its windows almost seem like eyes.

Not all haunted houses are home to ghosts. Well, that's not entirely true—not all haunted houses are haunted...wait, let's try that again. Not all haunted houses are even *houses*!

There exists a strange type of abomination currently unknown to even the Rangers or Agency we like to call a "living house." This abomination is actually a living entity that resembles a house in all respects—it even has furniture, carpet, books, you name it. But the truth is, it's actually an enormous servant of the Reckoners.

Once a family takes up residence within, the house begins to produce effects that resemble those of a haunting.

The result is the same as that of a haunted house: the local Fear Level raises by one. Worse, the usual methods to cleanse a haunted house have no effect. The living house often gives investigators false clues and red herrings to distract them from its nature. It even secrets bodies away in hidden rooms, leading ghost hunters to believe the corpse is a spiritual anchor.

There are a couple of clues that all is not as it seems with a living house. First, while the house has a limited psychic ability to alter nearby folks' memories, no official records exist of its building or purchase. Furthermore, all living houses look exactly alike on the exterior—a posse may even recall having seen an identical "haunted house" elsewhere. Finally, the house has very little ability to alter the surrounding landscape, so yards, walkways and the like don't exist unless later occupants build them.

Because of these limitations, living houses are most often found on the distant outskirts of cities. There, enough folks are around to affect with false memories, yet record keeping is spotty at best. Since the houses literally spring up overnight, they also choose sites somewhat off the beaten path to avoid attracting attention.

Denver, Salt Lake City, and Shan Fan are known sites of living houses in the west. Back East, nearly every major city has been host to one at some time or another. Cities that have been ravaged by the fighting of the Civil War are especially prone to these entities.

Combat

The house has near complete control of its internal areas, able to modify humidity and temperature by as much as 20 degrees. It can move furnishings about at and even alter its inner structure at will, creating dead-end rooms, false doors, and so on to foil investigators—or even trap them to starve.

Thrown items (Su): The house can throw its own furnishings at heroes. Furniture does 1d3+3 damage, while knives, broken glass and other edged missiles do 1d4+3.

Climate control (Su): In addition to controlling temperature and humidity, the house can alter air flows. It can combine these abilities to create wavering heat waves that a cowpoke may mistake for a ghost unless he makes Spot skill check against DC 17. It also uses this control to create "cold spots" to further mislead investigators.

Memory fog (Su): This power affects the minds of neighbors. Every one within 5 miles of the house has vague "memories" of the house "always being there." These memories may even go so far as to recall former occupants, etc.

Dominion (Su): The house has complete control over doors, windows, furniture, and even the books that are a part of its interior. *Nothing* happens to these items that the house does not allow. However, only attacks against the structure of the house itself actually damage the thing. Breaking up the furniture and bric-a-brac simply makes the house mad.

Night Terrors: The house can inflict nightmares on the inhabitants of the house. Anyone subject to this attack must make a Fortitude save DC (15) or take 1d6 subdual damage due to uneasy sleep. This damage can only be healed by an undisturbed night's rest. The house often uses these dreams to give misleading visions of the creature's true nature.

Giants, Appalachian

Large Giant
Hit Dice: 23d8+7 (264 hp)
Initiative: +0
Speed: 55 ft.
AC: 9 (-1 size)
Attacks: Punch +23 melee; or by melee weapon type +23
Damage: Punch 1d3+7 (s), by melee weapon type
Face/Reach: 5 ft. by 10 ft./5 ft.
Special Qualities: Extra heads, rowdy
Saves: Fort +22, Ref +7, Will +7
Abilities: Str 24, Dex 11, Con 24, Int 7, Wis 10, Cha 16
Skills: Climb +7, Craft +4, Intimidate +8, Listen +5, Move Silently +5, Spot +5, Wilderness Lore +5
Feats: Cleave, Endurance, Great Cleave, Improved Bull Rush, Power Attack, Sunder
Climate/Terrain: Temperate Mountains
Challenge Rating: 20
Alignment: Always chaotic evil

Advancement: As rowdy character class

A giant looks like, well, a gigantic person. They are usually extremely ugly, and sometimes have multiple heads (as many as four).

Giants live in the very wildest and most remote backwoods of the Appalachians. Getting rid of them when you want to clear the land and farm it, or build a railroad, poses difficulties—they're rather big and strong, after all. Add in ill-tempered and it makes for quite the challenge for a posse.

Combat

Being none too bright, most giants simply try to hit their opponents with a rock or similar blunt item. Absent a weapon, their huge fists are nearly as formidable.

Extra heads (Ex): Increase a giant's Spot and Listen skill checks by +1 for each head after the first.

Rowdy (Ex): Giants have the Thick Skin and Tough as Nails 8 abilities as per the rowdy character class.

Giants of the Deep

Let's talk about some *slightly* more mundane critters. Sometimes the only thing you have to do to make a creature truly terrifying is make it BIG. That's the case with these next few monsters. (Of course, *regular* crocodiles, octopuses, and sharks are bad enough already.)

Although primarily saltwater animals, giant crocodiles can survive just fine in fresh water. These critters can survive even freezing temperatures and can swim *very* long distances. They might be encountered along any coastal area in the Weird West. Crocodiles can produce a loud bellowing roar, unlike alligators.

Giant octopuses are only encountered on the West Coast, especially in the ocean-ward fringes of the Great Maze and along the western coast of Mexico. They tend to lair up in caves and menace the local fisherman and trading vessels.

Giant sharks can be found wherever you want them to be found. After all, who's going to tell a 36' foot shark where to swim?

Giant Crocodile

Huge Beast
Hit Dice: 13d10+3 (110 hp)
Initiative: +1 (Dex)
Speed: 30 ft., 50 ft. swim
AC: 9 (-2 size, +1 Dex)
Attacks: Bite +13 melee, tail slap +13 melee
Damage: Bite 2d6+6, tail slap 1d8+6 (special)
Face/Reach: 10 ft. by 20 ft./10 ft.
Special Attacks: Improved grab, , lockjaw, tail slap
Special Qualities: Damage reduction 10/-
Saves: Fort +11, Ref +9, Will +3
Abilities: Str 22, Dex 13, Con 16, Int 6, Wis 8, Cha 9
Skills: Intimidate +5, Move Silently +5, Spot +5, Swim +14, Wilderness Lore +5
Feats: None
Climate/Terrain: Aquatic
Challenge Rating: 10
Alignment: Always neutral
Advancement: 14-26 HD (Huge), 27-39 HD (Gargantuan)

This is a REALLY big crocodile, up to 30' long in fact, with jaws that can crush small water craft into matchsticks.

Combat

Usually, giant crocodiles bite their victims and lock their jaws, doing damage each round until the victim dies or escapes. The croc often submerges once it has grabbed an enemy. Its tail attack is used literally to guard its backside.

Lockjaw (Ex): Once a croc has a victim in its jaws, it continues to inflict its bite damage to the poor cowpoke each round.

Tail slap (Ex): If the crocodile hits with this attack, the target is knocked off their feet and stunned. The victim must make a Fortitude saving throw against DC 10 to recover. This attack can only be used against victims to the critter's rear.

Giant Octopus

Gargantuan Beast
Hit Dice: 26d10+7 (325 hp)
Initiative: +2 (Dex)
Speed: 40 ft. swim
AC: 8 (-4 size, +2 Dex)
Attacks: 8 tentacles +19 melee, central beak +14 melee
Damage: Tentacle 1d3+4, central beak 2d6+2
Face/Reach: 20 ft. by 20 ft./20 ft.
Special Attacks: Fear, improved grab, constrict 1d3+4, ink jet
Special Qualities: Water jet
Saves: Fort +24, Ref +19, Will +8
Abilities: Str 19, Dex 15, Con 24, Int 5, Wis 9, Cha 8
Skills: Listen +6, Move Silently +5, Spot +6, Swim +12, Wilderness Lore +5
Feats: None
Climate/Terrain: Aquatic
Challenge Rating: 25
Alignment: Always neutral
Advancement: 27-52 HD (Gargantuan), 53-78 HD (Colossal)

Giant octopuses have large, bulbous heads about 10' in diameter and eight, tentacles each up to 20' or more in length. They are most often a mottled brown or gray in color, but are capable of limited chameleon-like color changes. They often feed on beasts that other creatures wouldn't think of tangling with like sharks and killer whales (oh, and unfortunate sailors, of course).

Combat

Giant octopuses grab and squeeze their prey into unconsciousness with their tentacles, but they are limited to one tentacle attack per target unless the victim is at least Large Size. The octopus can also bite with its central beak, but it usually only does so once a victim is incapacitated.

Fear (Ex): Anyone catching sight of this monster must make a Will saving throw against DC 19.

Ink jet (Ex): If seriously threatened, the octopus can spray a cloud of inky fluid into the water to cover its escape. This covers an area nearly 150 feet in diameter and completely obscures all vision. This takes a round to perform.

Water jet (Ex): The octopus can also expel a jet of water, giving it a Speed 105 for 1d4 rounds.

Giant Shark

Huge Beast
Hit Dice: 19d10+6 (218 hp)
Initiative: +1 (Dex)
Speed: 85 ft. swim
AC: 14 (-2 size, +1 Dex, +5 natural)
Attacks: Bite +19 melee
Damage: Bite 2d8+10
Face/Reach: 10 ft. by 20 ft./10 ft.
Special Qualities: Rough hide, damage reduction 5/-
Saves: Fort +17, Ref +12, Will +6
Abilities: Str 25, Dex 12, Con 22, Int 6, Wis 9, Cha 10
Skills: Listen +7, Move Silently +7, Spot +7, Swim +15, Wilderness Lore +7
Feats: None
Climate/Terrain: Aquatic
Challenge Rating: 17
Alignment: Always neutral
Advancement: 20-38 HD (Gargantuan), 39-57 HD (Colossal)

This creature looks like a really big shark (35'+ long) with a really big mouth (6'+ across) filled with a lot of really big teeth (6"+ long). Swimming with them is not advised.

Combat

Sharks this size require a huge amount of vittles, and eat any moving thing they come across. Blood in the water induces a berserk-like state in these beasts, during which they take a bite out of anything in range.

Rough hide (Ex): Any cowpoke who brushes bare skin against a giant shark's rough hide takes 1d3 hit points of damage.

Hangin' Judges

Marshal, you probably remember the hangin' judges we presented in the *Deadlands: The Weird West D20 Rulebook*—at least we hope so, because they're one of our favorite abominations. In that book, we gave you a standard profile to use for all hangin' judges because space prevented us from giving each of one of the abominations his own write-up.

Well, now we've got the space, so here they are. With the added detail, the judges form a cabal of powerful foes worthy of a campaign to defeat!

As you no doubt remember, the hangin' judges started out as five corrupt Confederate judges who hatched a scheme to make a land grab and ruin their enemies along the Chisolm Trail back in the 1860s. The judges' schemes were uncovered and they were each hunted down and lynched by angry mobs of Texans. They rose as horrific abominations, and stalk the Chisolm to this day. That's the gist of how things went, but if you read the individual judge's descriptions carefully, you can get a little more insight into exactly how they hatched their scheme.

You'll notice the judges below are even tougher than the ones detailed in the *Deadlands: The Weird West D20 Rulebook*. Additionally, although the only way to destroy a hangin' judge is still a good old-fashioned lynching, each one has his own special weakness, so a posse that discovers one judge's Achilles' heel doesn't have the inside track on wiping out all of them. A diligent posse that does a *lot* of research into the judges' history should discover clues pointing them at the particular weaknesses of each abomination (the finer points of each one's hanging requirements, for example).

We've also given each one individual powers more in line with the original circuit judge's personalities to further confound posses. Each judge now conveys its own coup power. That way, a Harrowed who takes it upon themselves to cleanse the Chisolm Trail of these monsters doesn't end up with five pairs of the judges' signature revolvers. The weapons of those without coup powers fade away within hours of their defeat. Or, if you've got a trophy-hunting party, Marshal, you might want to let them decay into corroded, useless lumps of metal so the heroes have a souvenir.

If you want to continue to use the judges as described in the *Deadlands: The Weird West D20 Rulebook*, by all means do so, but we've provided you with an alternative so those sets of statistics aren't wasted. The ringleader of the original judge's scheme, Hiram Jackson has the ability to create lesser judges. So those nasty rascals still can come in handy.

Read on to find out more about that. Without further ado, here are the five chief justices of Hell on earth, the hangin' judges.

Hiram Jackson

Medium-Size Undead
Hit Dice: 10d12 (65 hp)
Initiative: +1 (Dex)
Speed: 30 ft.
AC: 11 (+1 Dex)
Attacks: 2 Colt Army revolvers +11 ranged (+9 and +5 when used in tandem); or 2 scythes +13 melee (+11 and +7 when used in tandem)
Damage: Colt Army revolver 2d6, scythe 1d8+3
Face/Reach: 5 ft. by 5 ft./5 ft.
Special Attacks: Fear, recruit
Special Qualities: Damage reduction 25/see weaknesses, fast healing 25, arcane weapons, ringleader, fearless, undead, weaknesses, coup
Saves: Fort +5, Ref +8, Will +6
Abilities: Str 16, Dex 13, Con —, Int 12, Wis 16, Cha 15
Skills: Hide +7, Intimidate +7, Knowledge (Chisolm Trail) +7, Listen +8, Move Silently +7, Ride +7, Sense Motive +8, Spot +8, Use Rope +7, Wilderness Lore +7
Feats: Dead Eye, Exotic Weapon Proficiency (scythes), Point Blank Shot, Track, Two-Weapon Fighting
Climate/Terrain: Warm Hill and Plains
Challenge Rating: 9
Alignment: Neutral evil
Advancement: As gunslinger character class

Jackson dresses in a completely black outfit, including the hood shrouding his features. His ebon clothing distinguishes him from his unholy colleagues.

Jackson was the ringleader for the whole scheme. He was the first to see the potential represented by the Chisolm Trail and lust for a way to get his hands around it. Unfortunately, he lacked the charisma and legal knowledge to accomplish it.

However, what talents he lacked, he made up for with his keen sense of human nature and organizational skills. He simply kept an eye out for readily corruptible peers with the abilities he needed. Jackson soon found just the right mix to pull off his scheme: Cyrus Call for popular support, Luther Kirby for legal knowhow, Moses Moore for respectability, and Marcus Lafayette for brute force.

Combat

Jackson was the true power behind the original plan, although no one realized it until the very end. As a hangin' judge, he is the most cautious and scheming—in many ways the most dangerous, even though he lacks some of the formidable powers available to the other abominations. Jackson holds law-abiding folk in particular contempt. Being an honest lawmen (Marshal's call on this one) is always a hanging offense in his "court."

Fear (Su): Anyone catching sight of Jackson must make a Will saving throw against DC 19.

Arcane weapons (Su): Jackson's revolvers reload themselves 1 round after they're empty.

Recruit (Su): Once a month, Jackson can create a lesser hangin' judge if he gets his hands on a dishonest (Marshal's call) attorney, judge or lawman. This takes a night—and a hanging—to accomplish, but not consent.

Ringleader (Su): Jackson can summon any of the other hangin' judges (lesser or superior) to his side. Regardless of the distance, it arrives the next night. However, he can only summon one at a time.

Weaknesses (Su): Stringing Jackson up sends him to Boot Hill, but a legitimate judge must preside over the hanging. Bullets fired from a real lawman's gun can put him down—but only for a single night. Jackson's fast healing ability is ineffective against either such type of damage.

Coup: Harrowed gain the power to command walkin' dead—to an extent. They can only control one walkin' dead and must maintain concentration (i.e., only take simple actions) while doing so. Also, they must be able to see and communicate with the zombie at all times

Cyrus Call

Medium-Size Undead
Hit Dice: 9d12 (58 hp)
Initiative: +1 (Dex)
Speed: 30 ft.
AC: 11 (+1 Dex)
Attacks: Scattergun +10 ranged
Damage: Scattergun 1-4d6
Face/Reach: 5 ft. by 5 ft./5 ft.
Special Attacks: Fear, mob justice
Special Qualities: Damage reduction 25/see weaknesses, fast healing 25, arcane weapon, fearless, undead, weaknesses, coup

Saves: Fort +4, Ref +7, Will +4
Abilities: Str 15, Dex 13, Con –, Int 10, Wis 12, Cha 15
Skills: Hide +4, Intimidate +6, Knowledge (Chisolm Trail) +5, Listen +5, Move Silently +4, Ride +5, Ridicule +6, Sense Motive +6, Spot +5, Use Rope +5, Wilderness Lore +5
Feats: Dead Eye, Point Blank Shot, Track, Weapon Specialization (scattergun)
Climate/Terrain: Warm Hill and Plains
Challenge Rating: 9
Alignment: Neutral evil
Advancement: As gunslinger character class

Call wears an impressive black cloak over his features. His voice is deep and rumbling—even for a hangin' judge

Cyrus Call's claim to fame was as a demagogue. He was the glue that held the group of crooked judges together in life and Jackson's first accomplice.

Call had a knack for stirring up otherwise decent folk into an angry lynch mob. He used his rabble-rousing abilities to remove landowners that the judges knew would never be convicted in a court.

Combat

Call's persuasive nature has followed him to the Netherworld, allowing him to call forth his own mob of undead to back his plays, and he never hesitates to press any numerical advantage.

Whenever possible, Call preferred to see cases "settled" before trial. In his opinion, if a man wasn't guilty, he wouldn't have been arrested in the first place. Any cowpoke who's currently wanted for a crime, no matter how minor, gets himself a sentence of "hanged until dead" from Call.

Fear (Su): Anyone catching sight of Call must make a Will saving throw against DC 19.

Arcane weapon (Su): Call's sawed-off double barrel reloads itself 1 round after becoming empty.

Mob justice (Su): Call never goes into a fight outnumbered. He is always accompanied by twice as many walkin' dead (each having maximum Hit Dice; see the *Deadlands: The Weird West D20 Rulebook*) as there are heroes. He can also raise those killed by himself or his "mob" as walkin' dead, although this takes one round per zombie raised.

Weaknesses (Su): If a group of heroes outnumbers Call and his "lynch mob" (see above) by at least two-to-one, the cowpoke with the highest Cha can affect him with normal weapons—even to the extent of killing him for a single night. The next night, though, he's gunning for the "opposition leader." The only way to put Call for good is to hang 'im high with at least four folks present. Kirby's fast healing is ineffective against damage inflicted by either such attack mode.

Coup: Harrowed gain the Unholy Host feat. If the hero has that power, raise the Harrowed's Cha by 2 instead.

Luther Kirby

Medium-Size Undead
Hit Dice: 10d12 (65 hp)
Initiative: +1 (Dex)
Speed: 30 ft.
AC: 11 (+1 Dex)
Attacks: 2 Colt Army revolvers +11 ranged (+9 and +5 when used in tandem); or 2 scythes +13 melee (+11 and +7 when used in tandem)
Damage: Colt Army revolver 2d6, scythe 1d8+3
Face/Reach: 5 ft. by 5 ft./5 ft.
Special Attacks: Fear, restraining order
Special Qualities: Damage reduction 25/see weaknesses, fast healing 25, arcane weapons, fearless, undead, weaknesses, coup
Saves: Fort +5, Ref +8, Will +3
Abilities: Str 16, Dex 13, Con –, Int 15, Wis 11, Cha 13
Skills: Hide +6, Intimidate +7, Knowledge (Chisolm Trail) +6, Listen +7, Move Silently +6, Profession (law) +8, Ride +6, Sense Motive +7, Spot +7, Use Rope +6, Wilderness Lore +6
Feats: Dead Eye, Exotic Weapon Proficiency (scythes), Improved Critical (scythe), Point Blank Shot, Track, Two-Weapon Fighting,
Climate/Terrain: Warm Hill and Plains

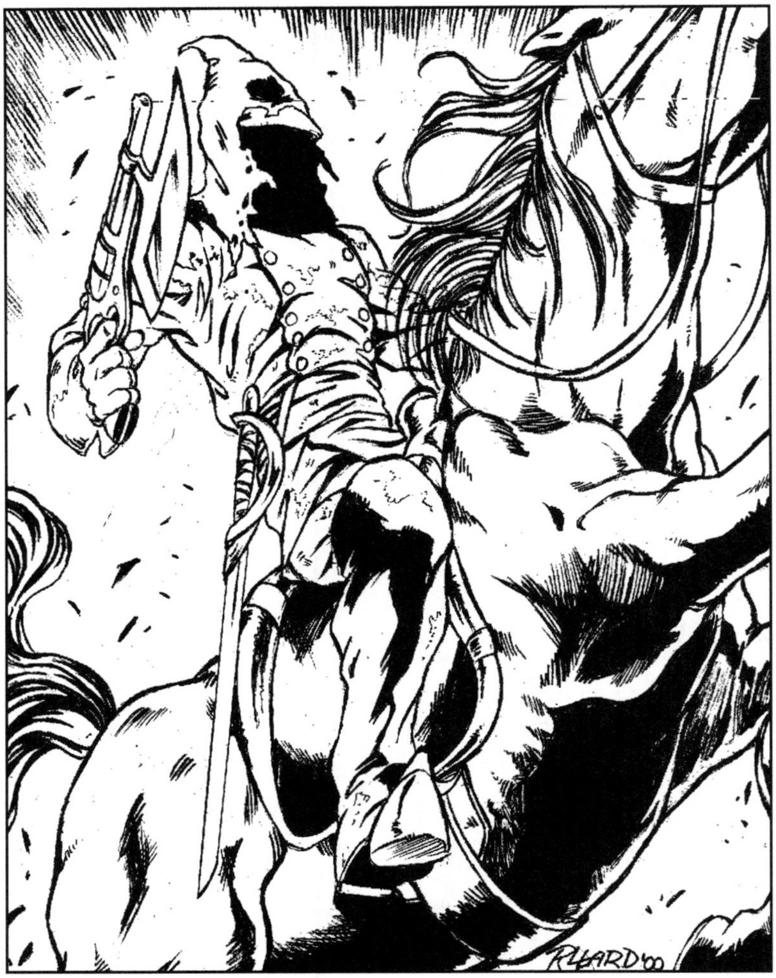

Challenge Rating: 9
Alignment: Lawful evil
Advancement: As gunslinger character class

Kirby is the shortest of the judges. He wears a dark brown, shoulder-length cowl to cover his head.

Luther Kirby was the judge responsible for the legal shenanigans the group undertook. He spent months pouring over Texas legal code looking for a loophole that would allow the judges to seize the valuable land along the Chisolm Trail.

He discovered that the judges had reasonable precedent to seize the lands of executed criminals under a state receivership until they could be offered for public sale. "Public sale" meant purchase by the judges themselves for less than a penny an acre.

Combat

Despite Kirby's formidable powers, his letter-of-the-law approach hinders him in his incarnation as an abomination. He doesn't pursue victims over what his twisted mind perceives as "jurisdictional boundaries" in the course of a single evening. A hero can shake his pursuit by crossing a county line or running water (a common property line marker in the Weird West), but only for that night. The next evening, he appears within the same "jurisdiction" as his victim.

Being an attorney or judge is always considered a hanging offense in Kirby's court.

Fear (Su): Anyone catching sight of Kirby must make a Will saving throw against DC 19.

Arcane weapons (Su): Kirby's revolvers reload themselves 1 round after they're empty.

Restraining order (Sp): Kirby can impose a "restraining order" on anyone opposing him within 30 feet. If the victim fails a Will saving throw against a Difficulty Class of 15, they can't move from that spot until they make another such saving throw, which they can attempt once each round on their initiative.

Weaknesses (Su): Hanging destroys Kirby for good, but only if a hero bests him in an opposed Profession (law) skill check prior to the event. Kirby's fast healing is ineffective against damage inflicted by such a hanging.

Other than that, only crossing "jurisdictions" or beating his total in a mutual check of Profession (law) skills can shake him from a victim's trail for a night. The next sundown he's back on his victim's trail, however, with a good supply of rope.

Coup: Harrowed gain the ability to open handcuffs, jail cells and the like, as long as they are used to restrain them. They can't simply open a cell and free a companion unless they're locked up with the Harrowed as well. This takes the Harrowed a round to perform. Attempts to influence honest lawmen, attorneys, and judges (with Intimidate skill, for instance) are at –2 however, because the Harrowed seems somehow "slippery."

Moses Moore

Medium-Size Undead
Hit Dice: 10d12 (65 hp)
Initiative: +2 (Dex)
Speed: 30 ft.
AC: 12 (+2 Dex)
Attacks: 2 Colt Army revolvers +12 ranged (+10 and +6 when used in tandem); or 2 scythes +13 melee (+11 and +7 when used in tandem)
Damage: Colt Army revolver 2d6, scythe 1d8+3
Face/Reach: 5 ft. by 5 ft./5 ft.
Special Attacks: Fear
Special Qualities: Damage reduction 25/see weaknesses, fast healing 25, arcane weapons, fearless, undead, horseman, weaknesses, coup
Saves: Fort +5, Ref +9, Will +4
Abilities: Str 16, Dex 15, Con –, Int 10, Wis 12, Cha 14
Skills: Hide +6, Intimidate +6, Knowledge (Chisolm Trail) +6, Listen +7, Move Silently +6, Ride +7, Sense Motive +6, Spot +7, Use Rope +6, Wilderness Lore +6
Feats: Dead Eye, Exotic Weapon Proficiency (scythes), Track, Two-Weapon Fighting
Climate/Terrain: Warm Hill and Plains
Challenge Rating: 9
Alignment: Neutral evil
Advancement: As gunslinger character class

Moore wears an old, dusty Confederate Army uniform. A hood drapes over his head, hiding his features in shadow. He rides a dark gray stallion.

Moses Moore was a snake-in-the-grass Confederate guerrilla up in Missouri and Kansas during the early years of The War, but after he made a name as a "war hero," he headed down to Texas to cash in on his fame. He quickly secured a judgeship and set about finagling that into as much power and money as possible.

When Hiram Jackson approached him with the scheme, he immediately realized the potential. After all, he'd spent enough time in Kansas to realize the money to be made moving cattle into the Disputed Lands for resale to Northerners. Jackson, on the other hand, wanted the "respectability" Moore's name would bring to his group.

Combat

An expert cavalryman before ever taking up a judge's gavel, Moore is the most dangerous gunfighter of the five. Moore always considers all Northerners, even deserters, capital criminals. Southerners consorting with Northerners are just as bad to Moore.

Fear (Su): Anyone catching sight of Moore must make a Will saving throw against DC 19.

Arcane weapons (Su): Moore's revolvers reload themselves 1 round after they're empty.

Horseman (Su): Moore's mount, a dark gray stallion, cannot be harmed while he's on it. It has a Speed 100 ft. while he's riding and he suffers no movement penalties to his attacks on horseback.

Weaknesses (Su): The only way to destroy Moore for good is to hang him by pulling a horse out from under him. Bullets from a firearm manufactured in the Union (including the ammunition) wielded by a U.S. (not Confederate) citizen can wound and even "kill" Moore. He returns the next evening to hunt down his "killer." Moore's fast healing is ineffective against damage inflicted by either such attack mode.

Coup: Harrowed gain use of Moore's twin pistols. They vanish in the hands of the living, however.

Marcus Lafayette

Medium-Size Undead
Hit Dice: 10d12 (65 hp)
Initiative: +1 (Dex)
Speed: 30 ft.
AC: 11 (+1 Dex)
Attacks: 2 Colt Army Revolvers +11 ranged (+9 and +5 when used in tandem); or axe-handle with barbed wire +15 melee
Damage: Colt Army Revolver 2d6, axe-handle with barbed wire 2d6+5
Face/Reach: 5 ft. by 5 ft./5 ft.

Special Attacks: Fear
Special Qualities: Fearless, damage reduction 25/see weaknesses, fast healing 25, berserk, coup, arcane weapons, undead, weaknesses
Saves: Fort +5, Ref +8, Will +3
Abilities: Str 20, Dex 13, Con –, Int 9, Wis 11, Cha 14
Skills: Hide +5, Intimidate +6, Knowledge (Chisolm Trail) +5, Listen +5, Move Silently +5, Ride +5, Sense Motive +5, Spot +5, Use Rope +5, Wilderness Lore +5
Feats: Dead Eye, Power Attack, Track, Two-Weapon Fighting
Climate/Terrain: Warm Hill and Plains
Challenge Rating: 9
Alignment: Neutral evil
Advancement: As gunslinger character class

Lafayette is the largest of the judges, standing nearly 7' tall. He carries a wire-covered club in one big, beefy hand.

Marcus Lafayette got his start as a bad-tempered rancher in central Texas. Lafayette fenced any land he laid claim to—legal or not—and dared trespassers to set foot on it. He had a reputation for rapacious land-greed and a rage like a prairie thunderstorm when balked by smaller landowners. The rancher once beat a cow to death with his bare hands in a fit of anger.

His influence and power in that region was so great that the other four judges decided not to risk a fight with the cattleman. Instead, they conspired to bring him into their fold. With Jackson's influence and Kirby's legal fancy-footwork, Lafayette was appointed a circuit judge in a matter of weeks.

Lafayette's legal knowledge was sadly lacking, but he served the group primarily as an enforcer. Word had it no man had ever stood up to Lafayette in a fair fight—or at least not for long—and most folks didn't think to question his decisions for fear of his anger. Lafayette's creed was to talk loudly *and* carry a big stick.

Combat

While he is not hesitant to use his revolvers, Lafayette takes special pleasure from using his barbed-wire-covered axe-handle. He always considers any rancher or cowboy a rustler a horse thief—a hanging offense, of course.

Fear (Su): Anyone catching sight of Lafayette must make a Will saving throw against DC 19.

Arcane weapons (Su): Marcus' revolvers reload themselves 1 round after they're empty.

Berserk (Ex): As soon as anyone takes a shot at Lafayette, or even just questions his "authority" he goes insane with rage, raising his Str and Dex by 2 and reducing his Int and Wis by the same amount. He attempts only melee attacks each round if an opponent is in range and charges them if not. He can fire his pistols while charging.

Weaknesses (Su): Stretching his neck with a noose of barbed wire ends Lafayette's reign of terror for good. Shooting or otherwise attacking him directly from behind does normal damage. Marcus' fast healing is ineffective against damage inflicted by either such attack mode.

It's the Marshal's call as to what is "directly behind" him or not. Unfortunately for the hero, the judge comes back the next night gunning for his "murderer."

Coup: Harrowed who put down Lafayette for good gain the Berserk feat. If they already have that power, raise their Str by 2 instead.

Headless Horseman

Medium-Size Undead
Hit Dice: 5d12 (32 hp)
Initiative: +2 (Dex)
Speed: 30 ft.
AC: 12 (+2 Dex)
Attacks: Double-action Colt revolver +4 ranged; or cavalry saber+2 melee
Damage: Double-action Colt revolver 2d6, cavalry saber 1d6
Face/Reach: 5 ft. by 5 ft./5 ft.
Special Attacks: Fear, pumpkin head

Special Qualities: Undead, fearless, blindsight
Saves: Fort +1, Ref +3, Will +5
Abilities: Str 9, Dex 14, Con –, Int 11, Wis 12, Cha 12
Skills: Hide +7, Intimidate +7, Intuit Direction +6, Move Silently +7, Ride +7, Ridicule +6, Spot +6, Wilderness Lore +6
Feats: Exotic Weapon Proficiency (cavalry saber), Track
Climate/Terrain: Any land
Challenge Rating: 5
Alignment: Always chaotic evil
Advancement: By character class

The headless horseman looks pretty much like a normal rider (with exception of not having a head, of course) on a wild-looking black horse. It performs increasingly impressive antics meant to inspire fear and is usually successful. It carries a glowing jack-o-lantern in one hand.

This creature is an abomination created when someone dies from decapitation. Chances are increased if the person was riding at the time of death or was a professional rider such as a Pony Express rider or a cavalry soldier.

When the poor unfortunate is transformed into a headless horseman, he is assigned the task of causing dread along the roads and trails of North America. The thing performs its job by doing increasingly frightening things, hoping to get someone to ride away from it.

Combat

While it creates fear to feed the Reckoners, it thrives on the thrill of the chase. Of course, if it actually catches someone, the horseman it more than willing to take their head. The abomination is not all that happy about its headless state, and vainly hopes to find a suitable replacement for the one it had in life.

Pumpkin head (Su): Besides being animated by the horseman, the pumpkin head bursts into flames when thrown. It does 4d6 damage and ignites flammable materials.

Fear (Su): This abomination uses various methods to terrify its victims, each of which requires a Will saving throw against the DC in the parenthesis following. The horseman starts with an invisible gallop, during which he can be heard but not seen (DC 10). The next step is to make the horse rear and shriek (DC 15). Then, the pumpkin head he carries begins to grimace horribly (DC 18). After that, he causes the pumpkin head to laugh (DC 20). Finally, he can throw the pumpkin head (DC 20).

In addition, the rider can shout (using the pumpkin as sort of an unholy vent figure), or shoot or perform riding tricks to use skills like Intimidate or Ridicule.

Undead (Su): Focus-Being on horseback; If he can be knocked off his horse, he loses his undead status and can be killed or wounded normally.

Hellfish

Medium-Size Beast
Hit Dice: 2d10 (11 hp)
Initiative: +0
Speed: 20 ft. swim
AC: 10
Attacks: Tentacle +1 melee
Damage: Tentacle 1d4 and poison
Face/Reach: 5 ft. by 5 ft./5 ft.
Special Attacks: Poison
Special Qualities: Tentacle range, heat vulnerability, gelatinous form
Saves: Fort +3, Ref +3, Will -2
Abilities: Str 9, Dex 10, Con 9, Int 7, Wis 6, Cha 7
Skills: Hide +5, Listen +5, Move Silently +5, Spot +5, Swim +8, Wilderness Lore +5
Feats: None
Climate/Terrain: Aquatic
Challenge Rating: 3
Alignment: Always neutral
Advancement: 3-4 HD (Medium-Size), 5-6 HD (Large)

These creatures look like reddish man o' wars nearly 5' tall. They have a bulbous, nearly transparent upper body with a crested ridge, and translucent tentacles over 100' long that dangle beneath them in the water. Dead fish and other sea-life are often trapped in these tentacles waiting to be pulled into the upper body for digestion.

The hellfish can actually manipulate its tentacles to a limited degree above water, and one of the most horrifying sights a seagoing hero can see is a hellfish that has recently caught a human victim. The body is pulled into the monster's semitransparent upper body where it slowly dissolves in the creature's digestive fluids. Unfortunately, the details of the process are all too evident to an outside observer.

Combat

Hellfish are also much smarter than a normal man o' war—although that's probably not saying a lot. These monsters are found only in saltwater, where they swim about in search of prey, which it seizes and holds in its tentacles prior to actually consuming it.

Tentacle range (Ex): The hellfish's tentacle attack per round can strike at opponents up to 100' away.

Poison (Ex): The hellfish's stinging tentacles inject a victim with a lethal toxin. The target must make a Fortitude saving throw against DC 17. Success means the victim takes 1d6 hit points and is -2 to all rolls for 1d6 days. Failure results in death in 1d6 minutes! Short of a magical cure, there is no known antidote for a hellfish's poison. This poison can be harvested, but remains potent only 24 hours.

Gelatinous form (Ex): Because of the hellfish's odd biology, no normal attack can inflict more than 6 hit points.

Heat vulnerability (Ex): All heat-based attacks do an extra 1d6 damage.

Skills: Hellfish receive a +2 bonus at all Hide, Listen, Move Silently, Spot and Wilderness Lore skill rolls.

Horned Serpent

Large Magical Beast
Hit Dice: 8d10+1 (52 hp)
Initiative: +1 (Dex)
Speed: 30 ft., 15 ft. swim
AC: 10 (-1 size, +1 Dex)
Attacks: 2 horns +9 melee, bite +7 melee
Damage: Horn 1d6+2, bite 1d4+1 and poison
Face/Reach: 5 ft. by 10 ft./5 ft.
Special Attacks: Poison, improved grab, constrict 1d3+2
Special Qualities: Shapeshift
Saves: Fort +7, Ref +7, Will +2
Abilities: Str 14, Dex 12, Con 12, Int 6, Wis 10, Cha 12
Skills: Intimidate +8, Listen +8, Move Silently +8, Spot +8, Swim +10, Wilderness Lore +8
Feats: Multiattack, Track
Climate/Terrain: Aquatic, Any Warm land
Challenge Rating: 7
Alignment: Always chaotic evil
Advancement: 9-16 HD (Large), 17-24 HD (Huge)

Horned serpents are huge, about twice the length of a normal man's height. The creature's belly is solid black, while the rest of its long body is covered with scales of multiple shades of green and blue. The coloration gives it great camouflage underwater. The head of a horned serpent is viper-like, similar to that of a rattlesnake or water moccasin. From the crown to the base of the neck, however, runs a series of small, bony horns. On either side of this crest of protrusions is a long, sharp horn, each about two feet long.

These creatures dwell in the deeper rivers of the Southwest, and while they are naturally dangerous predators, the most insidious quality the serpent possesses is its ability to change shape. It can take the form of anything it wraps in its coils. A perfect physical likeness is assumed: size, shape, bad breath—it's all there. The serpent's only flaw is that it doesn't get any smarter (it can't speak). It also smells a bit funny, something animals pick up on really quick. You never see a horned serpent in the saddle. While there are ways to pick up on the ruse, the serpent is crafty.

Combat

Horned serpents hunt by waiting beneath the surface of the river, watching for prey to come and drink. When it does, the serpent strikes, delivering a poisonous bite, then coiling about the prey to hold it while it eats. The venom is not especially deadly, but it does cause a temporary paralysis. Mercifully for most victims, they tend to sleep through dinner.

The horned serpent uses its shape-changing ability to hunt outside its normal domain (especially when large prey is scarce near its river), and if it is discovered while imitating one of its victims, it reverts to its true form and attempts to escape. If it's cornered, it never gives up without a fight. However, it always fights with a view towards beating a hasty retreat. One of its favorite tactics is to paralyze as many people as possible and head for the hills. These serpents are firm believers in living to fight another day, but if there is no way out, they'll try to take down as many people with them as possible.

Poison (Ex): Anyone bitten by the serpent must make a Fortitude saving throw against DC 17. Those who succeed lose 2d6 hit points, and those who fail are rendered unconscious for 1d4 hours (plenty of time to become a meal for the hungry serpent).

Shapeshift (Su): The serpent can take the form of any creature it has wrapped in its coils in the past hour. The shapechange lasts 24 hours, unless ended before that. If the serpent resumes its old form, the effect cannot be reassumed.

Skeptics may attempt a Spot skill check against DC 17 to realize there is something wrong. Most animals (dogs, horses, etc.) catch the scent of the serpent and know the truth. Their DC is 7.

Skills: Horned Serpents receive a +4 bonus to all Intimidate, Listen, Move Silently and Wilderness Lore skill rolls.

Humbug

Tiny Vermin
Hit Dice: 1d8 (4 hp)
Initiative: +2 (Dex)
Speed: 5 ft. climb, 70 ft. fly (good)
AC: 14 (+2 size, +2 Dex)
Attacks: Bite +0 melee
Damage: Bite 1d4-2
Face/Reach: 2 1/2 ft. by 2 1/2 ft./0 ft.
Special Attacks: Sonic attack
Special Qualities: Camouflage
Saves: Fort +2, Ref +2, Will -1
Abilities: Str 5, Dex 15, Con 10, Int -, Wis 7, Cha 5
Skills: Climb +6, Hide +10, Listen +3, Move Silently +2, Spot +3, Wilderness Lore +3
Feats: None
Climate/Terrain: Any Temperate or Warm land
Challenge Rating: 1
Alignment: Always neutral
Advancement: 2-3 HD (Tiny)

The mercifully rare humbug is related to the common cicada. It mostly keeps to itself, but when it gets the urge to mate it lets out an terrible screeching whine intended to attract a mate. Unfortunately, few other creatures can take the noise, which covers a huge range of frequencies at a ridiculously high volume.

The humbug's mating call is so loud that it disturbs everyone within five miles, keeping them awake. Towns usually go into a tizzy if they've got a humbug nearby, because almost nobody can get any sleep.

Combat

The humbug is a cowardly little critter that loves to hide in hard-to-reach places. If attacked, the humbug can modify its mating call to be downright deadly. However, if all else fails to get rid of the creature, it finds a mate after 2d20 days and finally shuts up.

Sonic attack (Ex): The humbug's cry shatters glass within one mile, and everyone in that radius suffers a -2 penalty to all die rolls. Those who approach within 300 feet of the critter must make a Fortitude saving throw against DC 17 every minute or lose 1 hit point. Nothing as simple as ear plugs prevents these effects, which are caused by the physical vibration of the sound more than the noise.

If anyone attacks the humbug, it changes the sound of its drone to an angry buzzing that can shatter bone and burst eardrums. Everyone within 30 feet (except for other humbugs) must make a Fortitude saving throw against DC 17 or take 1d6 damage. There's no other way to avoid this damage (unless some mad scientist manages to build a white-noise generator), except by moving away from the annoying little noisemaker. If more than a round goes by without the humbug being attacked successfully, the critter goes back to the drone that's only loud enough to torment.

Camouflage (Ex): Humbugs can change colors like a chameleon, and all attempts to Spot the creature are at -2 when it changes colors to match its surroundings.

Joaquin Murieta

Medium-Size Undead
Hit Dice: 7d12 (45 hp)
Initiative: +4 (Dex)
Speed: 30 ft.
AC: 14 (+4 Dex)
Attacks: 2 Colt Dragoon revolvers +11 ranged (+9 when used in tandem); or melee attack +9
Damage: Colt Dragoon 2d6; or melee attack +2
Face/Reach: 5 ft. by 5 ft./5 ft.
Special Attacks: Fear, decapitation
Special Qualities: Fearless, undead, coup, arcane weapons, blindsight
Saves: Fort +4, Ref +9, Will +3
Abilities: Str 14, Dex 18, Con –, Int 10, Wis 13, Cha 14
Skills: Climb +8, Hide +10, Intimidate +8, Move Silently +10, Ride +10, Sense Motive +7, Spot +7
Feats: Ambidexterity, Dead Eye, Point Blank Shot, Two-Weapon Fighting
Climate/Terrain: Any land
Challenge Rating: 7
Alignment: Chaotic evil
Advancement: As gunslinger character class

Joaquin is a headless corpse dressed in black clothing. His shirt is stained with blood from his decapitation and he's sometimes seen riding a black stallion as well. His head has long hair, a faint beard, and is pale and pickled in a large, screw-top jar.

According to legend, Joaquin Murieta came to California with his young wife Rosalita hoping to strike it rich in the gold rush of the late 1840s. The territory was ceded to the U.S. in 1848 and the U.S. government passed a law in less than two years that made it virtually illegal for Mexicans to mine gold in the region. Joaquin, however, filed for all the legal paperwork he needed to stake a claim and he and Rosalita set up a small and comfortable homestead not far from his newly legal mine.

That wasn't good enough for other miners in the region who felt he was somehow "stealing" their rightful bounty. They beat him into unconsciousness, raped and killed his wife, and later, after whipping Joaquin to death's door, hung his brother in front of him. Needless to say, this got Joaquin riled.

He rounded up a band of other angry Mexicans and a few bandits from the U.S. and started a reign of bloody terror in southern California. Many of the poorer workers saw Joaquin and his band as a modern day Robin Hood, but the California government had a different opinion. Especially since Joaquin and his band were rumored to have murdered over 300 men.

Captain Harry Love led a band of California lawmen against Joaquin and his band. They surprised the bandit leader away from camp one day with only a few men and quickly dispatched the group. To prove he'd bagged Joaquin—and to claim the $1000 reward offered by the California governor—Love chopped off the bandit's head and returned it to the governor.

Unfortunately for folks in the Maze and the rest of the Southwest, Joaquin's come back looking for his missing head. His head currently soaks in formaldehyde in a jar in a Shan Fan bar called the *Ivory Palace*, owned by one of Harry Love's descendants.

Combat

Murieta appears near mining camps, asking for his head. If no one produces it (which hasn't happened yet), he "liberates" the heads of Confederate or U.S. miners and tries them on for size. Joaquin never harms folks of Mexican descent or women of any nationality.

Arcane weapons (Sp): Joaquin's twin single-action Colt Dragoon revolvers completely reload themselves one round after they're emptied. They crumble to rust after Joaquin is destroyed.

Decapitation (Ex): Joaquin has a unique and terrible ability—he can literally tear a man's head off with his bare hands! To do so, he must successfully grapple with an opponent and then Pin them. Once he does so, he's gotten a grip on the head and the victim must make a Fortitude save against DC 18 on each subsequent round. Each failure inflicts 1d6 damage on the character. When the victim reaches 0 hit points, the head tears free.

Fear (Ex): Anyone catching sight of Murieta tearing off a victim's head (with accompanying sickening squelch) must make a Will saving throw against DC 18.

Undead (Su): Focus—Head. This might cause the heroes some problem since the abomination's head is several hundred miles away! Pouring liquor of any sort down Joaquin's neck stump causes the abomination to stop attacking and leave peacefully. This requires a touch attack against AC 24 to accomplish.

Coup: Destroying Joaquin nets the Harrowed the ability—or curse—to get drunk once again. It might not sound like much, but if you were a moldering corpse, you'd want to tie one on now and again!

Kangee

Gargantuan Outsider (Chaotic Evil)
Hit Dice: 16d8+3 (120 hp)
Initiative: +1 (Dex)
Speed: 30 ft.
AC: 7 (-4 size, +1 Dex)
Attacks: 6 tentacles +17 melee
Damage: Tentacle: 1d3+5
Face/Reach: 20 ft. by 20 ft./20 ft.
Special Attacks: Fear
Special Qualities: Animal control, surveillance, vulnerability
Saves: Fort +13, Ref +11, Will +11
Abilities: Str 21, Dex 12, Con 16, Int 11, Wis 13, Cha 15
Skills: Diplomacy +19, Languages (Apache, English, Sioux, Spanish), Intimidate +20, Listen +19, Move Silently +19, Sense Motive +18, Sleight of Hand +19, Spot +19
Feat: Power Attack
Climate/Terrain: Any land
Challenge Rating: 10
Alignment: Chaotic evil
Advancement: 17-32 (Gargantuan), 33-48 HD (Colossal)

The entity which calls itself "Kangee" (the Sioux word for "raven", not to confuse this being with *the* Raven) is a diabolical, shape-shifting carnivorous spirit from near-forgotten Indian legends. Currently, it is masquerading as the town of Bonasco in the New Mexico Territory. In that guise, it appears to be a typical Western boomtown, with a saloon, casino, brothel, etc.

The stories once told by the Indians tell of a village ravaged by a spirit so foul that every hut echoed with the screams of the souls devoured inside them. No one who entered the village left alive.

Kangee lay dormant for centuries, until the Reckoning awakened it in 1863. The spirit found itself in what today is the New Mexico Territory, and there it fashioned crude dwellings from its spiritual form to lure unwary travelers. All who chanced upon this quaint little "community" became vittles for Kangee.

Eventually, after a few experiences with overly suspicious folks, Kangee hit upon the idea of allowing people to settle there. Using its unholy abilities, the spirit provided food and water for the residents, much like a farmer tending its livestock.

Recently, an unscrupulous fellow by the name of Webbekiah J. Trapp avoided becoming an after-dinner mint for Kangee by somehow managing to make contact with it and successfully proposing a deal to it. Trapp convinced the spirit to remake itself in the image of a free-wheeling gambling town—dubbed Bonasco—which brings easy profits for Trapp (the nominal "owner" of the town's casinos) and bigger meals for Kangee. In exchange for staying off the spirit's bill of fare, Trapp also helps Kangee to maintain its "cover".

Combat

When it hungers, Kangee's primary method of attacking prey is its tentacles. After luring a victim inside one of the evil spirit's buildings, they (and any of their cohorts) are subject to attack by them. From the victims' perspective, they are strangled by a "lamp post", or drowned in a "well", or decapitated by a "cupboard". (Thus, people slain by Kangee appear to have died in accidents.)

Depending on how ravenous it is, Kangee may attempt to use its mortal pawns (like Trapp) to run suspicious visitors out of town if they seem too clever or formidable. However, if Kangee's tummy is growling, these people usually jump to the top of the menu.

Fear (Ex): Anyone catching sight of Kangee's true form, i.e. sees one of its tentacles or is somehow attacked by an inanimate object under the spirit's control, must make a Will saving throw against DC 19.

Animal control (Su): Kangee can control at will normal animals that are dog-sized and smaller. He mainly uses this to ensure that there is enough game around to feed his "pets", as Kangee's after bigger game.

Surveillance (Su): Whenever the Posse's carrying on a conversation inside one of Kangee's buildings, there's a chance the spirit may be eavesdropping. If the evil spirit makes a Listen skill check against DC 13, it becomes privy to the heroes' words. The DC becomes 17 if the posse's part of a crowd, and 7 if Kangee is specifically looking for them.

The posse's as likely as anyone to wind up on Kangee's menu, but the heroes may notice the hungry spirit checking them out beforehand. A Spot skill check against DC 10 gives a Posse member a "hunch" that they're being watched. If that hero looks fast enough (a Spot skill check against DC 20), they can catch a glimpse of a blood-red eye over the mounted moose-head, or a fleshy feeler nudging the roulette ball, or a slimy stalk slipping under the floorboard.

Should Kangee discover the heroes suspect that something is not right about the town, it either uses its human pawns to have them run out of town or it arranges for them to meet with an "accident." It also keeps a very close eye on the area around its "heart" (see below).

Vulnerability (Su): The profile above represents only an individual manifestation of Kangee (i.e., one building), and destroying any of the spirit's buildings only forces it to go dormant for a period of 1d12 hours. The only way to slay it permanently is to destroy its "heart", which is a large lump of smoky quartz. For obvious reasons, Kangee keeps this well-hidden. Currently, it's at the bottom of Bonasco's town well, but if heroes start nosing around this area it may have Trapp move the object to a new location.

Mexican Dragon

Medium-Size Magical Beast
Hit Dice: 4d10+3 (34 hp)
Initiative: +1 (Dex)
Speed: 35 ft.
AC: 16 (+1 Dex, +5 natural)
Attacks: Tail slap +6 melee, bite +1 melee
Damage: Tail slap 1d8+2, bite 1d4+1
Face/Reach: 5 ft. by 5 ft./5 ft.
Special Attacks: Breath weapon, improved grab
Special Qualities: Stubborn, roll-over
Saves: Fort +7, Ref +5, Will +3
Abilities: Str 14, Dex 13, Con 16, Int 9, Wis 9, Cha 11
Skills: Climb +8, Hide +8, Intimidate +8, Listen +8, Move Silently +8, Spot +8, Wilderness Lore +8
Feats: Dodge
Climate/Terrain: Any Warm land
Challenge Rating: 5
Alignment: Always neutral

Advancement: 5-8 HD (Medium-Size), 9-12 HD (Large)

This creature is a huge iguana with the ability to breath fire. The dragon is mostly orange in color, with black stripes on the tail and belly, and gray and white patches on its head and belly.

While iguanas are native to Mexico, a few of these creatures have crossed the border into the Southern States and can be found in southern Texas and the New Mexico and Arizona Territories.

The Mexican dragon is relatively peaceful and does not seek trouble. Still, the creatures, both male and female, are fiercely territorial. Also, while some of their smaller cousins are purely vegetarian, the Mexican dragon has a taste for meat, preferably warm. Carrion, if not too old, works too. Whatever it eats, the Mexican dragon aggressively attacks its chosen meal and defends it from interlopers as well.

Combat

If a Mexican dragon is startled, it may respond with a warning display, bobbing and shaking its head. If this does not work, it turns to present its side to its opponents, glaring at them with one baleful, orange eye (treat both these movements as an attempt at using its Intimidation skill against opponents).

If molested, threatened, or attacked, the Mexican dragon might strike in one of three ways. Its first choice is to sweep with its tail if an opponent is in range. The tail makes up half the creature's length (about 12 feet in total) and can slap one or two opponents if they are close to the creature's hindquarters. The dragon's second preferred attack is breathing fire. Finally, if the opponents remain, the iguana attacks with its bite.

Improved grab (Ex): Mexican dragons can grab any target equal in Size or smaller.

Breath weapon (Sp): The Mexican dragon can breathe fire once per round, up to 10 times per encounter. It recharges the ability by eating meat and a variety of minerals found in the desert. The creature's flame jet shoots out 30 feet, inflicting 2d6 damage and also lighting anything flammable on fire.

Roll-over (Ex): When entangled by lariats, whips, or similar weapons, the giant iguana uses a Partial action to roll over, barely changing its location. The creature can pull the other end of a whip or lariat out of an opponent's hands unless they make a Strength ability check against DC 16.

Stubborn (Ex): The dragon is persistent, and receives a +2 to all Will saves.

Skills: Mexican dragons receive a +4 bonus with all Climb, Hide, Intimidate, Listen, Move Silently, Spot and Wilderness Lore skill rolls.

Mourning Mist

Large Aberration
Hit Dice: 6d8+3 (45 hp)
Initiative: +6 (Dex, Improved Initiative)
Speed: 85 ft. fly (perfect)
AC: 11 (-1 size, +2 Dex)
Attacks: 3 touches +4 melee
Damage: Touch 2d6
Face/Reach: 5 ft. by 10 ft./5 ft.
Special Attacks: Psychic pain, chilling touch, hellish cry
Special Qualities: Damage reduction 25/melee attacks, spirit anchor
Saves: Fort +5, Ref +4, Will +5
Abilities: Str 13, Dex 14, Con 17, Int 8, Wis 11, Cha 11
Skills: Hide +7, Move Silently +9, Spot +8
Feat: Improved Initiative
Climate/Terrain: Any land
Challenge Rating: 6
Alignment: Always chaotic neutral
Advancement: 7-12 HD (Large), 13-18 HD (Huge)

A mourning mist appears as a cloud with a dark-red core between 8 and 10 feet in diameter. The entire mass pulses and flows on the breeze. The cloud is amorphous with thick tentacles and thin tendrils extending far beyond the core. Mourning mists hover a few feet off the ground and aren't slowed by material objects.

The mist pales in color beyond the center, eventually trailing into sickly pinks and leprous whites at the edges. Puffs of sooty smoke and streaks of silver move through the mass, ghostly reminders of cannon bursts and saber slashes. A study of the mist from closer than 10 feet reveals shadows of human faces twisted in screams of agony moving throughout the creature's body.

The most striking and memorable thing about the mourning mist is the sound it produces. The mist's chilling cry is comprised of several different elements: the moans and sighs of dying soldiers, the sharp retort of rifle fire, the low rumble of cannons, the shriek of wounded horses. These battle sounds combine to form a low, haunting drone that can be heard for several miles when the mist is active. (They are largely, but not exclusively, nocturnal.)

Because of the cry's supernatural nature, it is usually impossible to locate its source. The sound seems to emanate from everywhere and nowhere. But when the mist is attacked, the cry's source becomes obvious, and the noise can grow to unnerving loudness.

Mourning mists are born at the sites of particularly ignoble battles, places where cowardice or treachery of an extreme nature caused a disastrous defeat or the loss of many lives. The first such creature appeared in 1864 after the Battle of Jenkin's Ferry, Arkansas, after a regiment of Federals showed the white feather and allowed an entire Union army to be flanked and routed, and it remains there to this very day.

Each mist is linked to a specific inanimate object, an "anchor" that embodies the nefarious act that first brought the mist into existence—the bugle that sounded a craven retreat, for example, or even the corpse of the officer who issued the retreat order (as is the case at Jenkin's Ferry). The anchor is always within 10 miles of the mist to which it is linked. Most often, the item remains on the infamous battlefield, but mists have been known to follow an anchor that has been removed from the place of its disgrace.

The mourning mist is driven by its desire: to free itself from its weird existence by prompting someone to destroy the anchor to which the mist is

linked. To this end, the mist seeks to draw people into the empty trenches and blackened craters of its battlefield. The mist may roam far and wide, questing vainly for someone that can understand it. The mist prefers lone targets.

Combat

When a target nears, the mist reaches out with up to six tentacles, each of which can extend 20 feet in any direction. The phantasmal limbs do not cause damage directly at first, but they touch the victim's mind, projecting a nightmare vision of the event that created the mist into the victim's mind.

This usually has the unfortunate effect of driving the victim insane—or at least scaring the Hell out of them.

While the mist can reform on the following day if it is destroyed, this causes the critter an extreme amount of pain, and it defends itself vigorously against any physical attack. While the mist always uses at least one of its tentacle attacks to "share its pain" with a victim, when physically threatened it uses at least half its other attacks to defend itself.

Psychic pain (Sp): If the mist makes a successful touch attack, the victim must make a Will saving throw against DC 17. If they are successful, the mist's touch causes only a strong uneasiness and terrible sense of doom that renders the victim unable to act for a round. If the target fails their save, their mind floods with images of the inglorious battle that created the mist. These images are chaotic, surrealistic, and nightmarish, but hold hints as to the nature and location of the anchor that must be destroyed to free the mist. The victim cannot act for two rounds as they are bombarded by psychic images. Once the visions end, the victim must make a Will saving throw against DC 13 or lash out at the mist with their bare hands for 1d4 rounds.

Chilling touch (Sp): The mist can attack up to three targets in a single round, doing 2d6 cold damage as it inflicts the chill of the grave on its opponents. Non-magical Armor does not help against this attack.

Hellish cry (Sp): Once a battle turns against a mourning mist, its cry becomes frighteningly loud within a 60-foot radius. Everyone within that radius must make a Will saving throw against DC 5 or be unable to act for a round. The check need be made only once, regardless of how long the character stays in the screech's area of effect. The screech also deafens all characters within range for 1d4 hours afterwards, but those who make a Fortitude saving throw against DC 13 suffer only a -2 penalty to all rolls that involve listening ability.

Spirit anchor (Su): If the creature's anchor is discovered and sanctified by a blessed character, the mist disperses forever. Unless its anchor is destroyed, the mist always reappears at the next sunset, even if it was "killed" the day before.

Mummies

Many cultures treated their dead with great respect and prepared their bodies so they would better serve their owners in the afterworld. Unfortunately, upon the Reckoners' escape, some of these began to serve again in the world of the living.

Although mummification can result from climatic conditions, reanimation of those corpses only produces desiccated dead (see page 118 for all the details). Also, lesser mummies—those of servants and the like—are treated as desiccated dead as well. Only a rare few powerful individuals arise as true mummies.

Aztec Mummy

Medium-Size Undead
Hit Dice: 7d12 (45 hp)
Initiative: +0
Speed: 30 ft.
AC: 10
Attacks: Macahuitl +8 melee
Damage: Macahuitl 2d6+3
Face/Reach: 5 ft. by 5 ft./5 ft.
Special Attacks: Fear, spells
Special Qualities: Fearless, undead, jade stone
Saves: Fort +5, Ref +2, Will +5
Abilities: Str 16, Dex 11, Con –, Int 10, Wis 12, Cha 13
Skills: Black Magic +6, Climb +5, Hide +5, Intimidate +6, Knowledge (arcana, Aztec culture/history) +6, Listen +5, Move Silently +5, Spot +5
Feats: Cleave, Power Attack
Climate/Terrain: Any land
Challenge Rating: 6 (7 with jade stone)
Alignment: Always chaotic evil
Advancement: As black magician character class

The appearance of an Aztec mummy varies according to the freshness of its heart. With a new heart, the mummy is similar to a Harrowed—only detectable as undead with some effort. As the heart weakens, the mummy's skin begins to dry and tighten, until, on the last day, it becomes little more than a dried-up, withered bag of walking bones.

The Aztec culture relied on two methods to prepare their dead for the afterworld. The first, cremation, left little to later reanimate and plague ancestors. However, during certain periods of their history, the Aztecs practiced a form of mummification, particularly for those who were consider specially blessed or important.

Occasionally, one of these mummies—usually that of a mighty king or priest—returns to the world of the living. These revenants usually inhabit ruins or other areas tied to their past, and surround themselves with items appropriate to their history. Abominations of this sort often attract their own cult of human followers as well.

Combat

Unlike Egyptian mummies, one of the Aztec variety tends to be fairly nimble and quick. It uses this to its advantage in a melee, as it seeks to remove its victim's hearts in an effort to continue its unnatural existence. They are typically buried with an obsidian-bladed sword called a *macahuitl*, which they wield with deadly effect.

Fear (Su): Anyone catching sight of an Aztec mummy must make a Will saving throw against DC 19.

Spells (Sp): Commensurate with their Hit Dice levels, Aztec mummies have access to a wide range of black magic.

Jade stone (Su): Some mummies of this sort possess a small jade stone that protects them from all forms of attack. As long as a mummy has its jade stone, it has the Special Abilities damage reduction 25/- and fast healing 25. These mummies carry the stone underneath their tongues

Undead (Su): Focus—heart; Aztec culture placed a great value on the sacrifice of human hearts to their gods, and mummies rely on the power of those sacrifices to continue their existence among the living. Every twenty days, an Aztec mummy must remove the heart from a living person—which, of course, kills the victim. It then places the organ in its own chest cavity. The still beating heart then preserves the mummy's undead state for another twenty days. At the end of the period, the sacrifice must be repeated.

Egyptian Mummy

Medium-Size Undead
Hit Dice: 6d12 (39 hp)
Initiative: -1 (Dex)
Speed: 15 ft.
AC: 9 (-1 Dex)
Attacks: Punch +8 melee
Damage: Punch 1d3+4 (s)
Face/Reach: 5 ft. by 5 ft./5 ft.
Special Attacks: Spells, improved grab, constrict 1d6+4
Special Qualities: Fearless, undead, damage reduction 5/-, fast healing 5
Saves: Fort +5, Ref +1, Will +4
Abilities: Str 19, Dex 8, Con –, Int 9, Wis 13, Cha 14
Skills: Black Magic +6, Climb +5, Hide +4, Intimidate +5, Knowledge (ancient Egyptian history, arcana) +5, Listen +5, Move Silently +4, Spot +5
Feats: Cleave, Power Attack
Climate/Terrain: Desert and Underground
Challenge Rating: 8
Alignment: Always chaotic evil
Advancement: As black magician character class

In their natural form, Egyptian mummies look very much like desiccated corpses wrapped in ancient cloth bandages. Their skin is tightly drawn across their features and tanned by the passage of centuries. However, a mummy usually relies on an illusion to appear as a normal Arabic person.

This undead horror only arises from the embalmed corpse of an ancient Egyptian high priest or sorcerer. Such persons were usually buried in well-appointed tombs—tombs that are just now beginning to draw the interest of archaeologists and fortune hunters. After such a long rest, few Egyptian mummies take kindly to being disturbed.

These undead are normally buried with great riches and other, lesser mummies for servants in the afterworld. A mummy hunts down any who desecrate—or worse, rob!—its tomb. Often the abomination is aided by its former servants; these take the form of desiccated walkin' dead.

A posse's not too likely to run across one of these things roaming the desert outside Tombstone, so an Egyptian mummy should be a truly rare encounter. However, enough individuals and organizations have an active interest in the occult (or just ancient treasures) that somebody's sure to draw the ire of one at some point.

Combat

Mummies are have had centuries to perfect their patience and always carefully plot their revenge. The mastery of black magic (particularly illusion) allows them options not available to most undead.

Spells (Sp): Commensurate with their Hit Dice levels, Egyptian mummies have access to a wide range of black magic.

Improved grab (Ex): Egyptian mummies can grab any target equal in Size or smaller., and employ this ability to strangle (constrict) victims without the use of a weapon.

Undead (Su): Focus—burial scroll. If a mummy's burial scroll is destroyed, the monster crumbles to dust. For that reason, this scroll is *always* well hidden and protected.

Should a posse succeed in doing enough damage to actually kill the creature, it rises again the next night to pursue its victim. Even burning the corpse to ashes won't prevent its return.

Nagual

Medium-Size Shapechanger
Hit Dice: 4d8+1 (22 hp)
Initiative: +3 (Dex)
Speed: 30 ft., 15 ft. climb
AC: 13 (+3 Dex)
Attacks: 2 claws +5 melee; or by melee weapon type +5; or by ranged weapon type +6
Damage: Claw 1d6+2, by melee weapon type +2, by ranged weapon type
Face/Reach: 5 ft. by 5 ft./5 ft.
Special Qualities: Damage reduction 5/obsidian, scent, obsidian weakness
Saves: Fort +5, Ref +7, Will +6
Abilities: Str 14, Dex 16, Con 13, Int 9, Wis 14, Cha 14
Skills: Climb +10, Hide +6, Listen +6, Move Silently +6, Spot +6, Swim +5, Wilderness Lore +6
Feats: Track

Climate/Terrain: Any land
Challenge Rating: 2
Alignment: Usually chaotic evil
Advancement: By character class

Naguals are superficially similar to werewolves, humans able to transform themselves into animals—specifically jaguars. Their appearance is unremarkable in their normal forms, but once transformed they resemble large, anthropomorphic jaguars.

The naguals are creatures out of the ancient history of Central America. In the last days of the Aztec Empire, the emperor's most powerful sorcerer-priests attempted to concoct a suitable revenge against the Spanish soldiers that had ravaged the Aztecs once-mighty empire.

Nine of the emperor's best warriors were chosen to undergo a ritual to give them the power of the jaguar. In the

darkness of the new moon, the sorcerers tore out the warriors' hearts with obsidian knives and replaced them with the hearts of jaguars, sealing the powers of the great cats in the breasts of the nine.

The warriors fought well in the guise of jaguars, waging a nightly war against the invaders until only three were left and their Empire was no more. These three agreed they must fade into the shadows and produce children who could carry on the fight for subsequent generations.

Eventually, some of the descendants of the original warriors, who held the essence of the jaguar within their breasts, migrated northward, settling in the lands that would eventually become the Confederacy and the United States of America. Here, the naguals changed form but rarely, always using their abilities to aid the poor and oppressed around them.

Then came the Reckoning. The arcane energies released from the Hunting Grounds warped and twisted some naguals, turning them into creatures of sinister cunning with a dark hatred of humanity.

Even the naguals that still fight for causes they feel to be right cannot help but generate fear in their victims and enemies, and so feed the Reckoners like any abomination. As a result, they eventually become tainted by evil and begin to terrorize the innocent.

Combat

Like lycanthropes, naguals are affected by phases of the moon, and are forced to assume their jaguar forms on the dark nights of the new moon, which provide cover for their actions. Unlike standard were-forms, though, the nagual retains all its human intelligence and cunning in all its forms.

Naguals are very patient stalkers, striking only when their prey is at its most vulnerable. Surprise, stealth and speed are the hallmarks of all their attacks. Naguals can use any normal weapons, but most prefer their natural ones

Obsidian weakness (Su): Weapons made of obsidian do full normal damage to naguals.

Nibblers

Diminutive Beast
Hit Dice: 1d10-1 (4 hp)
Initiative: +1 (Dex)
Speed: 65 ft. swim
AC: 15 (+4 size, +1 Dex)
Attacks: Bite +1 melee
Damage: Bite 1 hit point
Face/Reach: 1 ft. by 1 ft./0 ft.
Special Attacks: Swarm
Saves: Fort +1, Ref +3, Will -2
Abilities: Str 3, Dex 12, Con 7, Int 5, Wis 6, Cha 5
Skills: Hide +13, Listen +3, Move Silently +3, Spot +3, Swim +5, Wilderness Lore +4
Feats: None
Climate/Terrain: Aquatic
Challenge Rating: 1/2
Alignment: Always neutral
Advancement: 2-3 HD (Diminutive)

These fish resemble their larger, South American cousins, the piranha. They are about 3" to 4" in length and fairly narrow. Their scales are a blood red color and their mouths have large, jutting, lower jaws filled with needlelike fangs.

Due to the influence of the Reckoning, these ferocious little biters can live in either fresh or salt water, and freely travel between the two. They normally travel in schools of 300 or more, and waters infested with them may contain thousands of the creatures.

Combat

Any creature entering such waters is likely to survive only a few moments before being stripped bare! In sufficient numbers, these tiny abominations are even capable of gnawing through boat hulls, to get to the "tasty filling" inside.

Swarm (Ex): Every group of 10 nibblers in a feeding school does 1d4 damage.

Night Raven

Tiny Magical Beast
Hit Dice: 2d10 (11 hp)
Initiative: +4 (Improved Initiative)
Speed: 70 ft. fly (average)
AC: 12 (+2 size)
Attacks: Claws +2 melee
Damage: Claw 1d3-2
Face/Reach: 2 1/2 ft. by 2 1/2 ft./0 ft.
Special Attacks: Inflict nightmares, fear, gaze attack
Saves: Fort +3, Ref +3, Will +1
Abilities: Str 5, Dex 9, Con 11, Int 8, Wis 12, Cha 12
Skills: Hide +8, Intimidate +5, Listen +5, Move Silently +5, Spot +5
Feats: Improved Initiative
Climate/Terrain: Any land
Challenge Rating: 2
Alignment: Always neutral evil
Advancement: 3-6 HD (Tiny)

Night ravens are nearly indistinguishable from common ravens. However, while feeding, a night raven takes on a dark glow that suggests its evil nature.

Everyone has nightmares, particularly in the Weird West. Indian legend tells that bad dreams are sometimes brought by dark birds in the night. These night ravens then feed off the fear generated by their victims' nightmares. Unfortunately for those prone to bad dreams, the Reckoners have brought these monsters of legends to life.

Night ravens can sense a sleeper's unconscious activity. They are attracted to vivid dreams and establish a psychic link with the dreamer. The raven then alters the content of the dream by drawing upon the sleeper's worries and fears, changing the dreams to generate even more anxiety on which it feeds.

Ironically, night-raven feathers can be used to make powerful dream catchers. Any such item made with a night raven's feathers prevent anyone sleeping under them from having nightmares, whether natural or otherwise.

Night ravens have been known to work as servitors of other abominations and even human sorcerers. These night ravens usually inflict nightmares on enemies of their masters.

Combat

A night raven chooses a victim to whom it can return for several nights. At first, the changes it makes in the sleeper's dreams are minor, but with each visit the terror increases. Night ravens never physically attack and they flee from dangerous situations. When threatened, the night raven tries to make eye contact and frighten the attacker into inaction long enough to allow escape.

Gaze attack (Sp): The night raven tries to make eye contact with anyone who would dare try to threaten it. A person who meets the raven's stare must immediately make a Will saving throw against DC 14 or fall victim to the Fear Special Ability due to the awful

sense of supernatural horror conveyed by the creature's eyes abnormally black eyes.

Inflict nightmares (Sp): When a night raven first selects a new victim, the sleeper must make a Will saving throw against DC 15. If the sleeper wins, the raven tries again the next two nights before seeking an easier target.

However, if the raven wins, it can alter the sleeper's dreams. The first night, the nightmares are relatively mild and require the victim to make a Will saving throw roll against DC 10. On each subsequent night, the power of the nightmare increases, and the DC rises by +2. The dreams become more and more vivid, and when the DC reaches 14, the victim begins to suffer the physical effects of the nightmare. For example, if the dreamer was wounded in the nightmare, the damage is applied to his waking form. Damage from the nightmares, however, is usually limited by the raven, who prefers the victim to succumb to the terror. The night raven's visits continue until the monster is killed or the victim dies of fright

Fear (Su): Any waking person who sees a feeding raven must make a Will saving throw against DC 10 or be affected by this Ability.

Patchwork Monsters

Not all threats of the new science come wrapped in steel and powered by steam. It didn't take long for mad scientists to start experimenting with reanimation and grafting processes. But, for years, no one was able to bring get the parts to function as a whole-or even by themselves. Then, along came Dr. Wilma Meister.

Meister figured out that by putting a portion of a single brain in each of the attached parts, reanimation was possible. What she didn't know was that she was creating a type of walkin' dead that has brains everywhere in its body—not just the head! Now, a small group of mad scientists experiment with Meister's findings, creating amalgams of human and animal parts.

Patchwork surgery is a branch of mad science that, thankfully, isn't too popular in the current thought. That's probably because the idea of stitching an assortment of parts and pieces to a corpse just strikes most folks the wrong way. Yeah, right—like there's a *right* way for that to strike someone!

(Dr. Meister wasn't actually the first to pioneer patchwork science, of course. Check out page 35 for the true modern Prometheus).

Patchwork Men

Medium-Size Undead
Hit Dice: 4d12 (26 hp)
Initiative: +0
Speed: 30 ft.
AC: 10
Attacks: Bite +3 melee
Damage: Bite 1d3+1
Face/Reach: 5 ft. by 5 ft./5 ft.
Special Attacks: Enhancements, disease
Special Qualities: Fearless, undead, enhancements
Saves: Fort +1, Ref +1, Will +4
Abilities: Str 13, Dex 11, Con –, Int 7, Wis 9, Cha 8
Skills: Climb +6, Hide +5, Listen +4, Move Silently +5, Spot +4, Swim +5
Feats: Power Attack
Climate/Terrain: Any land
Challenge Rating: 3 (4 with enhancements and/or disease)
Alignment: Usually lawful neutral
Advancement: 5-12 HD (Medium-Size)

Patchwork men are obviously artificial creations. Large sewing and grafting scars crisscross their bodies and the abominations often have very nonhuman parts attached. They seldom display the decay or other signs of death that walkin' dead do.

Most mad scientists drawn to this unsavory practice focus their endeavors on the human body. Patchwork men are largely human in design and function, with a few "extras" thrown in every now and then to make them interesting.

Combat

As a general rule, patchwork men are bound by their creator's will, and in combat tend to follow whatever instructions have been laid out for them. Those with a measure of independent thought tend to be brutal killers using whatever deadly parts have been sewn onto their forms.

Disease (Ex): Sometimes a patchwork scientist isn't careful about where he "harvests" his materials, and as a result a few patchwork creations may carry any number of diseases. If infected, the patchwork man can pass on a disease by making a successful attack (touch or otherwise), and the victim must then make a Fortitude saving throw against DC 10 to avoid contagion.

Enhancements (Ex):. Claws, extra-sharp teeth, horns, and the like are added to some patchwork men, giving them a 1d3+2 damage attack. Others have animal sensory organs (ears, eyes, noses, etc.) attached to give them a +2 (or higher) bonus to Spot and Listen skill checks–or even entirely new senses like radar, sonar, etc. which confer the Special Ability Blindsight. Extra muscle can be added to patchwork men, boosting their Str to superhuman levels.

Undead (Su): Focus–patchwork; The creature can only be killed if all its individual parts are completely destroyed by fire, acid or the like.

Patchwork Wasp

Small Undead
Hit Dice: 1d12 (6 hp)
Initiative: +0
Speed: 30 ft., 40 ft. fly (poor)
AC: 11 (+1 size)
Attacks: Sting +1 melee
Damage: Sting 1d4 and poison
Face/Reach: 5 ft. by 5 ft./5 ft.
Special Attacks: Poison
Special Qualities: Multifaceted eyes, undead, fearless
Saves: Fort +0, Ref +0, Will +1
Abilities: Str 9, Dex 11, Con –, Int 6, Wis 7, Cha 5
Skills: Climb +4, Hide +4, Listen +4, Move Silently +4, Spot +8
Feats: Flyby Attack
Climate/Terrain: Any land
Challenge Rating: 2
Alignment: Usually lawful neutral
Advancement: 2-3 HD (Small)

Although it uses mostly human parts for its construction, this little horror is about as alien as you can get. The core of the body is a human head and torso. Attached to the torso like an insect's legs are six arms, complete with hands. A small, hollowed-out cow's horn on the backside is the stinger, with extra, external human stomachs serving as poison sacs. The wings are a disgusting marvel of bio-construction, made from hollow human forearm bones and thinly stretched human skin.

If patchwork men are the norm for patchwork scientists, then this critter is probably the far end of the patchwork

science spectrum. It's design is so unusual—and disgusting—that most mad scientists steer clear of it. However, it does serve as a good example of just how extreme a patchwork creation can get when designed by a scientist with absolutely no scruples.

Combat

See the Patchwork Men entry on page 72.

Poison (Ex): A cowpoke stung by a patchwork wasp is injected with a strong toxin. Its statistics are: Type Injury, DC 17, Initial Damage 2d6, Secondary Damage paralysis for 3d6 minutes.

Multifaceted eyes (Ex): The wasp has a mass of human eyes grafted into each socket, giving it a +4 bonus to all Spot skill checks.

Undead (Su): Focus—patchwork; The creature can only be killed if all its individual parts are completely destroyed by fire, acid or the like.

Piasa

Large Beast
Hit Dice: 8d10+1 (52 hp)
Initiative: +1 (Dex)
Speed: 30 ft., 85 ft. fly (poor)
AC: 14 (-1 size, +1 Dex, +4 natural)
Attacks: Beak +9 melee, 2 claws +4 melee
Damage: Beak 2d6+4, claw 1d6+2
Face/Reach: 5 ft. by 10 ft./5 ft.
Special Attacks: Improved grab
Special Qualities: Light weakness
Saves: Fort +7, Ref +7, Will +2
Abilities: Str 19, Dex 12, Con 12, Int 6, Wis 11, Cha 8
Skills: Climb +8, Listen +9, Move Silently +9, Spot +9, Wilderness Lore +8
Feats: None
Climate/Terrain: Temperate Hill and Mountains
Challenge Rating: 5
Alignment: Always neutral
Advancement: 9-16 HD (Large), 17-24 HD (Huge)

The piasa is like a cross between a bat and a woodpecker—with a little lizard thrown in for spice. It stands 7' tall at the shoulder and has a nearly 35' wingspan. The monster's wings are modified hands, like a bat's. Its feet end in long, gray talons and its otherwise bat-like face has a narrow, piercing beak. Its hide is black as the deepest night.

Piasas are normally solitary hunters, but nested pairs are fiercely loyal and fight to the death to protect each other. It favors hilly and rocky terrain that allows it to swoop onto its prey from above. Piasas are found along the central Mississippi and Missouri Rivers, and as yet, it hasn't spread further west than the Rockies, north of the Great Lakes or east of western Tennessee and Kentucky.

Combat

Piasas hunt at night, diving onto their prey from the dark sky and pinning them to the ground with their enormous wing membranes. Once its victim is so trapped, the abomination uses its hard beak to puncture the skull, allowing it to lap out brain matter—the monster's only food. The piasa hunts any creature up to Large Size, but favors cows, horses, and, of course, humans.

Light weakness (Ex): In any light brighter than a torch, the piasa suffers -2 to all rolls.

Skills: Piasas receive a +4 bonus to all Climb, Listen, Move Silently, Spot and Wilderness Lore skill rolls.

Pit Wasps

Medium Vermin
Hit Dice: 1d8-1 (3 hp)
Initiative: +0
Speed: 5 ft. climb, 40 ft. fly (good)
AC: 12 (+2 size)
Attacks: Sting +1 melee
Damage: Sting 1d6-1
Face/Reach: 2 1/2 ft. by 2 1/2 ft./0 ft.
Special Attacks: Poison
Special Qualities: Maneuverability, hive mind, subtypes
Saves: Fort +1, Ref +0, Will +0
Abilities: Str 7, Dex 11, Con 8, Int -, Wis 10, Cha 8
Skills: Climb +7, Hide +8, Listen +3, Move Silently +3, Spot +3, Wilderness Lore +3
Feats: None
Climate/Terrain: Temperate Forest and Underground
Challenge Rating: 1
Alignment: Always neutral
Advancement: 2 HD (Small), 3 HD (Medium-Size)

The pit wasp is a gigantic version of the smaller, namesake insect. Its spiky exoskeleton is predominantly red, so some people unfortunate enough to live close to a hive of the critters call them "red coats." The things range from about 2 to 6 feet long.

Pit wasps consume wood, and have been known to demolish small towns in search of sustenance. The wasps transform some of the cellulose into building material for their nests. Normally found in wooded areas, these nests are usually 12 to 30 feet tall and 20 to 90 feet across, with tunnels and pits dug beneath them. The tunnels branch out into the ground, and the entrance to the nest can be located up to a mile from the main body of it. These underground passages sometimes run close to the surface, and it isn't unheard of for a person or animal to fall through the ceiling of a tunnel.

Fortunately for any wasp hunters, the nests burn easily, being composed of paper, more or less. However, the closer a person gets to the nest, the more wasps he meets, in three convenient sizes. The smallest are the workers, which make up about two thirds of the hive's population. Each of these critters is about 2 feet long and very strong, able to fly while carrying up to 40 pounds. The workers gather food and other necessary materials for the hive's survival and do all the building necessary.

Guarding the workers are the warriors, which make up most of the remaining third of the hive. Each of these nasty beasts measures about 3' in length. Warriors are fast and smart; they can solve problems creatively, and are difficult to trap or capture. Warriors have stingers connected to glands that secrete a powerful tranquilizer. Warriors guard the nest, the workers, and the queen.

Running the whole hive is the queen, a rarely seen critter. She usually stays underground, attended by a few males (useless critters incapable of attacking) and a handful of workers and warriors. The queen also produces a lot of eggs, and a hive that has only a dozen members one week might have a much larger population when next approached.

Combat

The pit wasp queen directs the rest of the hive by some unknown form of communication, and in battle does so efficiently and ruthlessly. She lends her wisdom to the other members of the hive. Under her direction, the wasp warriors make short work of most intruders.

Poison (Ex): Warriors and queens have poison stings. Any victim stung by one of these pit wasps takes 1d4 points

of subdual damage at the beginning of every round thereafter for 10 rounds or until unconscious. The effect of multiple stings is cumulative, so someone who gets stung twice takes 2d4 hit points at the beginning of the next round.

Hive mind (Ex): Pit wasps within 300 feet of the queen are assumed to be in communication with her (even if separated by solid material) and use her Wis and Cha Ability scores.

Maneuverability (Ex): When flying, a pit wasp increases its Dex by +2.

Subtypes (Ex): *Queen:* The hive's mother and director has Wis 11 and Cha 9.

Warrior: They have a flying Speed of 50 ft.

Worker: A worker pit wasp has a Strength of 9.

Poison Woman

Medium-Size Undead
Hit Dice: 6d12 (39 hp)
Initiative: +0
Speed: 15 ft.
AC: 10
Attacks: Kick +4 melee
Damage: Kick 1d6+1
Face/Reach: 5 ft. by 5 ft./5 ft.
Special Attacks: Poison, spells
Special Qualities: Damage reduction 25/-, fast healing 5, coup, vulnerability
Saves: Fort +2, Ref +2, Will +5
Abilities: Str 13, Dex 9, Con –, Int 17, Wis 11, Cha 14
Skills: Black Magic +7, Bluff +7, Climb +6, Craft +6, Knowledge (Indian lore) +6, Hide +6, Listen +6, Pick Pocket +7, Sleight of Hand +7, Spot +6, Wilderness Lore +6
Feats: Cleave, Great Cleave, Improved Bull Rush, Power Attack, Sunder
Climate/Terrain: Any land
Challenge Rating: 5 (6 with Spells)
Alignment: Always chaotic evil
Advancement: By character class

A poison woman looks exactly as she did in life except that her legs are much thicker and stronger than before, the top of her skull is missing, and part of her brains are exposed. She wears a hat or something to cover up her brain, since it is her only weakness.

An old Sioux legend claims that once upon a time, women could pull their brains out of their heads and use the old gray matter to brew poisons. While some might simply dismiss this as a misogynistic tale, there is a bit of truth to it–at least since the Reckoning.

Whenever a woman kills a man with poison within the borders of the Sioux Nations (including Deadwood), there is a chance she becomes a poison woman. (Any female guilty of such a deed returns to life as a poison woman rather than becoming Harrowed.) If she does in fact attract the attention of the Reckoners, they imbue her corpse with a seed of supernatural energy, blowing the top of her head off. Men, by the way, are not subject to this particular curse.

The truly grotesque part of the resurrection is that afterwards the newly-arisen abomination can pick out pieces of her brain and use them to poison foods. The poison woman attempts to do just that to any unwary travelers who accept her offer of a home-cooked meal, which usually turns out to be their last.

Combat

Poison women who possess black magical abilities use whatever black arcana they have learned against their enemies. More mundane varieties of this abomination rely on devastating kicks delivered with their preternaturally powerful legs.

Poison (Su): This abomination can pick out pieces of her brain and use them to poison foods. She takes no damage from doing this, and the lost brain matter regenerates within an hour or so. Once in the food, a Spot skill check against DC 17 is required to detect it. Its relevant statistics are: **Type:** Ingested, **DC:** 17, **Initial Damage:** 1d2 Con, **Secondary Damage:** 1d4 Con. If the target rolls a natural one on any of their saving throws, they die immediately.

Spells (Sp): Commensurate with their Hit Dice levels, some poison women can use black magic.

Vulnerability (Su): The only way to harm a poison woman is to attack her through the hole in her noggin. Unfortunately, it is nearly impossible to hit her brain. Attackers must hit the hole's AC 20, and then only if they manage to position themselves so they can see the hole. Her fast healing ability is ineffective against this type of damage.

Coup: Any Harrowed who absorbs the essence of a poison woman can scoop out some of their own brains and use them to poison the walkin' dead. Any walkin' dead smelling the stuff drop whatever they're doing and chow down on the brains for 1d4 rounds, after which they must make a Will saving throw against DC 18 or drop dead (for good, this time) on the spot. This little stunt causes 1d4 damage points to the Harrowed character, which can't be cured by magic or first aid, though the Harrowed Stitchin' feat still works, as does normal Harrowed healing.

Pox Walker

Medium-Size Undead
Hit Dice: 6d12 (39 hp)
Initiative: +0
Speed: 20 ft.
AC: 10
Attacks: Short bow +6 ranged; or large knife +7 melee
Damage: Short bow 1d6 plus disease, large knife 1d4+2 plus disease
Face/Reach: 5 ft. by 5 ft./5 ft.
Special Attacks: Disease, spatter, virulent breath
Special Qualities: Coup
Saves: Fort +5, Ref +3, Will +3
Abilities: Str 13, Dex 10, Con –, Int 9, Wis 12, Cha 10
Skills: Climb +5, Hide +5, Knowledge (local) +5, Listen +5, Move Silently +5, Ride +6, Spot +5, Wilderness Lore +5
Feats: Killing Shot, Mounted Combat, Power Attack, Track
Climate/Terrain: Any land
Challenge Rating: 4
Alignment: Always chaotic evil
Advancement: As brave character class

A pox walker appears as an Indian whose skin is pocked with pus-filled sores oozing yellow fluid, with flesh hanging limply where sores have burst. Its eyes are milky, and its body wracked by tremors. Froth gathers at the corners of its mouth, and it dribbles gobbets of sputum as it exhales.

When a particularly angry brave or shaman dies of smallpox or some other disease brought by the white man, there is a chance the Reckoners take notice of this fact and give the body new life as an abomination so it can spread the pestilence. After all, there's nothing like a good plague to cause a panic.

Pox walkers are solitary creatures who use stealth and vicious cunning to spread the disease among those they feel have wronged them. Fortunately, thus far, the appearance of a pox walker has been an incredibly rare event in the Weird West.

Combat

Pox walkers shun firearms, preferring to fight their prey close up (the better to spread the disease). However, some pox walkers, particularly Apaches and those from the Coyote Confederation, have been known to stab themselves with arrows, covering the arrowheads with their infected pus before firing them.

Pox walkers choose a white man over all others—and anyone else before an Indian—as an opponent. Some have thrown themselves off cliffs or into rivers rather than attack the native peoples, but these are few and far between. Woe betide any brave who thinks himself safe because of his race.

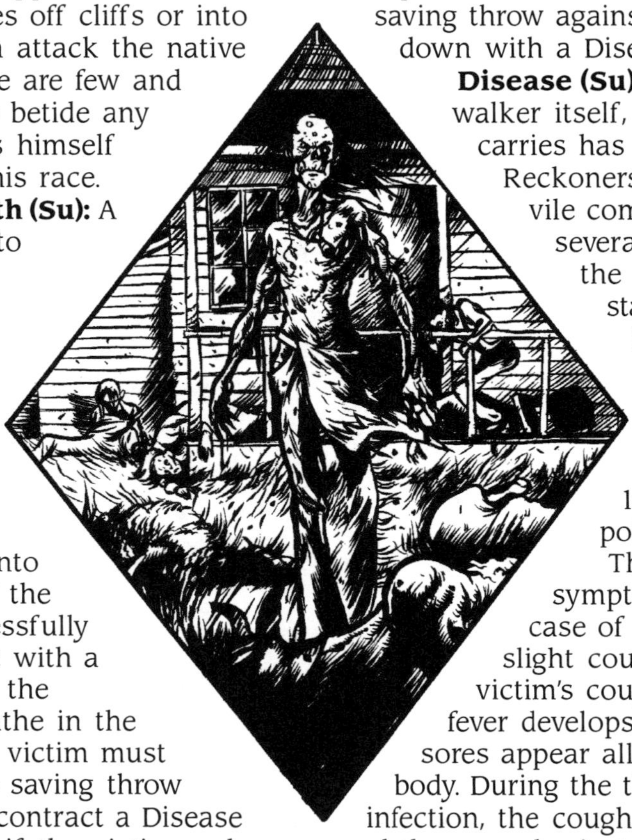

Virulent Breath (Su): A pox walker tries to grapple with antagonists whenever possible, attempting to breathe its foul, disease-tainted breath into the face of whoever comes into contact with it. If the pox walker successfully Pins an opponent with a Grappling attack, the monster can breathe in the victim's face. The victim must make a Fortitude saving throw against DC 13 or contract a Disease (see below). Even if the victim makes the saving throw, they take 1d6 damage and receives a -2 to all rolls for the next two rounds, due to the noxious smell of the pox walker's breath. The effect is cumulative if the same victim gets breathed on again before recovering.

Spatter (Ex): Any time the pox walker is hit in combat, it attempts a Fortitude saving throw against DC 19. If it fails, one of the sores on its body bursts, spattering pus in a 10-foot radius. Anyone within that radius must make a Reflex saving throw against DC 13 . Those that fail must make a Fortitude saving throw against DC 17. Failure indicates they contract a Disease.

The pox walker usually carries at least a knife and a bow and arrows, both of which it coats with the toxin from the sores on its body. This coating is good for one hit, and the pox walker can reapply the toxin with a Partial action. Anyone hit with one of these weapons must make a Fortitude saving throw against DC 13 or come down with a Disease.

Disease (Su): Like the pox walker itself, the disease it carries has been altered by Reckoners, changed into a vile combination of several diseases. It has the following statistics—**Infection:** Inhaled, Injury, Contact, **DC:** 17, **Incubation:** 1 hour, **Damage:** 1d4 Str, 1d4 Dex, 1d4 Con and 1d4 hit points.

The earliest symptoms are merely a case of the chills and a slight cough, then the victim's cough gets worse, a fever develops, and bright red sores appear all over the victim's body. During the third day of infection, the cough and fever worsen, and the sores begin to itch and fill with pus. The victim also becomes contagious, as if he had the pox walker's Virulent Breath (as described above).

In the fourth day of infection, the victim's body is wracked by constant tremors and chills. The coughing is almost constant, and the victim's vision blurs. The sores begin to burst, oozing pus, and the victim gains the pox walker's Spatter ability. Ultimately, a victim killed by the disease is wracked by a final, great spasm as they die. After death, instead of potentially becoming Harrowed, the victim must check to see if they become a pox walker.

Harrowed characters are immune to the effects of the disease, but if subjected to it (through either spatter or virulent breath), they must make a Will saving throw against DC 17 or become carriers of the disease, as described in the Coup section.

Once the victim (or the pox walker itself) is dead, the body must be burned immediately, or else there is a good chance that flies or other vermin may carry the disease elsewhere.

Coup: A Harrowed who counts coup with a pox walker can thereafter try to absorb any disease (be it a cold, smallpox, or even gangrene) from an infected person by making a Con check against DC 13. If successful, the Harrowed absorbs the disease, and the victim is "cured;" otherwise, there is no change in either's condition. If the Harrowed rolls a natural one, not only is the victim not cured, but their condition actually worsens, and the Harrowed becomes a carrier anyway.

Only one disease can be carried (and one victim cured) at a time. To stop being a carrier of the disease, the Harrowed must deliberately pass the disease on to someone else (as if they had the pox walker's Virulent Breath, described above). If the Harrowed decides not to pass on the disease and simply holds it, after about three weeks, the disease starts to bleed off into the air around her and affect people anyway. After a number of people equal to half the Harrowed's Con (round down) have been affected—or a period of two months goes by without any living human contact—the disease fully dissipates.

Prairie Tick Queen

Small Vermin
Hit Dice: 6d8+4 (51 hp)
Initiative: +1 (Dex)
Speed: 20 ft., 10 ft. climb
AC: 22 (+1 size, +1 Dex, +10 natural)
Attacks: 4 hooks +6 melee, bite +1 melee
Damage: Hook 1d4+1, bite 1d3
Face/Reach: 5 ft. by 5 ft./5 ft.
Special Attacks: Improved grab, blood drain
Special Qualities: Hive mind
Saves: Fort +9, Ref +3, Will +2
Abilities: Str 13, Dex 13, Con 18, Int —, Wis 10, Cha 11
Skills: Climb +9, Hide +4, Listen +4, Move Silently +4, Spot +4
Feats: None
Climate/Terrain: Underground
Challenge Rating: 6
Alignment: Always neutral
Advancement: 7-12 HD (Small), 13-18 HD (Medium-Size)

Queens resemble a dog-sized prairie tick, with an elongated and swollen abdomen. An ovipositor extends from the lower rear portion of her abdomen. Her mouth parts are larger and are able to penetrate skin, unlike those of drone ticks. A small horde of hatchlings often cling to her body as she moves around the egg chamber depositing her pasty, grub-like eggs.

Prairie tick queens evolve from "drone" prairie ticks. This usually occurs in two instances—if the tick is carried far from its nest before its host succumbs, or the nest grows too large and some members are forced out. This migration/evolution process makes prairie ticks very prolific.

Prairie tick warrens are usually labyrinths of small, 2' diameter tunnels that may stretch as far as a quarter mile in any direction. Rooting prairie ticks out of the ground is therefore very difficult. The queen's egg chamber is much larger than other chambers—often more than 20' in diameter—and usually located near the center of the warrens.

Within an egg chamber are as many as 40 eggs and 20 or more prairie tick hatchlings, depending on how successful the drones have been in securing blood. A queen's reproductive cycle depends entirely on the amount of blood she receives.

The queen is a fat and lazy creature, seldom leaving the nest's egg chamber. She remains underground and feeds from her bloated drones. She give birth to all of the tick on the nest, and her children protect her fiercely. All

members of a nest converge to protect the queen should she be threatened.

Combat

When threatened, the queen directs the hatchlings, which ride, massed on her thorax and distended abdomen, to swarm the nearest warm body. (After all, she can always spawn more should the "babies" be killed!) If a queen is forced to defend herself, she employs her hooks against multiple enemies and blood drain against singular threats.

Improved grab (Ex): Queens can use improved grab against Medium-Size targets or smaller.

Blood drain (Ex): Once a queen bites a victim, she drains their blood and inflicts 1d4 damage per round.

Hive mind (Ex): The queen can communicate with all prairie ticks in the nest out to a range of 300 feet. This allows here to coordinate the nest's defensive efforts and ambushes of nearby prey.

Prairie Tick Hatchlings

Diminutive Vermin
Hit Dice: 1d8 (4 hp)
Initiative: +1 (Dex)
Speed: 35 ft., 15 ft. climb
AC: 17 (+4 size, +1 Dex, +2 natural)
Attacks: None
Damage: None
Face/Reach: 1 ft. by 1 ft./0 ft.
Special Attacks: Swarm, invasion
Saves: Fort +2, Ref +1, Will -2
Abilities: Str 3, Dex 12, Con 9, Int –, Wis 6, Cha 6
Skills: Climb +5, Hide +13, Listen +2, Move Silently +2, Spot +2, Wilderness Lore +1
Feats: None
Climate/Terrain: Underground
Challenge Rating: 1/2
Alignment: Always neutral
Advancement: See the prairie tick profile in the *Deadlands: The Weird West D20 Rulebook*

Hatchlings are miniature prairie ticks about the size of a lady's palm when their legs are fully extended. They are a paler shade of red, almost pinkish in hue. These tiny arachnids often ride on the queen's body, massed on her thorax and distended abdomen.

Combat

When the queen is threatened, she directs the hatchlings to swarm the nearest warm body. (After all, she can always spawn more should the "babies" be killed!) The hatchlings then attempt to crawl down a victim's mouth and feed, just like a full-grown tick.

Swarm (Ex): Every 6 prairie tick hatchlings do 1d6 damage.

Invasion (Ex): After being successfully hit by a prairie tick in melee, a victim must attempt a Reflex saving throw against DC 5. Failure means one of the little buggers has scuttled down the target's throat, unless the hero took precautions against this sort of thing. Each tick then drains 1 hit point per hour, up to a maximum of 25 points, when it is sated.

Once full, the hatchling is driven by the same compulsion to return to the nest to feed the queen. However, hatchlings lack the strength to burst out of host like a full-grown tick. Instead, they must crawl back up the throat (or in the other direction, if you're feeling *really* sadistic, Marshal). This is an extremely painful process that takes 2d4 rounds and does 1d4 damage to the host every round until the swollen bug gets free. Castor oil treatment, as described in the *Deadlands: The Weird West D20 Rulebook*, is just as effective against hatchlings.

Replicant

Medium-Size Shapechanger
Hit Dice: As original victim
Initiative: As original victim
Speed: As original victim
AC: As original victim
Attacks: As original victim
Damage: As original victim
Face/Reach: 5 ft. by 5 ft./5 ft.
Special Attacks: Replication
Special Qualities: Fearless, emotionless
Saves: As original victim (use replicant's Con and Wis when figuring bonuses)
Abilities: Str *, Dex *, Con 14, Int *, Wis 12, Cha * (*Same as the victim)
Skills: As original victim
Feats: As original victim
Climate/Terrain: Any land
Challenge Rating: 1 plus original victim's Level
Alignment: Always chaotic evil
Advancement: By victim's character class

Replicants begin life as bulbous green seed pods nearly 6' in length. After they've duplicated someone, they look and act exactly like their victims. Close acquaintances may be uncomfortable around them after extended periods, but average observers can find nothing out of the ordinary.

Replicants are a more dispassionate and inhuman sower of discord. These abominations are actually a form of

intelligent plant life. While still a pod, it forms a psychic connection with the nearest human mind and a replicant begins to grow within the husk. Initially, it is a featureless humanoid, but when the process is complete, the replicant is a perfect physical copy of the victim. The one difference is that replicants do not bleed as such—instead, a thick, whitish liquid leaks from deep wounds for a short period of time.

Once the copy is complete, the replicant must make physical contact with its victim to gain access to his memories and personality., and afterwards replicants are capable of mimicking their victims almost perfectly. Close friends or relatives do notice a few inconsistencies in the replicant's behavior, however.

Fortunately, replicants reproduce slowly. Each abomination can produce a new seedpod each month. These monsters are usually discovered long before they have the chance to overrun a settlement—which is exactly what the Reckoners want.

Combat

Replicants almost always duplicate people while they sleep. Once they have fully assimilated their victim's form and memories, they use the skills and weapons acquired from them to defend themselves as best they can in a fight.

Replication (Su): To use this special ability, a replicant has to touch its victim for 5 minutes and then the victim must fail a Will saving throw against DC 17. The monster usually waits until the victim is asleep to attempt this. The creature then kills its victim and places the body in its seed pod, which releases a powerful acid destroying both the cadaver and itself. This transfer must happen within 24 hours or the abomination perishes, rapidly melting into a puddle of greenish goo.

Perhaps the abomination doesn't hold its fork the right way or smiles just a little off kilter. Whatever the cues, they're not easy to notice even for loved ones, and a Spot skill check against DC 17 is allowed only once every day. Replicants also cannot recreate any sort of arcane abilities.

Emotionless (Ex): Although they can fake emotional responses, replicants have no true feelings. They are immune to all skills or magic that influence emotions in any way.

River Leviathan

Gargantuan Beast
Hit Dice: 20d10+4 (304 hp)
Initiative: +1 (Dex)
Speed: 110 ft. swim
AC: 7 (-4 size, +1 Dex)
Attacks: Beak +15 melee
Damage: Beak 2d6+4
Face/Reach: 20 ft. by 20 ft./20 ft.
Special Attacks: Improved grab, swallow whole
Special Qualities: Blindsight, artificial armor, fire vulnerability
Saves: Fort +16, Ref +13, Will +7
Abilities: Str 18, Dex 13, Con 19, Int 6, Wis 12, Cha 13
Skills: Listen +5, Move Silently +5, Spot +5, Swim +12, Wilderness Lore +5
Feats: None
Climate/Terrain: Aquatic
Challenge Rating: 23
Alignment: Always neutral
Advancement: 21-40 HD (Gargantuan), 41-60 HD (Colossal)

As might be expected in the Weird West, this is a strange beast. The river leviathan, sometimes known as a river fiend, is an octopus altered by the Reckoners into a monster about 40 feet across, with tentacles about 20 feet in length.

Most of the time, this critter sits on the bottom of a river, tentacles extended upward to grab prey. It can also rise to the surface of the water and sometimes adopts a wrecked ship or other large object as an improvised shell and then goes off in search of prey.

The leviathan locates targets by sensing heat with patches on its long tentacles. As a result, the critter equates greater heat with larger prey (so long as the source is moving), and might be duped into attacking a torch or other fire source.

Much like the octopus that it resembles, the leviathan can exhale clouds of ink into the water to mask its retreat. It can also exhale this ink into the air as plumes of black smoke. This helps its imitation of a steam-powered ship, and allows it to blind and confuse prey.

Combat

Whether the leviathan goes hunting, or lies in wait for its prey, it attacks first with its long tentacles. In fact, many victims see nothing of the critter but the tentacles and think they're dealing with a bunch of black, eyeless snakes. Those who live past their capture, though, might just catch a glimpse of the leviathan's body before the tentacle deposits them in the thing's mouth.

Swallow whole (Ex): The leviathan can swallow opponents that it bites with its central mouth, provided the victim is no larger than Medium-Size. A swallowed person (if they live) is also in a position to inflict great damage to the abomination, because the creature's vital organs can be struck from inside the stomach. Any successful attack made by someone in the stomach hits the leviathan's unarmored gizzards. However, besides worrying about drowning and any wounds already suffered, the gut-diver also takes 1d6 damage per round from the critter's digestive juices.

Improved grab (Ex): The abomination needs three rounds to drag a grabbed victim to the central mouth.

Blindsight (Ex): The leviathan can "see" with its tentacles, sensing heat from living creatures. It's possible to distract the tentacles into attacking a big enough heat source if it moves like

it's alive. If someone tries to distract the beast like this, they must make a Dex ability check against DC 10.

Artificial armor (Ex): A river leviathan sometimes makes a home for itself in a shipwreck or even in a house that has collapsed into the water. From its protected location, it can still attack with its tentacles. The value of the armor depends on the material used (see page 65 in the *Deadlands: The Weird West D20 Rulebook*). Fortunately, there are usually gaps in armor of this sort.

Fire vulnerability (Ex): The leviathan is especially sensitive to fire and takes an additional die of damage from any fire-based attack. If the critter is using a ship as armor, and that ship is set ablaze, it usually breaks off any attacks and dives for safety—though some especially persistent individuals will dive only long enough to extinguish the flames, then continue attacking.

Saddle Burrs

Fine Beast
Hit Dice: 1d5-1 (2 hp)
Initiative: +2 (Dex)
Speed: 5 ft.
AC: 20 (+8 size, +2 Dex)
Attacks: Sting +6 melee
Damage: 1d3-2 plus poison
Face/Reach: 1 ft. by 1 ft./0 ft.
Special Attacks: Poison
Special Qualities: Proliferation
Saves: Fort +1, Ref +4, Will -1
Abilities: Str 5, Dex 14, Con 7, Int 6, Wis 7, Cha 6
Skills: Hide +18, Listen +3, Move Silently +4, Tumble +4, Spot +3
Feats: None
Climate/Terrain: Any land
Challenge Rating: 1
Alignment: Always neutral
Advancement: 2-3 HD (Fine)

Saddle burrs are about the size of walnuts, with brown quills sticking out of them like a prickly pear. They are light enough to be carried by the wind, which means they can be found almost anywhere.

These creatures stick to anything that touches them until smashed or attached to something else—a cowpoke who picks the critters off his horse's legs only finds the danged things stuck to his glove. Anyone who tries to squish a burr pushes the quills into her hand, getting a little jolt of poison unless something sturdier than hardened leather is used as protection. Not only can their poison cause swelling and pain for a few days, but the things multiply very fast, apparently in response to quick motions.

Rarely are the burrs enough to make anyone water their boots, but the consequences of a burr bite might. Burrs should be used to add a little humor to the campaign or to cause special problems for the posse—like not being able to use a gun hand in a duel the next day. Running from a lynching party to find that your horse can barely stand or that you can't use your trigger finger might also be cause for alarm and consternation.

Combat

Once a burr is kicked up by a cowpoke's horse or by the wind, it tries to attach itself to the first thing it touches. Once it gets hooked into something, it bends its quills so it can't be pulled out easily. It would take a great many of them to fatally harm anyone, but their sting causes soreness for days afterwards.

Poison (Ex): If the hero touches a burr, the critter gets to make a to-hit roll to jab them with a quill. If a character grabs and pulls a burr, they force the quills into their own skin, giving the critter an automatic hit. Once a quill has pierced skin, it sucks up a drop or two of blood (not enough to cause damage) and injects a mild poison. The poison makes the spot swell up and become very tender for 1d4 days.

While the spot is sore, the victim receives a -4 penalty to all rolls that require the use of the hand (or other stung area). An extra sting to the same area causes an additional -2 penalty. A horse that is stung gets ornery for a few days, and is much more likely to throw anyone trying to ride it.

Proliferation (Ex): Saddle burrs reproduce using kinetic energy. Someone who tries to shake off a burr soon has two burrs. If a burr is shaken for a round, it duplicates itself, and the new burr attaches right next to its prickly sire.

Sand Vipers

Small Beast
Hit Dice: 2d10 (11 hp)
Initiative: +0
Speed: 5 ft., 5 ft. burrow, 20 ft. swim
AC: 21 (+1 size, +10 natural)
Attacks: Sting +3 melee
Damage: Sting 1d6+1 plus poison
Face/Reach: 5 ft. by 5 ft./5 ft.
Special Attacks: Poison, fluid drain
Saves: Fort +3, Ref +3, Will -1
Abilities: Str 12, Dex 9, Con 10, Int 6, Wis 7, Cha 5
Skills: Hide +4, Listen +5, Move Silently +4, Spot +5, Swim +9, Wilderness Lore +4
Feats: None
Climate/Terrain: Aquatic, Underground
Challenge Rating: 3
Alignment: Always neutral
Advancement: 3-4 HD (Small), 5-6 HD (Medium-Size)

A sand viper looks like a 3' long greenish-black conch. A long, spike projects from the narrow end of the shell when it's attacking, and small tentacles emerge from the crown to pull the abomination through the sand.

The sand viper is really a large, saltwater mollusk that buries itself in sand just offshore, and are usually found in large colonies of 20 or more. Once an area becomes alerted to the colony's baleful presence, it moves to another site elsewhere along the coast.

Sand viper victims may be mistaken for those of vampires or other, blood-drinking abominations. Due to the nature of the sand viper's attack, witnesses may not even be able to tell what killed a victim.

Combat

This creature uses its spear-like appendage to inject a powerful paralytic toxin into a victim. Once paralyzed, the sand viper uses the same organ to drain the victim's vital fluids, leaving a nearly completely desiccated corpse.

Poison (Ex): A successful Fortitude saving throw against DC 17 indicates the victim shakes off the venom's effects; failure means she's paralyzed for a number of minutes equal to the amount by which she missed the roll.

Fluid drain (Ex): A sand viper can drain 1d4 hit points per round from a paralyzed victim.

Skills: Sand vipers receive a +2 bonus to all Listen, Move Silently, Spot and Wilderness Lore skill rolls.

Scarecrow

Medium-Size Monstrous Humanoid
Hit Dice: 3d8 (13 hp)
Initiative: +2 (Dex)
Speed: 35 ft.
AC: 12 (+2 Dex)
Attacks: By melee weapon type +4
Damage: By melee weapon type +1
Face/Reach: 5 ft. by 5 ft./5 ft.
Special Qualities: Damage reduction 5/ slashing damage, fire vulnerability
Saves: Fort +1, Ref +5, Will +3
Abilities: Str 12, Dex 14, Con 10, Int 8, Wis 11, Cha 10
Skills: Climb +5, Escape Artist +6, Hide +6, Listen +5, Move Silently +6, Spot +5
Feats: Simple Weapons Proficiency
Climate/Terrain: Any Warm or Temperate land
Challenge Rating: 1
Alignment: Always chaotic evil
Advancement: 4-9 HD (Medium-Size)

A scarecrow is made from clothing once worn by a person, stuffed with corn husks or straw. The head is often a pumpkin or dried gourd, but it might be a grain sack with buttons for eyes and a stitched mouth. While normal scarecrows don't often have hands or feet, this abomination has both. These extremities look like ears of corn from which the kernels have been stripped: flaky, dry, and pocked.

These abominations are malevolent creatures animated by the Reckoners to scare more than just crows. They are active only at night during the growing season, spending the rest of the time hanging on a pole, pretending to be normal scarecrows. Once night falls, they become animate and look to spread fear and mayhem.

Once a scarecrow has taken a life, it can reproduce. It starts by growing seeds (like giant, black kernels of corn) in rows along its belly, one seed for each of its victims. Once these seeds

get to be about the size of a fist (in about a month), they can be planted. The next night, a lesser scarecrow, sometimes called a "corn stalker" sprouts (see page 86).

Combat

When scarecrows come to life, they stalk their fields, attacking anyone and anything that trespasses in their domain, sometimes traveling short distances from the fields to find other victims. Scarecrows favor sharp farming tools like sickles (treat as Bowie knives) and scythes or pitchforks (treat as sabers and tridents).

Fire vulnerability (Ex): Fire causes damage to scarecrows as normal. If it causes enough damage to kill the scarecrow, the thing's death is permanent. Otherwise, any damage taken is completely healed while the abomination sleeps the next day.

Skills: Scarecrows receive a +2 bonus to all Escape Artist, Hide and Move Silently skill rolls.

Corn Stalker

Tiny Monstrous Humanoid
Hit Dice: 3d8 (13 hp)
Initiative: +1 (Dex)
Speed: 30 ft.
AC: 13 (+2 size, +1 Dex)
Attacks: 2 claws +5 melee
Damage: Claw 1d4
Face/Reach: 2 1/2 ft. by 2 1/2 ft./0 ft.
Special Qualities: Go to ground, fire vulnerability
Saves: Fort +1, Ref +4, Will +3
Abilities: Str 9, Dex 12, Con 10, Int 6, Wis 10, Cha 9
Skills: Climb +4, Escape Artist +5, Hide +8, Listen +4, Move Silently +5, Spot +4
Feats: Simple Weapons Proficiency
Climate/Terrain: Any Warm or Temperate land
Challenge Rating: 1
Alignment: Always chaotic evil
Advancement: 4-6 HD (Tiny), 7-9 HD (Small)

After being planted by a scarecrow (see page 85), a corn stalker seed quickly grows to around 2 feet in height, with sharp claws, a scrawny body that looks like twisted corn husks, a head that resembles a pumpkin with a leering face, and sharp claws.

If the corn stalker takes a life, it leaves its home field in search of a field with a normal scarecrow. Once it finds one, the corn stalker nestles inside, spreading its evil essence through the thing and animating it, becoming a full-fledged scarecrow itself. If instead the scarecrow is destroyed, the first corn stalker to take a life grows into a scarecrow in that same field.

Combat

A corn stalker obeys the scarecrow, aiding and abetting its bloody schemes, until it takes a life or the scarecrow is destroyed. It behaves and fights in a similar manner to its sire and fights to the death to protect it.

Go to Ground (Su): The corn stalker can spend a standard action to enter the soil as if sucked into the ground. In the next round, it can reappear anywhere in its home field.

Fire vulnerability (Su): Fire damages corn stalkers as normal. If it causes enough damage to kill the stalker, the thing's death is permanent. Otherwise, any damage taken is completely healed while the abomination sleeps in the earth the next day.

Skills: Corn stalkers receive a +2 bonus to all Escape Artist and Move Silently skill rolls.

Sin Eater

Medium-Size Shapechanger
Hit Dice: 6d8+4 (51 hp)
Initiative: +0
Speed: 30 ft.
AC: 10
Attacks: Punch +5 melee; or by melee weapon type +5; or by ranged weapon type +4
Damage: Punch 1d3+1 (s), or by melee weapon type +1, or by ranged weapon type
Face/Reach: 5 ft. by 5 ft./5 ft.
Special Qualities: Damage reduction 15/slashing damage, imitation, fast healing 1, weaknesses
Saves: Fort +9, Ref +5, Will +5
Abilities: Str 13, Dex 11, Con 18, Int 10, Wis 10 Cha 9
Skills: Bluff +5*, Climb +5, Hide +5, Intimidate +5*, Listen +5, Move Silently +5, Perform (acting) +6*, Ridicule +6*
Feats: Power Attack, Sunder
Climate/Terrain: Any land
Challenge Rating: 5
Alignment: Always chaotic evil
Advancement: 7-18 HD (Medium-Size)

The sin eater looks like a large, clear sack of translucent jelly with shadowy, writhing forms inside. Occasionally, a hand or face comes to the surface of the creature's skin, as if attempting to escape its awful prison. The sin eater can take on the physical appearance of any person whose corpse it has devoured, but usually can only hold this shape for an hour, after which it reverts to its original form.

This fearmonger is generated by the Reckoners to take advantage of the superstitious beliefs of some folk. Among the people of the Ozark Mountains, it is believed that apples placed on the graves of the recently deceased absorbs the loved one's sins. The apple is then devoured by the sin eater, which gains the departed admission to Heaven free of mortal transgressions.

In truth, all this abomination requires to work its malicious evil is the grave of a person buried in unconsecrated ground. Once it finds such a grave, the sin eater absorbs the corpse, and can then call upon its memories and knowledge and can even take on its appearance for short periods of time. It uses these powers to cause fear among the enemies of the deceased, as well as to cause grief for the departed's family.

The sin eater is able to "read" the souls it has absorbed, allowing it to know personal details about that person's life, down to accent, manner of speech, and any painful secrets or facts in the person's history. The sin eater visits the people close to the person absorbed, causing as much psychological pain and suffering as possible.

Combat

If attacked, the sin eater strikes back, fighting until it kills at least one person close to the soul that it has devoured. If driven off, it continues to return in the form of the devoured soul until it claims at least one life. Then it moves on.

Damage Reduction (Su): Slashing damage is unaffected by this ability. The sin eater can be put down by normal weapons, but it always arises at the site of the next body buried in unhallowed ground. The only way to permanently destroy the sin eater is to cut it to pieces and bury each piece in consecrated ground. This can be difficult, because many graveyards throughout the West have never seen a practicing minister and thus have not been blessed. Sacred Indian burial grounds would do just fine, but Indians are likely to be upset to find a paleface burying grisly pieces of some slimy critter in their holy ground and try to stop them.

Imitation (Su): A sin eater in "disguise" has a +4 bonus to all Bluff, Intimidate, Perform (acting) and Ridicule skill checks. Anyone who was close to an individual mimicked by a sin eater has a chance of noticing a fault in the creature's performance with a Sense Motive skill check against DC 17. If its disguise is penetrated and the sin eater knows it, it reverts to its true form (to cause one last bit of fear) and oozes away into the night.

After dropping a disguise, the sin eater must rest for eight hours before trying a new one.

Siren

Huge Beast
Hit Dice: 10d10+1 (65 hp)
Initiative: +1 (Dex)
Speed: 70 ft. swim
AC: 9 (-2 size, +1 Dex)
Attacks: Bite +8 melee
Damage: Bite 2d6+4
Face/Reach: 10 ft. by 20 ft./10 ft.
Special Attacks: Lure
Saves: Fort +8, Ref +8, Will +3

Abilities: Str 16, Dex 12, Con 13, Int 9, Wis 11, Cha 9
Skills: Listen +5, Move Silently +5, Perform (lure) +5, Spot +5, Swim +11, Wilderness Lore +5
Feats: None
Climate/Terrain: Aquatic
Challenge Rating: 6
Alignment: Always neutral
Advancement: 11-20 HD (Huge), 21-30 HD (Gargantuan)

The siren is a large, dull green fish, nearly 25′ long, with a wide body and oversized, fang-filled mouth. Its "lure" normally dangles about 5′ in front of the monster's mouth, but the appendage that holds it can extend up to 15′ when in use.

Sirens are only found in saltwater bodies and are becoming more common in the Great Maze. This abomination is an enormous, carnivorous fish that has a unique "lure" that it uses to attract humans to it. Similar to an angler fish, the siren dangles its lure—in this case another "human"—near its mouth to draw its prey close enough to capture.

The lure itself is a human corpse that the abomination controls by way of a long appendage inserted into the base of the skull. The siren's attachment prevents the corpse from decaying and allows it some simple muscular control. This appendage, a 4″ thick tendril, is usually only visible from behind the lure. The creature can't produce intelligible sounds through the corpse's vocal cords and is limited to screams, wordless shouts or tonal songs.

Combat

The monsters use their lures to ambush unsuspecting swimmers, draw boats into dangerous waters, or even coax a lone longshoreman near the edge of a pier. Those who stray too close get bitten.

Lure (Ex): In addition to bait, the siren can use the lure in combat. Treat the lure as a walkin' dead, but with no skills other than those possessed by the siren. The lure has no Int, Wis or Cha, instead using the siren's values for these as well. Sirens seldom use lures for this purpose, for fear of damaging a valuable tool.

Skinshifter

Medium-Size Monstrous Humanoid
Hit Dice: 3d8 (13 hp)
Initiative: +1 (Dex)
Speed: 35 ft.
AC: 11 (+1 Dex)
Attacks: 2 claws +4 melee
Damage: Claw 1d6+1
Face/Reach: 5 ft. by 5 ft./5 ft.
Special Attacks: Soul drain
Special Qualities: Shadow teleport, coup
Saves: Fort +1, Ref +4, Will +3
Abilities: Str 12, Dex 12, Con 10, Int 11, Wis 11, Cha 10
Skills: Craft +6, Hide +6, Intimidate +6, Knowledge (Indian lore) +6, Listen +6, Move Silently +6, Wilderness Lore +6
Feats: Track
Climate/Terrain: Any land
Challenge Rating: 2
Alignment: Always chaotic evil
Advancement: By character class

Skinshifters appear as frail shadows of men, with pasty white skin that hangs from their bones. Their eyes glow with an evil, purplish light.

These creatures are created from Indians who have sold their souls to the Reckoners in exchange for power. As part of the ritual to become a skinshifter, an Indian must devour the heart of an innocent, usually a child. After this act, the Reckoners transform the criminal into a creature of legend.

Skinshifters hide in their caves by day, where they perform rituals with sand paintings depicting foul deeds perverse by the standards of even the nonreligious. They emerge at nightfall to hunt for victims, driven by the fact that the power of the Reckoners poisons the skinshifter's body, and its life force must be replenished from that of others.

After feeding, the skinshifter gains certain physical characteristics from the victim. It is from this ability that these creatures get their name.

Combat

Skinshifter victims are usually solitary people lost in the wilderness. When a camped group is encountered, the skinshifter tries to lead one of them away to a place where he is isolated and vulnerable. There it attempts to drain away the poor unfortunate's soul.

Soul drain (Sp): After making a successful melee attack, this abomination can drain 1d6 hit points from any victim who fails a Will saving throw against DC 15. The skinwalker must drain one victim each week or die. When the skinshifter has completely drained a victim, it can assume some of the victim's characteristics. The Marshal rolls a d20, and the result is the DC to notice the skinshifter is not who he appears to be. A skinshifter retains a victim's form for 1d4 days afterwards. The critter assumes only the physical likeness, none of the personal quirks, so it's pretty easy for friends of the deceased to figure out this thing is nothing but an impostor.

Shadow teleport (Su): The skinshifter has the ability to teleport itself between shadows. The critter merely steps into a shadowy place and reappears in another such area within 90 feet. This is not an effortless action, and each use costs 1d4 hit points.

Coup: A Harrowed who defeats a skinwalker gains the Soul Eater feat.

Skinwalkers

Medium-Size Shapechanger
Hit Dice: 3d8 (13 hp)
Initiative: +2 (Dex)
Speed: 35 ft.
AC: 12 (+2 Dex)
Attacks: 2 claws +3 melee, bite +1 melee
Damage: Claw 1d6+1, bite 1d4
Face/Reach: 5 ft. by 5 ft./5 ft.
Special Qualities: Damage reduction 5/-, immunity, disguise
Saves: Fort +3, Ref +5, Will +3
Abilities: Str 13, Dex 14, Con 11, Int 13, Wis 11, Cha 9
Skills: Bluff +6*, Climb +5, Disguise +6*, Gather Information +6*, Hide +6, Listen +6, Move Silently +6, Spot +6
Feats: Multiattack, Power Attack
Climate/Terrain: Any land
Challenge Rating: 3
Alignment: Always neutral evil
Advancement: 4-9 HD (Medium-Size)

Skinwalkers are seldom seen in their natural form. They prefer to wear the skins of humans and hide among mankind. Their skeleton is made of a mutable cartilage-like substance and allows them to freely mimic any human from the size of a twelve-year-old child to the largest of adults. A skinwalker's "skinless" appearance is very similar to a skinless human body. Long, retractable claws extend from the index and middle fingers of each hand, and their tongues are rough and rasp-like.

Since few people intentionally remove their own outer flesh, skinwalkers usually have to take it from unwilling victims. They are very talented at this, able to accomplish the complete and flawless skinning of an adult in less than five minutes. Their claws are naturally suited for this task, and they use their coarse tongues to draw off the blood from their victims as they remove the skin. Being particularly malicious creatures, they often try to keep their victims alive for as long as possible during this process.

Finally, they insert their tongue's proboscis-like tube through the base of the skull and devour the brain of the subject. They are able to glean some of the subject's memories by this process. Needless to say, this final step of the procedure is invariably fatal.

Combat

Baron Simone LaCroix, owner of the Bayou Vermillion railroad, has formed a strange alliance with a number of these creatures and uses them for a variety of tasks, from spying to terrorism. In a fight, their claws prove just as efficacious at inflicting gaping wounds as they do at delicately skinning victims.

Immunity (Su): As long as a skinwalker wears another's skin, it is impervious to physical harm. Once a total of 30 hit points of damage has been dealt to it, however, it sloughs off the destroyed skin. This is a horrifying site in itself, and any witnesses must make a Will saving throw against DC 20 or be affected by the Fear Special Ability. Once its true form is exposed, it can be harmed by normal weapons.

Disguise (Su): A skinwalker in "disguise" has a +2 bonus to all Bluff, Disguise and Gather Information skill checks. A skinwalker can wear a skin for about a month before decay makes it unusable. The hide can be used indefinitely if maintained with vinegar or formaldehyde. They can also store skins for up to three months in solutions of either liquid. This preservative process gives the skin an odor, noticeable by anyone near the creature with a Spot skill check DC (13). Also, anyone closely examining a skinwalker from behind may notice a faint line or "seam" up the back with a Spot check DC (17).

Skills: Skinwalkers receive a +2 bonus to all Hide, Listen, Move Silently and Spot skill rolls.

Springheel Jack

Medium-Size Monstrous Humanoid
Hit Dice: 7d8+3 (52 hp)
Initiative: +5 (Dex)
Speed: 60 ft.
AC: 15 (+5 Dex)
Attacks: 2 claws +9 melee; or blue flame +12 ranged
Damage: Claw 1d8+2, blue flame 2d6
Face/Reach: 5 ft. by 5 ft./5 ft.
Special Attacks: Fear, blue flame
Special Qualities: Damage reduction 25/see weaknesses, fast healing 5, shadow teleport, weaknesses, coup
Saves: Fort +5, Ref +10, Will +7
Abilities: Str 14, Dex 20, Con 16, Int 11, Wis 14, Cha 16
Skills: Balance +7, Hide +7, Intimidate +6, Jump +9, Knowledge (arcana) +5, Listen +5, Move Silently +7, Ridicule +5, Spot +5, Tumble +7
Feats: Dodge, Mobility
Climate/Terrain: Any land
Challenge Rating: 7
Alignment: Chaotic evil
Advancement: 8-21 HD (Medium-Size)

Springheel Jack is generally human in appearance. His body is extraordinarily thin and tall—nearly 7'—and his flesh is a ghastly greenish white. His hands end in slender, extra-jointed fingers tipped with talon like claws. His face is stretched into a long, devil-like appearance, locked into an evil, toothy predatory grin. He has a pointed beard on his chin, but he is otherwise bald. His eyes protrude from their sockets almost as if they are going to pop out of his skull at any moment. Finally, his lanky body is covered with ancient clothing that somewhat resembles an oilskin suit, complete with tattered tails.

Jack is an old terror from across the seas in merry old England. The first sightings of this creature occurred in the late 1830s, and persist through the time of the Weird West. Jack is actually a nature spirit horribly corrupted by an addiction to ancient blood sacrifices. It ran amok in the English countryside for years prior to Roman conquest, but was eventually trapped in a warded tor (hill) by a band of druids. In the mid-1830s, the tor was accidentally excavated, and Jack was freed on the populace of that otherwise green and pleasant land.

Prior to the Reckoning, most of Springheel Jack's activities, while horrifying, were more mischievous than deadly. Now, all that has changed. Since the Reckoning, Jack's true evil has risen to the surface. Instead of merely tearing at clothing, Jack attempts to kill its victims after it has stunned them. If successful, it strings their entrails about the murder site like a grotesque cat's cradle.

Combat

Jack prefers to attack solitary victims and tries to run from any encounter where it's outnumbered. He first attempts to stun targets with his flame belch, and then to gut and kill them.

Fear (Ex): Anyone catching sight of Springheel Jack must make a Will saving throw against DC 19.

Blue flame (Sp): Jack can belch a blue flame into the face of an opponent within 5'. The flame does 2d6 damage, and a victim who fails a Fortitude saving throw against DC 10 falls stunned and helpless to the ground.

Shadow teleport (Su): Jack can teleport from one shadow to another shadow within 600 feet as long as it is not being directly observed. He must be able to see the destination shadow and both shadows must be of sufficient size to conceal it completely. If someone is directly watching Jack's actions, he can't use this ability

Weaknesses (Su): Springheel Jack takes full damage from weapons made from oak and half damage from weapons made from other woods. His fast healing ability is ineffective against this type of damage. He cannot open wooden doors or shadow teleport from an space enclosed completely by wood. Weapons enchanted by the spirit weapon favor do full damage to him.

Coup: Harrowed who put Springheel Jack down permanently gains the ability to leap his full Speed in a single bound. This gives the Harrowed a +2 to-hit on any attack that he can leap into. However, this can only be performed once per round.

Tarnished Phantasy

Medium-Size Undead (Incorporeal)
Hit Dice: 5d12 (32 hp)
Initiative: +3 (-1 Dex, Improved Initiative)
Speed: 15 ft.
AC: 11 (-1 Dex, +2 deflection)
Attacks: Touch +1 melee
Damage: Energy drain
Face/Reach: 5 ft. by 5 ft./5 ft.
Special Attacks: Energy drain
Special Qualities: Incorporeality
Saves: Fort +1, Ref +0, Will +5
Abilities: Str –, Dex 7, Con –, Int 11, Wis 12, Cha 15
Skills: Hide +7, Intimidate +8, Listen +7, Move Silently +8, Perform (acting) +8, Spot +7
Feats: Blind-Fight, Improved Initiative
Climate/Terrain: Any land
Challenge Rating: 4
Alignment: Always chaotic evil
Advancement: 6-15 HD (Medium-Size)

A tarnished phantasy looks much as she did in life. However, a casual glance reveals the ghostly etherealness of her new form.

This abomination is created when a woman of questionable virtue (like your typical saloon gal) dies while trying to save a man she truly loves. While a noble death such as this would hardly seem likely to generate an abomination, the powers of the Reckoners can twist good deeds to evil ends.

If the conditions are right, such a fallen woman returns to the world of the living as a tarnished phantasy, a phantasmal creature that drains the life energy of sleeping men by visiting them with erotic dreams. This creature seems to be a modern variation on fairy-tale hags, who used to "ride" mortal men to death in their sleep.

As a piece of delicious irony, the phantasy is first drawn to the very man who she sacrificed her life for—if he still lives. After destroying him, the tarnished phantasy turns fickle, "loving" almost any man she might encounter.

Combat

Tarnished phantasies have but one means of attack, but are almost completely safe from harm. If attacked and seriously threatened by the one capable of injuring her, she flees the scene.

Energy drain (Su): During her nocturnal visits to men, the tarnished phantasy drains them physically. Anyone "ridden" by a tarnished phantasy must make Fortitude saving throw against DC 15 to eliminate a negative level. A victim who dies as a result of this attack perishes from exhaustion.

Incorporeality (Su): A tarnished phantasy can manifest in the material world at will. She can only be harmed normally by her victim (if he can be convinced to attack her). She is also vulnerable to arcane damage from any quarter.

Terrantulas

Diminutive Vermin
Hit Dice: 1d4-2 (1 hp)
Initiative: +0
Speed: 35 ft., 15 ft. climb
AC: 14 (+4 size)
Attacks: None
Damage: None
Face/Reach: 1 ft. by 1 ft./0 ft.
Special Attacks: Swarm, poison
Saves: Fort +0, Ref +0, Will -2
Abilities: Str 3, Dex 10, Con 5, Int –, Wis 5, Cha 5
Skills: Climb +7, Hide +12, Listen +1, Move Silently +2, Spot +1, Wilderness Lore +2
Feats: None
Climate/Terrain: Warm Desert, Hill, Mountains
Challenge Rating: 1/2
Alignment: Always neutral
Advancement: 2 HD (Tiny), 3 HD (Small), 4 (Medium-Size), 5-9 HD (Large), 10-15 HD (Huge), 16-22 HD (Gargantuan)

Terrantulas resemble normal tarantulas in all respects except for a skull-shaped marking on the backs of their abdomens. They travel in hordes of up to 500, literally obscuring the ground with their rustling, scurrying numbers.

These voracious little arachnids are common to the southwestern Confederate Territories. They prey on anything they can get their mandibles over—even each other, if no other food source is available.

There is no upper limit to these monsters' growth. Left unchecked, the strongest in the group can reach the size of a horse—or sometimes even much larger!

Combat

When small, the monsters do use swarm tactics to overwhelm larger prey. As they increase in size, they become territorial and use methods similar to that of trapdoor spiders to capture their prey.

Swarm (Ex): A terrantula swarm does 1d4 damage for every 20 in the spider horde.

Poison (Ex): A successful Fortitude saving throw against DC 10 indicates the victim shakes off the venom's effects; failure means they're paralyzed for 1d6 hours. A small terrantula's poison is only effective when administered by a swarm; a single bite is painful, but nothing more. A saving throw is required only if a swarm damages the hero.

Texas Skeeters

Diminutive Vermin
Hit Dice: 1d4-1 (1 hp)
Initiative: +1 (Dex)
Speed: 5 ft. climb, 35 ft. fly (good)
AC: 15 (+4 size, +1 Dex)
Attacks: Bite +2 melee
Damage: Bite 1 hp plus blood drain
Face/Reach: 1 ft. by 1 ft./0 ft.
Special Attacks: Swarm, improved grab, blood drain
Special Qualities: Fire vulnerability
Saves: Fort +1, Ref +1, Will -1
Abilities: Str 5, Dex 12, Con 7, Int –, Wis 8, Cha 6
Skills: Climb +6, Hide +12, Listen +2, Move Silently +3, Spot +2, Wilderness Lore +3
Feats: None
Climate/Terrain: Marsh
Challenge Rating: 1/2
Alignment: Always neutral
Advancement: None

These hand-sized insects (6" long) are gigantic versions of normal mosquitoes. They travel in swarms, descending on warm-blooded victims to drain the blood that provides their sustenance.

The name Texas skeeter refers to the critter's size, not where it can be found. These nasty bloodsuckers have been sighted up and down the Mississippi, as well as further east. They prefer swampy terrain, as that is where they breed.

A swarm holds 12 to 20 skeeters. Unlike their smaller cousins, skeeters need a lot of blood to survive and tend to attack in such numbers that they kill their prey instead of just raising welts. A swarm that catches a person unaware can quickly drain them to a bloodless husk.

Combat

These relatively weak creatures rely on stealth and numbers. They are most active at dusk or later, using darkness to hide until they are close to their intended victims. They are very quiet as well. Since several skeeters often attack a single victim, it is not unusual for a victim to fall unconscious or even die from blood loss.

Swarm (Ex): Every group of 5 Texas skeeters in a horde does 5 hit points damage, and gets a +1 on their to-hit roll.

Improved grab (Ex): Texas skeeters can use improved grab against Medium-Size targets or smaller.

Blood drain (Ex): Once a skeeter sinks its proboscis into a victim, it stays there, draining blood at the rate of 1 hit point per round. Other Texas skeeters continue to attack until all are attached to victims. Once a skeeter is attached, the only way to remove it is to kill it, or to bring open flame up to it. Skeeters do eventually detach of their own accord. A skeeter's bloodlust is sated after it drains 4 hit points, at which time it flies away at half of its normal speed.

Fire vulnerability (Ex): Texas skeeters don't like fire and smoke and avoid them. The skeeters normally avoid such things. A person carrying a torch almost never gets attacked–almost.

The Thing Under the Bed

Medium-Size Monstrous Humanoid
Hit Dice: 2d8-1 (8 hp)
Initiative: +1 (Dex)
Speed: 35 ft.
AC: 11 (+1 Dex)
Attacks: 2 claws +3 melee
Damage: Claw 1d4+1
Face/Reach: 5 ft. by 5 ft./5 ft.
Special Qualities: Damage reduction 25/Magic weapons, shadow teleport, contortion, light vulnerability
Saves: Fort -1, Ref +4, Will +3
Abilities: Str 13, Dex 12, Con 7, Int 9, Wis 10, Cha 8
Skills: Climb +5, Hide +5, Intimidate +3, Listen +5, Move Silently +5, Open Lock +5, Pick Pocket +5, Sneak +5, Spot +5
Feats: Power Attack
Climate/Terrain: Any land
Challenge Rating: 1
Alignment: Always chaotic evil
Advancement: 3-6 HD (Medium-Size)

Things seldom exist in light long enough for folks to get a good look at them. Most people only see a clawed hand coming up the side of the bed or a hunched humanoid figure in the shadows behind hanging clothes. Exact descriptions vary from Thing to Thing, some seem skeletal while others are gray-skinned, warty, hairy, troll-like monsters.

Kids aren't being childish when they run in and jump on their bed at night—there really is a monster under there! And it's just waiting to snatch at the feet or hanging arm of a careless little one.

The Thing isn't just limited to beds, either. It can lurk in a dark closet, a musty attic corner, or behind the stairs to the basement. The monster takes great pains to keep its presence hidden from the older population. Adults seldom believe it exists, even after it has taken a child or two. This only heightens the kids' feelings of helplessness. Any disappearances are usually explained as runaways, wild animal attacks, or other, more mundane occurrences.

Combat

The Thing preys on the fears of a community's children, allowing kids to get a glimpse of it shifting under the bed or hiding in the back of a dark closet. It keeps them on edge by snatching a child every month or so. These little ones are taken to the abomination's lair—usually subterranean—and never seen again. The monster may gobble them up or, possibly more disturbing, turn them into Things themselves.

The monster further weakens the bond between adults and children by committing acts of theft or vandalism. It then frames the most outspoken children.

Shadow teleport (Su): The Thing can teleport from one shadow to another within 300 feet as long as it is not being directly observed. For example, it can blink from underneath the bed to the closet or any other darkened area. It must either see its destination or know that it is there and the shadow must conceal it (and remember its contortion ability, below). However, if anyone is watching it, the Thing can't use this ability.

Contortion (Su): Although the Thing is roughly adult-sized, it can wedge its body into areas normally accessible only to Small creatures.

Light vulnerability (Su): Direct exposure to light equal to that of a torch or greater does 2d6 damage to it each round.

Skills: The Thing receives a +2 bonus to all Climb, Hide, Intimidate, Listen, Move Silently, Open Lock, Pick Pocket, Sneak and Spot skill rolls.

Tommyknockers

Small Monstrous Humanoid
Hit Dice: 5d8+3 (37 hp)
Initiative: +0
Speed: 20 ft., 30 ft. burrow
AC: 11 (+1 size)
Attacks: 2 claws +8 melee
Damage: Claw 1d6+3
Face/Reach: 5 ft. by 5 ft./5 ft.
Special Attacks: Disorient
Special Qualities: Sabotage, traceless burrow, light sensitivity
Saves: Fort +4, Ref +4, Will +4
Abilities: Str 14, Dex 11, Con 16, Int 10 Wis 11, Cha 8
Skills: Climb +7, Disable Device +8, Hide +8, Listen +8, Move Silently +8, Profession (miner) +8, Spot +8
Feats: Power Attack, Track
Climate/Terrain: Underground
Challenge Rating: 4
Alignment: Always neutral evil
Advancement: By character class

Tommyknockers are 3' tall humanoids, with disproportionately large heads. They walk perpetually hunched-over, perhaps due to their subterranean nature, perhaps due to the weight of their enormous heads. Their skin is a mottled blackish-gray and their solid black eyes are as large as saucers. Their hands have only three fingers each and these end in thick, claw-nails.

Tommyknockers lurk in mine tunnels and shafts, slowly weakening supports and otherwise threatening miners. Because the Reckoners *want* ghost rock successfully mined, these monsters don't interfere with those mines until they're tapped out. Gold and silver mines are their usual haunts.

A mine known (or even just rumored!) to be plagued by a tommyknocker may have a Fear Level one point higher than the surrounding area. Seldom does more than one of these mischievous monsters infest a single mine.

Combat

These carnivorous abominations lurk deep in the mines and damage supports, mine-car tracks, and other important structures during the night. Miners and watchmen sometimes hear the creature tapping away down in the depths after the work force has left for the evening. Should the creature succeed in causing a cave-in, it begins to systematically hunt down and feed on any trapped miners, picking them off one by one as lack of food and oxygen weakens them.

Disorient (Su): A tommyknocker can cause limited confusion in a target if the victim fails a Will saving throw against DC 10. If the abomination wins, the victim loses her sense of direction and may become lost in the mine tunnels. This lasts a number of hours equal to the amount by which the victim failed the saving throw.

Sabotage (Ex): The creature can damage mine equipment, supplies, and even structures. Exactly how much is up to the Marshal, but the larger the destruction, the longer it takes. A cave-in, for example, usually requires a week or more of work on the monster's part.

Light sensitivity (Ex): In any light brighter than a torch, the tommyknocker is -2 to all rolls.

Traceless burrow (Su): A tommyknocker leaves no tunnel or evidence of its passing when burrowing; it literally passes through the earth. It uses this to sneak up on prey.

Skills: Tommyknockers receive a +3 bonus on all Climb, Disable Device, Hide, Listen, Move Silently, Profession (miner) and Spot skill rolls.

Tunnel Critters

Tiny Vermin
Hit Dice: 1d8 (4 hp)
Initiative: +0
Speed: 30 ft., 15 ft. climb
AC: 17 (+2 size, +5natural)
Attacks: Bite +2 melee
Damage: Bite 1d3 plus paralysis
Face/Reach: 2 1/2 ft. by 2 1/2 ft./0 ft.
Special Attacks: Improved grab, paralysis, egg-laying
Special Qualities: Tremorsense
Saves: Fort +2, Ref +0, Will -1
Abilities: Str 9, Dex 11, Con 9, Int –, Wis 7, Cha 6
Skills: Climb +8, Hide +8, Listen +2, Move Silently +3, Spot +2, Wilderness Lore +2
Feats: None
Climate/Terrain: Underground
Challenge Rating: 1
Alignment: Always neutral
Advancement: 2 HD (Small), 3-6 HD (Large), 7-10 HD (Huge), 11-16 HD (Gargantuan)

Tunnel critters are monstrous subterranean insects, typically the size of large dogs, with bodies like centipedes. They are armed with large mandibles and vestigial eyes in front. Each segment has 4 claw-tipped appendages, for movement, digging, or even limited manipulation.

These creatures are found in deep mines and caverns in the Weird West. Living in darkness, they are blind but have a highly developed sense of touch. They are attracted to mines for the ready supply of food.

Tunnel critters are sensitive to vibrations. Exceptionally large vibrations, like those generated by explosions, drive them off (even a tunnel critter doesn't want to get caught in a cave-in). Smaller vibrations draw the creature because it associates such sensations with food.

Very young tunnel critters are harmless, but after a month or so their shells harden and the poison glands develop. They feed on anything living (even each other) so old, large specimens are very rare. If one somehow lived long enough, it would eventually become too heavy to support itself on land and would have to dwell in underground lakes or rivers. No such specimens have been discovered—yet.

The larger tunnel critters get, the slower their reactions. Full-grown specimens can also tunnel (slowly) through earth. They are a bit faster in dirt and much slower in bedrock.

Combat

Tunnel critters attack by first grabbing their target. While holding a victim, the tunnel critter uses each of its actions to bite and inject poison.

Improved grab (Ex): Tunnel critters can grab any target equal in Size or smaller.

Paralysis (Ex): A target bitten by a tunnel critter is injected with a toxin and immediately paralyzed if they fail a Fortitude saving throw against DC 13. Each successive saving throw in that combat receives a cumulative +2 DC.

Egg-laying (Ex): Once a held target stops struggling, if the critter opts not eat them it bites one last time (causing damage and another Fortitude saving throw) and then lays eggs in them. The victim remains unconscious for 2d10 hours, and eggs hatch in about 12. If the eggs hatch while they're still inside, the victim dies. Removing all the eggs from a victim requires a Heal skill check against DC 15.

Two-Faces

Medium-Size Monstrous Humanoid
Hit Dice: 5d12+2 (42 hp)
Initiative: +1 (Dex)
Speed: 35 ft.
AC: 16 (+1 Dex, +5 natural)
Attacks: 2 claws +7 melee, 2 bites +5 melee
Damage: Claw 1d6+2, bite: 1d3+1
Face/Reach: 5 ft. by 5 ft./5 ft.
Special Attacks: Gaze attack
Special Qualities: Salt vulnerability, light sensitivity, unusual diet
Saves: Fort +3, Ref +5, Will +5
Abilities: Str 15, Dex 13, Con 14, Int 9, Wis 13, Cha 10
Skills: Climb +7, Craft +7, Hide +7, Intimidate +7, Knowledge (Indian lore) +7, Move Silently +7, Spot +7, Wilderness Lore +7
Feats: Multiattack, Track
Climate/Terrain: Any land
Challenge Rating: 4
Alignment: Always chaotic evil
Advancement: By character class

A two-faces appears as a lean and wiry Indian, with long fingers that end in sharp, black claws. It takes its name from part of its physical form. Its face, with feverish eyes twisted by hatred, has a twin on the back of its skull. This second face reminds the creature to pay attention to its surroundings, preventing it from being surprised. Both faces have mouths full of sharp teeth. The creature lacks ears because it refused to listen during its previous life.

This abomination is the spirit of an Indian who died because he failed to heed good advice and insisted on a foolhardy course. The spirit takes physical form at night because to appear in light would cause more shame than it could bear. As part of its penance for its ignoble death, it must feed on a diet of the ears of children who do not listen, washed down with their innocent blood.

While a small part of the two-faces' soul realizes the torment it inflicts, another part revels in its hatred of youth, innocence, and vitality. What the two-faces lost, it cannot stand for others to have.

Combat

This malevolent creature is a sly and elusive killer that attempts to surprise its victims, waking them and then paralyzing them with the power of its gaze. It feeds on some victims immediately, while taking others back to its lair where it can dine at its leisure.

Gaze attack (Sp): The gaze of the two-faces puts a Hold (as per the Special Ability) on victims who fail a Will saving throw against DC 15. The Hold lasts 2d12 hours.

Salt vulnerability (Su): A two-faces cannot abide the touch of salt. A handful thrown on one causes 1d6 damage. Larger amounts inflicts commensurately more damage. This is the only way to permanently destroy a two-faces. If it is "killed" any other way, it returns the next night to wreak havoc on its attacker.

Light sensitivity (Su): When a two-faces is in the presence of a light source (other than the moon or stars), it receives a -2 penalty to all rolls. A few shamans also know of a ritual of drum beats combined with the burning of fat that deters a two-faces from visiting the village.

Unusual diet (Su): The two-faces must devour at least one pair of ears per week or it starves to death. Some of the creatures kill several victims at once, stringing extra ears on a necklace to avoid starvation. It enjoys only fresh blood, however, and might keep a victim or two alive for many days so it has a ready supply of blood to draw on as well.

Skills: A two-faces receives a +3 to all Climb, Craft, Hide, Intimidate, Knowledge (Indian lore), Spot and Wilderness Lore skill rolls.

Uktena

Huge Magical Beast
Hit Dice: 14d10+3 (119 hp)
Initiative: +2 (Dex)
Speed: 85 ft. swim
AC: 10 (-2 size, +2 Dex)
Attacks: 2 horns +17 melee, bite +15 melee
Damage: Horn 2d8+5, bite 2d6+2
Face/Reach: 10 ft. by 20 ft./10 ft.
Special Attacks: Compulsion
Special Qualities: Invulnerability, crystal
Saves: Fort +12, Ref +11, Will +5
Abilities: Str 20, Dex 15, Con 17, Int 8, Wis 13, Cha 14
Skills: Intimidate +8, Listen +8, Move Silently +8, Spot +8, Swim +13
Feats: Cleave, Multiattack, Power Attack
Climate/Terrain: Aquatic
Challenge Rating: 10
Alignment: Always chaotic evil
Advancement: 15-21 HD (Huge), 22-28 HD (Gargantuan), 29-42 HD (Colossal)

The uktena is a 30' long snake as thick as a good-sized tree trunk. It strongly resembles a small Maze dragon with a few differences. It has a pair of horns on its head, between which rests a small, brilliant, diamond-like crystal. Its neck has seven faint bands of color, one for each in the spectrum. The heart lies under the violet band.

This beast (also called an unktehi) appears in the mythology of both the northern tribes of the Great Plains and in that of the southeastern groups. All these native peoples fear its power, but those with arcane abilities occasionally seek these monsters in an effort to secure its unique gemstone.

The crystal (which is about the size of a rifle cartridge) is imbedded in the uktena's skull. It serves as a conduit to the Hunting Grounds, constantly feeding the monster supernatural energies. Not only does this make the creature nearly immune to injury, but it also has a hypnotic effect on any human.

Combat

An uktena uses its hypnotic power to render its victims helpless, and then orders them to walk slowly towards it to their doom.

Compulsion (Su): Any hero looking at the uktena must make a Will saving throw against DC 13 at the beginning of each round. Failure means they're hypnotized and walk slowly toward the monster, completely helpless. They can attempt to break free of the spell each round by rolling another Will saving throw.

Invulnerability (Su): The only way to harm the uktena is to pierce the creature's heart, which lies underneath the seventh band on its neck. The heart has AC 16, assuming the hero knows the monster's weakness.

Crystal (Su): After the uktena is slain, the crystal can be pried from its skull, giving its owner easier access to the Hunting Grounds. The crystal provides a +2 bonus to a Blessed's Faith skill checks, a Shaman's Ritual skill checks, a Huckster's Hexslingin' skill checks and a Mad Scientist's Alchemy and Mad Science skill checks. Every seven days, the crystal must be soaked in the blood of a small game animal. If not, it completely and permanently loses its power and the owner suffers hazardously bad luck: anytime the target rolls a natural 1, the result is somehow life threatening. A cowpoke must possess the crystal for a week to be considered its owner.

Union Pride Ghost Train & "Ornery" Will

Medium-Size Undead
Hit Dice: 3d12 (18 hp)
Initiative: +3 (Dex)
Speed: 35 ft.
AC: 13 (+3 Dex)
Attacks: 2 Double-action Revolvers +6 ranged (+4 and +0 when used in tandem)
Damage: Spirit weapons 2d6+2
Face/Reach: 5 ft. by 5 ft./5 ft.
Special Attacks: Fear, spirit weapons
Special Qualities: Undead
Saves: Fort +2, Ref +6, Will +1
Abilities: Str 14, Dex 16, Con –, Int 9, Wis 11, Cha 11
Skills: Bluff +6, Climb +6, Intimidate +6, Knowledge (Iowa/Missouri border) +6, Ride +6, Ridicule +6, Spot +6
Feat: Two-Weapon Fighting
Climate/Terrain: Any land
Challenge Rating: 3
Alignment: Chaotic evil
Advancement: As gunslinger character class

The Union Pride Ghost Train manifests itself on every new moon, racing along a stretch of tracks with fire streaming from its boiler and screams coming from within. Its damned passenger, "Ornery" Will Jenkins, is perpetually ablaze, and screams almost constantly as if in great pain (which he is). His skin and Confederate uniform are still visible, but the closer it gets to sunrise, the more they burn away. Just before he and the train vanish, he is a skeleton with a chunk of ghost rock trapped within his rib cage.

The origin of the Ghost Train goes back to the early days of the Great Rail Wars, when a band of Confederate guerillas led by one "Ornery" Will Jenkins found a line of track laid by the Union Blue railroad across his native Missouri. Angered, Jenkins followed the track until he and his men came upon a train led by the ghost-rock powered Union Pride locomotive.

Jenkins and his men boarded the moving train, and in their rage killed everyone aboard, including all but one of the engineers. The lone survivor refused to obey Jenkins' orders, and threw the throttle wide upon, knowing in advance he'd likely die as a result.

As the train hit the end of the tracks, it smacked the dirt so hard Jenkins was thrown against the boiler, which burst from the impact. The ghost rock inside exploded, immolating Jenkins.

At the site of the wreck, the Union Pride boiler burns with ghost rock fire to this very day. The explosion tore open the engine, and although the rest of the train has been salvaged for parts and materials, the locomotive is still there, ablaze until the ghost rock burns itself out.

However, the Union Pride continues to make its bloody run over and over again, no longer tied to the site of its horrible crash and roaming freely on the tracks owned by Union Blue. Anything on the tracks had better watch out, as the spectral train has derailed at least three trains in the last year.

So far the train only stops when it arrives at a town. On those occasions, "Ornery" Will and his "men" have debarked for a short time to terrorize the town with their looting and pillaging, only to climb back onto the train and vanish by sunrise.

Combat

Most folks are terrorized by the very site of "Ornery" Will and the Union Pride, which makes them easy targets for Jenkins' spectral shooting-irons. Jenkins and his gang fights without both fear or mercy. (Treat each of the 12 gang members as walkin' dead; refer to the *Deadlands: The Weird West D20 Rulebook* for statistics.)

Fear (Su): Anyone catching sight of "Ornery" Will must make a Will saving throw against DC 19.

Undead (Su): Focus-head; The only way to put the apparition of the Union Pride to rest is to kill "Ornery" Will and all of his men in one night. If all are not killed, the Union Pride appears again on the next full moon with any killed gang members brought back to unlife.

Spirit weapons (Sp): Any firearm wielded by "Ornery" Will never needs to be loaded, because it fires small arcane bolts, which do 2d6+2 damage

Vampires

No book of monsters could be complete without a few of everyone's favorite bloodsucking freaks. Below, you'll find ravenous nosferatu, disgusting penanggalen, creepy little ustrel and a few other varieties to allow you to choose the style of *chupasangre* best suited to your campaign.

Of course, we're not saying you've got to choose just one, either. Nothing is more disappointing than finding out what worked on the last vampire *doesn't* work on the one that's trying to gnaw off your head this time!

Vampires of all sorts are a form of undead pestilence. After all, vampirism itself is a contagious, fatal disease that spreads even after death!

However, a vampire's food supply is hard to sustain in the sparsely populated West. The smarter bloodsuckers take this into account when planning their lairs and hunting trips. Others, like nosferatu and wampyr, are likely to exhaust the local population quickly—or draw the attention of the Rangers or Agency.

It bears mentioning that Harrowed are immune to the effects of a vampire's contagion. To be honest, the bloodsuckers usually ignore these graveyard rejects unless they attack them first. No self-respecting vampire wants to get a mouthful of that sludge that passes for a Harrowed's blood anyway.

Bottom line: the Harrowed (and any other undead) can't contract any form of vampirism. Plain and simple, they're already dead and can't double-dip on the unlife pool. Any Harrowed somehow killed by a vampire's bite is just dead.

Cinematic Vampire

Medium-Size Undead
Hit Dice: 8d12 (52 hp)
Initiative: +4 (Dex)
Speed: 60 ft.
AC: 14 (+4 Dex)
Attacks: 2 claws +9 melee; bite +7 melee

Damage: Claw 1d6+5, bite 1d4+2 plus energy drain
Face/Reach: 5 ft. by 5 ft./5 ft.
Special Attacks: Improved grab, energy drain
Special Qualities: Blood drain, undead, vampiric weaknesses
Saves: Fort +2, Ref +6, Will +8
Abilities: Str 20, Dex 19, Con –, Int 11, Wis 15, Cha 16
Skills: Climb +11, Hide +10, Intimidate +10, Listen +9, Move Silently +11, Sense Motive +9, Spot +9
Feats: Dodge, Multiattack
Climate/Terrain: Any land
Challenge Rating: 7
Alignment: Usually chaotic evil
Advancement: By character class

Vampires appear much like normal humans until they attack. Then, their eyes turn black, sometimes with a faint red gleam, and their fangs and nails lengthen. The facial features of some vampires taken a bestial look at this point. However, much of the terror generated by this sort of bloodsucker comes from the aura of sheer malevolence than shrouds it once revealed.

Vampires of this sort are best used as recurring villains than one-shot encounters. These undead are more concerned with the "long view" of their unlife than those of folklore, whose entire existence usually revolves around the next drink. As such, they make good long-term opponents for a posse—especially since they can generate hordes of lesser vampires to throw at the heroes nearly at will!

Combat

Vampires use their superior speed and strength to subdue their prey. Their are loath to kill outright or vampirize their victims, as both present a threat to the available food supply.

Improved grab (Ex): Vampires can grab any target equal in Size or smaller.

Energy Drain (Sp): Anyone bitten by a vampire must make Fortitude saving throw against DC 17 to eliminate a negative level. Anyone slain by a vampire's bite rises as a lesser vampire (use the statistics for a nosferatu). Often, the lesser vampire is controlled by its creator.

Blood drain (Su): Every three hit points inflicted by a vampire's bite heals one hit point of damage it has suffered.

Undead (Su): Focus—heart. Beheading or a wooden stake through the heart kills the vampire. Reducing the vampire to 0 hit points or less simply incapacitates it.

Vampiric Weaknesses (Su): A pint of holy water thrown at it does 1d6 damage. A vampire takes 2d6 damage each round it has any flesh exposed to sunlight. Damage from these sources can kill the vampire also.

Nachtzehrer

Medium-Size Undead
Hit Dice: 5d12 (32 hp)
Initiative: +0
Speed: 30 ft., 30 ft. burrow
AC: 10
Attacks: Bite melee +3, 2 claws melee +1
Damage: Bite 1d3+1, claw 1d6
Face/Reach: 5 ft. by 5 ft./5 ft.
Special Attacks: Fear, infection
Special Qualities: Undead, vampiric weaknesses
Saves: Fort +1, Ref +1, Will +4
Abilities: Str 13, Dex 11, Con —, Int 8, Wis 9, Cha 10
Skills: Climb +5, Hide +5, Listen +5, Move Silently +6, Knowledge (local) +6, Spot +5
Feats: Brave, Multiattack
Climate/Terrain: Any land
Challenge Rating: 5
Alignment: Always chaotic evil
Advancement: By character class

This monster resembles a walkin' dead or ghoul more than a vampire. The two exceptions are its gnawed-upon hands and limbs and a bloodstained mouth. The nachtzehrer doesn't cast a reflection in a mirror or other such surface.

This creature is a part of German folklore; nachtzehrer means "night waster" in its native language. Other terms for the grisly abomination are nachttoter ("night killer") and bluatsuager ("blood sucker").

Although it's a form of vampiric undead, many of its habits resemble those most associated with ghouls. Nachtzehrers seem to prefer to feast on the blood of the recently dead. They lack the characteristic fangs associated with common vampires, and have to chew at a body to open up the sluices, if you'll forgive the imagery. That's probably why they choose to feast on the dead; most normal folks aren't going to sit still long enough for the thing to gnaw through to a vein!

A nachtzehrer's hunger for blood, and to a lesser extent, flesh is nearly overwhelming. It begins by chewing at its own extremities and clothing when first risen from the dead. This leaves the monster's hands and other limbs looking torn and ragged when it finally does emerge from the grave to feed.

A victim of a nachtzehrer may appear at first to have been killed by a wild animal attack, and only closer examination reveals the abnormal absence of blood. There are also a couple of signs unique to a nachtzehrer's activity that a sharp-eyed cowpoke might pick up on.

First, the monster prefers to drink from the dead and a hero frequenting the local Boot Hill after dark might hear the sucking sounds under the ground. Also, the abomination is a bit of a glutton and tends to drink more than it needs. As a result, opening a nachtzehrer's coffin reveals the corpse soaking in a pool of excess blood that has been purged from its body.

Combat

This monster isn't above attacking the living for blood, but kills its prey before feasting. When attacking, it prefers to sate its hunger for flesh and bite rather than claw its opponents. The nachtzehrer is only active at night. Sunlight causes it no harm, but it is dormant (comatose) during daylight hours.

Fear (Su): Anyone catching sight of a nachtzehrer must make a Will saving throw against DC 19.

Infection (Su): A person killed by a nachtzehrer rises again as one of the

abominations herself after three days, unless they're removed from their funeral clothing before burial. This practice is likely to meet a *lot* of resistance in the Old West, by the way!

Undead (Su): Focus—heart; To permanently destroy the creature, it must be staked through the heart with a rosewood stake and its mouth filled with garlic, otherwise it eventually rises again.

Vampiric Weaknesses (Su): The nachtzehrer is repelled by garlic and roses. To approach them, it must make a Will saving throw against DC 18; if failed, it remains 10' from either. Also, for some reason, the monster is terrified by black dogs. It must make a Will saving throw against DC 12 when confronted with one or flee the canine's presence.

Nosferatu

Medium-Size Undead
Hit Dice: 2d12 (13 hp)
Initiative: +2 (Dex)
Speed: 35 ft.
AC: 12 (+2 Dex)
Attacks: Bite +5 melee, 2 claws +0 melee
Damage: Bite 1d3+4 plus energy drain, claw 1d4+2
Face/Reach: 5 ft. by 5 ft./5 ft.
Special Attacks: Odor, improved grab, energy drain
Special Qualities: Fast healing 25, vampiric weaknesses, undead
Saves: Fort +0, Ref +2, Will +2
Abilities: Str 18, Dex 14, Con –, Int 7, Wis 8, Cha 7
Skills: Climb +5, Hide +4, Intimidate +5, Listen +5, Move Silently +4, Spot +5
Feats: Dodge
Climate/Terrain: Any land
Challenge Rating: 5
Alignment: Always chaotic evil
Advancement: By character class

Nosferatu are bald and emaciated humanoids. Their eyes are solid black, with only a tiny spark of red visible in the center. Coarse, brown claws tip their fingers and toes, while chisel-like incisors protrude from between their withered lips.

Possibly the most voracious of any variety of bloodsucker, the nosferatu are certainly the least attractive. Only a bald, albino weasel could love one of these monsters—and then only if it was nearly blind. Nosferatu can speak in a lisping, sibilant voice, but most use their mouths only for feasting on their victims.

This variety of vampire is probably the most commonly encountered in the Weird West, thanks to Baron LaCroix's infamous "Night Trains." Originally found only in a few isolated areas of the American Southwest, trainloads of these monsters were released onto the network of railroads inside the Disputed Territories. Although efforts by the Texas Rangers and Agency have been fairly successful in eliminating the resultant nests, smaller packs of these bloodsuckers still exist in scattered pockets throughout both countries.

Combat

Driven solely by their bloodlust, these abominations seldom think beyond their next meal. Although possessed of an animal cunning at times, the most common tactic for the monsters is an overwhelming ambush. Any time spent planning beyond that cuts into valuable feeding time.

Improved grab (Ex): Nosferatu can grab any target equal in Size or smaller.

Energy Drain (Su): Anyone bitten by a nosferatu must make a Fortitude save DC (10) to eliminate a negative level.

Undead (Su): Focus—head/neck. The only way to permanently kill a nosferatu is decapitation or to expose it to sunlight.

Odor (Ex): Nosferatu smell so bad that all in a 9-foot radius of the creature must make a Will saving throw against DC 7 or be unable to act that round. The bloodsuckers themselves are immune to this effect.

Vampiric Weakness (Su): Nosferatu take 2d6 damage per round from sunlight. Their fast healing ability is ineffective against this type of damage. A wooden stake through the heart totally paralyzes a nosferatu until the stake is removed.

Penanggalen

Small Undead
Hit Dice: 7d12 (45 hp)
Initiative: +1 (Dex)
Speed: 55 ft. fly (average; unfed), 20 ft. fly (average; after feeding)
AC: 12 (+1 size, +1 Dex)
Attacks: Bite +6 melee
Damage: Bite 1d6+2
Face/Reach: 5 ft. by 5 ft./5 ft.
Special Attacks: Fear, improved grab, disease
Special Qualities: Damage reduction 5/-, undead, vampiric weaknesses
Saves: Fort +2, Ref +3, Will +6
Abilities: Str 14, Dex 13, Con –, Int 10, Wis 13, Cha 10
Skills: Hide +9, Intimidate +10, Listen +10, Move Silently +10, Spot +10
Feats: Dodge, Power Attack
Climate/Terrain: Warm Forest
Challenge Rating: 7
Alignment: Always chaotic evil
Advancement: By character class

A penanggalen is a particularly dangerous and revolting breed of vampire that has its origins in the jungles of Southeast Asia. This abomination actually separates its head and vital organs (lungs, heart, liver, intestines, etc.) from the rest of it's body and flies through the night skies in search of fresh blood. A nasty-looking head with intestines and such still attached floating a few feet above the ground—do you really need any more description?

The statistics above detail the abomination in its hunting (head and entrails) form. In that form, the monster is virtually invincible. The best a posse can hope to do is chase the monster away.

Almost all penanggalen are female. Kephn, the male form of this monster, are much rarer than the penanggalen.

Since this disgusting form of bloodsucker is normally found in the jungles of the South Pacific, you're probably wondering why we're telling you about it. Well, a few have made it to ports on the North American continent thanks to trading vessels, particularly those of the warlord Kang. Since penanggalen can move about freely in daylight, those few have traveled far and wide across the West.

Besides, they're just too cool to ignore.

Combat

Obviously, the creature prefers to hunt in isolated areas; not many folks are going to overlook a flying head dragging a pile of guts!

Fear (Su): Anyone catching sight of a penanggalen must make a Will saving throw against DC 19.

Improved grab (Ex): Penanggalen can use improved grab against Medium-Size targets or smaller.

Disease (Ex): Anyone contacting the foul bile on the monster's dangling entrails must make a Fortitude saving throw or else contact a serious illness. The disease has the following

statistics—**Infection:** Contact, **DC:** 18, **Incubation:** 1 day, **Damage:** 1d4 Con. Anyone who drops to 0 Con due to this disease dies a slow, wasting death.

Undead (Su): Focus—special (see vampiric weaknesses, below). Even if a hero succeeds in reducing it below 0 hit points, it isn't destroyed. Instead, it flees to its body.

Vampiric weaknesses (Su): A penanggalen cannot cross even the smallest branch of thorns. Should its dangling entrails become entangled in the prickly bush, it is trapped until daylight—and death under the sun's rays. While in hunting form, a penanggalen takes 2d6 damage each round it's exposed to direct sunlight. Also, when encountered during the daytime, it has no special abilities whatsoever.

While the head is separated, the penanggalen must keep its body immersed in vinegar to preserve it, and must return to it by daybreak. Once whole, it can move about freely in daytime. The creature's body can be destroyed normally, but note that this does not immediately kill the penanggalen. A penanggalen can sense when its body is disturbed, no matter the distance between head and body.

Shtriga

Medium-Size Fey
Hit Dice: 8d6+3 (52 hp)
Initiative: +1 (Dex)
Speed: 20 ft.
AC: 11 (+1 Dex)
Attacks: By melee weapon type +7
Damage: By melee weapon type +1
Face/Reach: 5 ft. by 5 ft./5 ft.
Special Attacks: Spells
Special Qualities: Unnatural toughness, polymorph, vampiric weaknesses, regeneration 1
Saves: Fort +9, Ref +3, Will +6
Abilities: Str 12, Dex 13, Con 16, Int 13, Wis 14, Cha 15
Skills: Black Magic +7, Climb +6, Concentration +8, Diplomacy +7, Hide +6, Intimidate +7, Knowledge (arcana) +6, Listen +7, Move Silently +6, Sense Motive +7, Spot +7
Feats: Brave, Dodge, Extend Spell
Climate/Terrain: Any land
Challenge Rating: 7
Alignment: Always chaotic evil
Advancement: As black magician character class

Shtriga appear to be normal, older woman of Central European descent. After a feeding, her skin takes on a bright red blush, her belly is distended, her lips bloodstained, her eyes crimson, and she appears much younger.

The shtriga is found in Central European folk-tales (especially Albanian), and is sometimes confused with the strigoi which is a Romanian vampire. Other names include striga, strigon, and vyeshtitza. Although the shtriga does have a thirst for blood, it differs from other "vampires" in one major point: it's not undead. A shtriga is very much alive.

This bloodsucker is actually a form of witch who's developed a taste for human blood and uses her powers to hunt her prey. The shtriga's living status makes her a particularly dangerous foe as most of the usual defenses against a vampire (garlic, crosses, sunlight, etc.) are completely useless against her.

The shtriga conceals herself in a community and, since she can travel freely in daylight, can be very difficult to detect. Furthermore, she has the ability to transform into an animal form to hide her nocturnal comings and goings. Top all that off with respectable black magic powers, and you've got a foe to challenge any posse, particularly since the shtriga is more than smart enough to disguise her feedings as the work of a more mundane vampire!

Her gluttony often leads her to consume more blood than she can assimilate, however, and a surefire way to tell a shtriga is haunting a community is a telltale pool of regurgitated blood near the site of the attack.

Combat

The witch is, like many of her undead cousins, particularly voracious in her feedings. Often she kills her victim in a single attack, instead of returning to feed over the course of time. As she lacks fangs, she's forced to use a knife, dagger, or other cutting instrument to draw the blood, though.

Spells (Sp): Commensurate with their Hit Dice levels, shtriga have access to a wide range of black magic.

Unnatural toughness (Su): Although she's still living, due to her unholy practices the shtriga is treated as Undead for the purposes of damage. She can be injured or even temporarily incapacitated by normal weapons and magic, the only way to kill a shtriga is to drive a wooden stake into her stomach.

Regeneration (Su): Only staking a shtriga (as described above) prevents her from regenerating.

Vampiric weaknesses (Su): For some reason, only a cross made from pig bones has any effect on a shtriga. When faced with one, she must make a Will saving throw against DC 18 or be forced to remain 10' away from the device. Also, a hero who recognizes the shtriga's activities can fashion an amulet using the blood she typically vomits as an ingredient with a Knowledge (arcana) skill check against DC 18. Such an amulet provides +4 to all saving throws and ability checks made to resist the witch's black magic.

Upir

Medium-Size Undead
Hit Dice: 7d12 (45 hp)
Initiative: +1 (Dex)
Speed: 30 ft.
AC: 11 (+1 Dex)
Attacks: 2 claws +9 melee
Damage: Claw 1d3+6
Face/Reach: 5 ft. by 5 ft./5 ft.
Special Attacks: Improved grab, constrict 1d3+6, gaze attack
Special Qualities: Fearless, undead, vampiric weaknesses
Saves: Fort +2, Ref +3, Will +6
Abilities: Str 24, Dex 13, Con –, Int 9, Wis 12, Cha 12
Skills: Climb +7, Hide +7, Intimidate +7, Listen +7, Move Silently +7, Knowledge (local) +8, Spot +7
Feats: Dodge, Power Attack
Climate/Terrain: Any land
Challenge Rating: 7
Alignment: Always chaotic evil
Advancement: By character class

The upir looks much like it did in life. However, its eyes never blink and two distinct curls appear in its hair. After feedings, its skin takes on a reddish cast, but it is otherwise slightly paler

than in life. The upir does cast a reflection when confronted with a mirror. The upir is another type of vampire from Central European legend, with reports dating back to the 16th century. This abomination is undead, unlike the shtriga, and one of the most powerful forms of bloodsuckers a posse is likely to run into, short of a ancient nosferatu or the legendary Dracula himself!

Upirs aren't given to traveling, and usually haunt the locale near their place of death or interment. An upir usually begins as a restless spirit or ghost, similar to a poltergeist, except that it attempts to smother folks or even domesticated animals. After a short period of plaguing the area, the spirit returns to its dead body and animates it as an undead vampire.

Combat

Once in corporeal form, the upir usually kills its victims by strangulation. This may lead initial vampire hunters astray, as the cause of death is suffocation or a broken neck. The abomination draws blood from the victim after the fact by biting the victim's tongue—an area often overlooked by 19th century doctors in a postmortem!

However, the upir has another weapon in its arsenal should old-fashioned choking fail. The monster can kill a person unlucky enough to simply meet its gaze!

Gaze attack (Sp): Once per day, the upir can force an opponent whose gaze has met its own stare to make a Fortitude saving throw against a DC of 20. If they fail, they suffer a heart attack and die.

Improved grab (Ex): Upir can grab any target equal in Size or smaller, and employ this ability to strangle (constrict) victims without a weapon.

Undead (Su): Focus—head; Only an iron spike driven through the upir's skull permanently destroys it. Completely burning the body has the same effect. Additionally, the creature has two hearts and is not slain by the staking experienced vampire hunters may rely upon to eliminate undead bloodsuckers.

Vampiric weaknesses (Su): If confronted with a line or trail of poppy seeds, the upir must make a Will saving throw against DC 9 to cross it. Otherwise, it must either go around or turn back. The upir is only active at night. Sunlight causes it no harm, but it is dormant (comatose) during daylight hours unless aroused. Then, it is -4 on all rolls.

Ustrel

Small Undead
Hit Dice: 3d12 (19 hp)
Initiative: +1 (Dex)
Speed: 30 ft.
AC: 12 (+1 size, +1 Dex.)
Attacks: Bite +3 melee
Damage: Bite 1d3+1 plus blood drain
Face/Reach: 5 ft. by 5 ft./5 ft.

Special Attacks: Improved grab, anesthetic saliva
Special Qualities: Invisibility, undead, fire weakness
Saves: Fort +1, Ref +2, Will +2
Abilities: Str 12, Dex 13, Con –, Int 7, Wis 8, Cha 8
Skills: Climb +5, Hide +6, Listen +6, Move Silently +6, Spot +6
Feats: Dodge
Climate/Terrain: Any land
Challenge Rating: 4
Alignment: Always chaotic evil
Advancement: By character class

An ustrel looks like a pale, human child or infant. Its eyes are vertically slit, like a cat's, and its hands and feet have long, curved nails for hanging onto host animals. Four large canine teeth protrude from its mouth; it has no other teeth.

These foul little monsters rise from the corpses of very young children (two years or younger) that have died due to abandonment or neglect. Unfortunately, this sad event happens more often in the Weird West than decent folk would like to believe.

Ustrel normally feed on cattle or other livestock, and their depredations are often mistaken for prairie ticks or some sort of disease. These abominations are voracious eaters, often causing the death of seven or eight steers in a single night.

Luckily for ranchers, ustrels are usually solitary in nature. Only rare instances occur that cause more than one to form in the same area at the same time—say, an unusually cruel orphanage or the like.

Once the livestock have been totally drained, an ustrel seldom moves on to feed on the human populace. Most vampires of this sort simply become dormant, awaiting the replenishment of the local herds.

Combat

Thanks to their supernatural abilities, most targets aren't aware of a ustrel's attack. Any victim who fights back is likely to cause an ustrel to beat a hasty retreat.

Improved grab (Ex): Ustrels can use improved grab against Medium-Size targets or smaller.

Blood drain (Ex): After successfully biting an opponent, ustrels can drain 1d3+1 hit points worth of blood from an opponent each round.

Anesthetic Saliva (Ex): Thanks to a side effect of the ustrel's spit, most victims don't even know they've been bitten. The victim must make a Spot skill check with DC 17 to even notice the wound as its being drained.

Undead (Su): Focus-heart.

Invisibility (Su): Ustrels are normally invisible.

Fire Weakness (Su): Exposure to a source of fire equal to a small bonfire or greater renders the monster visible.

Wampyr

Medium-Size Undead
Hit Dice: 4d12 (26 hp)
Initiative: +0
Speed: 20 ft.
AC: 10
Attacks: Bite +2 melee
Damage: Bite 1d3 plus energy drain
Face/Reach: 5 ft. by 5 ft./5 ft.
Special Attacks: Energy drain
Special Qualities: Undead, damage reduction 5/-, vampiric weaknesses
Saves: Fort +1, Ref +1, Will +3
Abilities: Str 11, Dex 10, Con –, Int 8, Wis 7, Cha 6
Skills: Climb +4, Hide +5, Listen +4, Move Silently +5, Perform (acting) +5, Spot +4
Feats: Endurance
Climate/Terrain: Any land
Challenge Rating: 4
Alignment: Always chaotic evil
Advancement: By character class

A wampyr resembles a walkin' dead in many respects, save that its flesh is full and bloated. Its eyes may have a vacant or glassy stare and its fingernails are often splintered and dirt-encrusted from its escape from the grave.

A wampyr is typical of the type of vampire found in the folklore of the Balkan region of Eastern Europe. This foul creature is also known as a vyrkolakas, upir, vampir and a host of other names.

Wampyrs are actually little more than undead plague carriers, spreading the disease of their form of vampirism among their former loved ones. Unlike some other vampires, wampyrs aren't terribly strong and the decay of death is obvious on their bodies. Those unfamiliar with this sort of bloodsucker often mistake it for a simple walkin' dead.

Corpses infected by wampyr retain some of their color, do not stiffen and often have spots of blood around their lips and fingernails. A recently fed wampyr may have a pool of blood in its coffin—these monsters are notorious gluttons. Others may have gnawed on their own appendages while trapped in their coffins.

Combat

Possessed of a crude, animal cunning, these vampires prefer to prey on weaker individuals, and usually attack by ambush. Another common tactic is for the monsters to return to the homes of their former families and feast on their bereaved kin. Due to the highly infectious nature of the wampyr's bite, this sort of vampirism often spreads very quickly through a community.

Energy drain (Su): Anyone bitten by a wampyr must make Fortitude saving throw against DC 10 to eliminate a negative level.

Undead (Su): Focus-heart

Vampiric weaknesses (Su): Garlic and roses both cause a wampyr 1d6 damage if they contact them—and the monsters find these plants abhorrent. Sunlight causes 2d6 damage each round to a risen wampyr; resting wampyr are immune to this. A wampyr can be destroyed by digging it up, beheading it and placing garlic in its mouth. Exposing a resting wampyr's corpse to sunlight does not harm it. On the other hand, if it's caught by the sun's rays before it reaches its coffin, it begins to burn rapidly.

Walkin' Fossil

Huge Undead
Hit Dice: 10d12 (65 hp)
Initiative: +2 (Dex)
Speed: 70 ft.
AC: 15 (-2 size, +2 Dex, +5 natural)
Attacks: Bite +7 melee; or 2 claws +7 melee
Damage: Bite 1d6+4, claw 1d8+4
Face/Reach: 10 ft. by 20 ft./10 ft.
Special Attacks: Trample 1d8+4, improved grab
Special Qualities: Undead, fearless, blindsight, scent
Saves: Fort +3, Ref +5, Will +7
Abilities: Str 18, Dex 14, Con —, Int 6, Wis 11, Cha 9
Skills: Jump +10, Listen +7, Move Silently +6, Spot +7, Wilderness Lore +6
Feats: Power Attack, Track
Climate/Terrain: Any land
Challenge Rating: 8
Alignment: Always neutral
Advancement: 11-30 HD (Huge)

In this case, the fossilized creature is an Utahraptor, a quick predator some 20 feet long (including 8' tail). Parts of these reanimated beasts may be missing, but the petrification creates armor for the ancient animal.

The whole creature appears to be made of stone, like a statue brought to life, except for its empty eye sockets, which glare with a bright, unholy light. The dinosaur has vicious teeth and fore-claws as well as great, curved, ripping claws on its hind legs. When moving, it sounds like rocks grinding together.

Whether animated by determined manitous that manage to find a trace of brain matter, or simply created as entirely new beings by the Reckoners, walkin' fossils are extremely dangerous predators. Fortunately, these creatures seem pretty difficult for the dark forces to animate. While other forms of fossilized dinosaurs may be animated, the Reckoners and their agents typically prefer large predators.

Combat

The walkin' fossil is a quick, dangerous hunter, a pack hunter, but very capable alone. The creature can track prey by smell and wait in ambush if necessary. Once it sees prey, the critter usually runs forward and leaps on it with fore-claws and mouth, then rakes with its hind claws. Once a victim is down, the critter turns to other prey, eating only when all prey is down or gone.

Trample (Ex): These creatures can leap up to 70 feet with a running start. A leap causes 1d8+4 damage to whatever it hits.

Undead (Su): Focus-head

Wave Shadows

Medium-Size Monstrous Humanoid
Hit Dice: 4d8+1 (22 hp)
Initiative: +1 (Dex)
Speed: 35 ft., 15 ft. swim
AC: 11 (+1 Dex)
Attacks: 2 claws +5 melee; or by ranged weapon type +5; or by melee weapon type +5
Damage: Claw 1d6+1, by melee weapon type +1, by ranged weapon type
Face/Reach: 5 ft. by 5 ft./5 ft.
Special Qualities: Shadow cloak
Saves: Fort +2, Ref +5, Will +5
Abilities: Str 12 Dex 12, Con 12, Int 10, Wis 13, Cha 13
Skills: Hide +8*, Listen +6, Move Silently +8*, Search +6, Swim +9, Spot +6
Feats: Endurance
Climate/Terrain: Aquatic
Challenge Rating: 2
Alignment: Always lawful evil
Advancement: By character class

In their non-obscured form, wave shadows appear as amphibious, reptilian humanoids. They equip themselves with items taken from their victims, making themselves grim parodies of the people they have killed. Normally, they conceal themselves behind a mystical cloak of darkness which makes them look like living shadows.

Wave shadows have been rumored to exist in the ocean depths for centuries and may in fact have existed prior to the Reckoning, giving rise to myths about mermaids and the like. Regardless of that, in the last fourteen years confirmed sightings have become increasingly common, usually in the Great Maze.

The creatures are aggressive, living in large clans and preying on small, isolated villages, lone travelers and occasionally fully-crewed ships. They raid not only for goods, but for food as well: They consume their victims.

Combat

Clans of wave shadows set up underwater camps near the isolated communities they have plundered. They leave spies hiding in the town, so they are aware if anybody enters the seemingly abandoned community.

Shadow cloak (Su): A wave shadow is shrouded in inky blackness between sunset and sunrise, giving opponents a -2 penalty on all attacks and granting the wave shadow a +2 on Hide and Move Silently skill checks.

Weeping Widow

Medium-Size Undead
Hit Dice: 8d12 (52 hp)
Initiative: +6 (Dex, Improved Initiative)
Speed: 35 ft.
AC: 12 (+2 Dex)
Attacks: Punch +7 melee
Damage: Punch 1d3+3(s) plus acidic tears
Face/Reach: 5 ft. by 5 ft./5 ft.
Special Attacks: Possession, acidic tears
Special Qualities: Blessed weakness, specific immunity
Saves: Fort +2, Ref +4, Will +8
Abilities: Str 16, Dex 14, Con –, Int 9, Wis 14, Cha 17

Skills: Climb +8, Hide +8, Intimidate +8, Knowledge (local) +7, Listen +8, Move Silently +8, Spot +8
Feats: Improved Initiative, Power Attack
Climate/Terrain: Any land
Challenge Rating: 6
Alignment: Always chaotic evil
Advancement: By victim's character class

A woman possessed by a weeping widow spirit always appears as the widow did when she died, dressed in culturally appropriate funeral clothing and often with a veil covering her face. Tears can be seen to streak her dress, and her gloves, handkerchief and so forth are wet with them. She speaks and weeps in the voice of her host body in a voice ranging from quiet sobbing to racking wails against fate.

This abomination is the grief-stricken spirit of a woman who has witnessed the violent death of at least one member of her immediate family, and then died herself soon after. These women never had time to mourn their loss, so the unfinished business of their grief and rage binds them to the physical world.

Normally, the spirit is invisible, wallowing in self-pity, despair and anger while wandering the vicinity of the tragedy. If an adult woman enters the spirit's domain, the weeping widow takes over her body and exacts revenge—even if her victims had nothing to do with her sorrow.

In her spirit form, a weeping widow can't do much but possess whatever woman enters her domain, so the above statistics refers to a typical woman possessed by a weeping widow. Feel free to substitute the appropriate Str, Dex and Con scores of a posse member or important non-player character who falls under the spirit's influence.

Combat

During combat, the possessed woman shrieks howls of rage and pain at the top of her lungs, cursing the murderers of her sons or husband. She attempts to wound anyone nearby with her acidic teardrops. Weeping widows always attack those farthest away from any blessed present. If the widow defeats her opponents, she weeps over the bodies of those she has slain as if they were her lost family, and remains there until her host dies of thirst or starvation, at which point she becomes incorporeal again.

Acidic tears (Su): The widow's tears, which cover her face and saturate her gloves and clothes, are extremely corrosive. Anyone whose bare flesh contacts the widow (or anyone she makes a successful touch attack against) immediately takes 2d6 acid damage. Likewise, if the widow punches a target, it inflicts an additional 2d6 damage. If the widow touches an item (or if an item touches her), the item loses 2 points from its Reliability (or the device now has Reliability of 18, if it didn't have a Reliability before).

Possession (Su): A weeping widow takes control of a woman if the target fails a Will saving throw against DC 13. The widow can attempt possession once per round until the potential victim either leaves the area or steps inside the radius of a protection miracle, where the widow can't sense her. A potential victim who makes her saving throw has visions of a horrible massacre (the death of the widow's family), but does not know exactly why these visions are occurring.

If the weeping widow can be incapacitated or bound, the blessed miracle exorcism can release the spirit into the afterlife and free the woman possessed. Killing the creature outright destroys it, but it also slays the woman it is possessing.

Specific Immunity (Su): The widow is immune to whatever weapon killed her loved one(s). While often guns, it can be any weapon the Marshal chooses, depending on how difficult you want to make it. If hit by such a weapon, the widow should give a clue, shrieking something about how those weapons can't take anything more away from her.

Blessed weakness (Su): The widow is -4 to all saving throws and ability checks against all blessed miracles, gifts and divine interventions. The widow is obviously afraid of any blessed, and actively seeks to avoid them.

Were-Sharks

Medium-Size Shapechanger
Hit Dice: 4d8+1 (22 hp)
Initiative: +1 (Dex)
Speed: 35 ft., 70 ft. swim
AC: 16 (+1 Dex, +5 natural)
Attacks: Bite +5 melee, 2 claws +3 melee; or by melee weapon type +5; or by ranged weapon type +3
Damage: Bite 1d4+2, claw 1d3+1, by melee weapon type +2, by ranged weapon type
Face/Reach: 5 ft. by 5 ft./5 ft.
Saves: Fort +5, Ref +4, Will +4
Abilities: Str 14, Dex 11, Con 12, Int 9, Wis 9, Cha 9
Skills: Climb +6, Hide +7, Intimidate +7, Listen +7, Move Silently +7, Spot +7, Swim +10
Feats: Multiattack
Climate/Terrain: Aquatic
Challenge Rating: 1
Alignment: Usually lawful evil
Advancement: By character class

In their humanoid form, were-sharks are, for all intents, normal humans. (These statistics are for the abominations' predatory form; otherwise, use more normal human numbers.)

In their beast form, these creatures stand almost 7' tall and are covered with a rough, gray, scaly hide. Thick webbing stretches between their clawed fingers and toes, and a small dorsal ridge hunches out of their backs. Their eyes become solid black and their lips harden over an abnormally wide mouth filled with razor-sharp, shark-like teeth in double rows. Rows of gills appear on their throats, just below their receded chins.

The term "were-sharks" isn't really accurate, as these monsters have no relation to true sharks. However, since the abominations can freely change between a human form and a form of carnivorous marine life, we'll overlook the finer details.

Combat

These abominations lurk in port cities, particularly in the Maze, and join ship crews. Once the vessel is at sea (or deep within the Great Maze's channels), they begin preying on the crew. At least one ship plying the waters between Shan Fan and Lost Angels (the *Edward Fitzhugh*) is crewed entirely by were-sharks.

Skills: Were-sharks receive a +3 bonus to all Climb, Hide, Intimidate, Listen, Move Silently and Spot skill rolls.

Will o' the Wisp

Tiny Aberration
Hit Dice: 3d8+2 (19 hp)
Initiative: +3 (Dex)
Speed: 55 ft. fly (perfect)
AC: 15 (+2 size, +3 Dex)
Attacks: None
Damage: None
Face/Reach: 2 1/2 ft. by 2 1/2 ft./0 ft.
Special Attacks: Compulsion
Special Qualities: Damage reduction 15/electricity, blindsight, electricity weakness, pain absorption
Saves: Fort +3, Ref +4, Will +3
Abilities: Str 7, Dex 16, Con 14, Int 12, Wis 10, Cha 11
Skills: Bluff +5, Diplomacy +5, Hide +8, Intimidate +5, Move Silently +5, Sense Motive +5, Spot +5
Feats: Dodge
Climate/Terrain: Marsh, Mountains, Underground
Challenge Rating: 4
Alignment: Always chaotic evil
Advancement: 4-6 HD (Tiny)

This abomination looks like a ball of light about the size of a person's head. It has been theorized they are the ghosts of those killed by quicksand, in mining accidents, or through other misfortunes common to the places where they are found. The truth is unknown, but they are a terrible hazard to any who encounter them.

The glowing beasts are found only in areas of great danger. They are commonly found in swamps of quicksand, but they have also been encountered in abandoned mines (especially those with explosive gasses in them), and even in the lairs of other abominations. They are nearly impossible to harm, but are incapable of causing any direct injury themselves. Instead, they have the ability to coerce others to follow them. They invariably lead the victims into danger, and then feast on the pain and suffering produced.

Wisps are intelligent and able to communicate via flashing patterns of light, and even in Morse code. They rarely communicate with humans, however, unless they are trying to manipulate the foolish mortals into making a possibly fatal mistake.

Combat

The will o' the wisp doesn't attack directly. Instead, it mesmerizes victims to manipulate them into doing what it wants. Invariably, the wisp tries to lead its victims into places where they can be hurt.

Compulsion (Sp): When someone first views a wisp, they must make a Will saving throw against DC 13. If the character wins, the wisp tries again on the next round. Should the wisp win, the creature controls the character's actions for the next 10 minutes.

The victim follows passively, even into obvious danger, at a normal walking speed, and responds with violence to any attempts to restrain them. The subject cannot speak or act normally.

A successful Diplomacy check by a companion against DC 13 allows a mesmerized victim another saving throw contest—but with a +2 to their roll. A wisp can mesmerize only one target at a time.

Electricity weakness (Su): An electrical attack of sufficient power can kill a will o' the wisp. If it is slain by other methods, it winks out of existence, only to reappear the next night.

Pain absorption (Su): Whenever something endures pain within 300 feet of a will o' the wisp, it feeds off the victim's pain. Each time a living being loses hit points, the wisp heals an equal amount on itself. The critter can also gain a surplus: an extra 20 hit points gained (and not used for healing) allow the wisp to reproduce itself.

Witches, Appalachian

Medium-Size Humanoid
Hit Dice: 5d6 (17 hp)
Initiative: +1 (Dex)
Speed: 20 ft.
AC: 11 (+1 Dex)
Attacks: By spell type
Damage: By spell type
Face/Reach: 5 ft. by 5 ft./5 ft.
Special Attacks: Drought, blight, spells, polymorph
Special Qualities: Silver weakness, blessed invocation
Saves: Fort +4, Ref +2, Will +4
Abilities: Str 9, Dex 13, Con 11, Int 12, Wis 13, Cha 12
Skills: Black Magic +5, Concentration +4, Diplomacy +5, Intimidate +5, Knowledge (arcana) +5, Listen +5, Move Silently +5, Ridicule +5, Sense Motive +5, Spot +5, Wilderness Lore +5 **Feats:** Dodge, Enlarge Spell, Extend Spell
Climate/Terrain: Any land
Challenge Rating: 3
Alignment: Usually chaotic evil
Advancement: As black magician character class

Witches are almost always women. They tend to fall into two categories: young, beautiful ones and ugly old crones. Warlocks—male witches—are much rarer, but they tend to be powerful. They also tend towards exceeding ugliness.

A young witch tends towards subtlety; she likes to take advantage of her good looks to get a man to fall in love with her. The hag-like witches typically live by themselves in backwoods cabins where they can work their devilments as they please.

Many witches are solitary, but sometimes they like to gather in groups called witch-gangs. Witch-gangs usually have 13 members, with the most powerful witch serving as the gang's leader. Witch-gangs hold their meetings in old, abandoned mills, hidden hollows, caves and other out-of-the-way places where they won't be disturbed. Sometimes they use their powers to drive folks away from a desired meeting place, making it seem haunted so no one ventures near the location.

Witches sometimes have special pets, which are called familiars back in the Old Country. These creatures are often used to spy on folks the witch wants to know about. Lizards and black cats are the most common creatures, but many others are possible.

Combat

Witches avoid face-to-face fights whenever possible, but in the event they find themselves in one they

defend themselves as best they can with black magic. When casting, they prefer subtler spells to big, flashy effects.

Spells (Sp): Commensurate with their Hit Dice levels, witches have access to a wide range of black magic.

Blight (Sp): A witch can curse crops, livestock and wells, causing them to sicken, wither and die. She can affect one acre of crops, one animal or one well per level she has (for many small Appalachian farmers, an acre or two is all it takes to ruin them). Once the power has been used, it takes effect over the course of about a week as the crops, animals, or people die or the well dries up. During this time characters can counteract the blight with hexes, miracles or the like, allowing the subject to start growing/living normally again. Failing that, only convincing the witch to remove the curse can end the suffering.

Drought (Sp): This power lets a witch control the weather, making it rain or not rain. The power's area of effect is a 5 mile radius. If she chooses drought, there will be no rain in that area for 1 week per level she has attained. If she chooses rain instead, it will rain steadily for one entire hour per level.

Anyone in the area of effect of rain is at a -2 to all actions while outdoors. She can increase the intensity of the rain (as well as the accompanying penalty) one step per three character levels attained, to a downpour (-4), a gullywasher (-6) or a toadstrangler (-8). Once the spell has been cast, the witch can leave the area without negating its effects.

Polymorph (Sp): Most witches can change their shape into one specific type of creature. A black cat is the most common form assumed, but pigs, black dogs, and crows are also possible. The witch can also change her appearance to that of any other person. The witch can make herself look just like a specific person, or simply look "different" (prettier, taller, different gender, and so on).

The change lasts for only an hour, though, and if the witch touches or is touched by anything silver, she instantly changes back to her true visage or form.

Silver weakness (Su): Only silver weapons can put a witch down for good: silver knives, silver bullets, silver hammers—anything like that will do. A witch killed by any other means automatically comes back Harrowed to continue her wicked ways; by contrast, one killed with silver cannot become Harrowed. For this reason, witches refuse to handle silver coins or objects, and flee from silver forcefully presented. The first order of those who do come back as Harrowed is to find the heroes responsible for her demise and invoke some retribution.

Blessed invocation (Su): A universally accepted way to cancel out witch-powers is to invoke the Lord. Saying "the Lord" or "my Lord" while a witch is casting a spell lowers the DC of all saving throws made against it by 4. After the spell is cast, invoking the Lord doesn't work. Similarly, the blessed have special protection against witchery, exactly as they have against black magic.

Zombies

These are the types of undead that can literally reach out and touch their victims. Fortunately, for posses of monster-hunting cowpokes, they're also the kind of undead you can plug with your trusty six-shooter.

Well, most of the time, anyway.

Zombies are a staple for most *Deadlands* campaigns, and why not? Everybody loves zombies, after all.

However, after a while, your posse might get a little tired of the same old walkin' dead. With that in mind, we've thrown together a funeral wagon full of different sorts of zombies to keep them jumping. These should keep your smarty pants heroes from thinking they know all there is to know about zombies. Once a walkin' dead exhibits a power they've never seen, they'll be a little less complacent.

Bloat

Medium-Size Undead
Hit Dice: 2d12 (13 hp)
Initiative: +0
Speed: 30 ft.
AC: 10
Attacks: Bite +2 melee; or by melee weapon type +2
Damage: Bite 1d3+1, by melee weapon type +1
Face/Reach: 5 ft. by 5 ft./5 ft.
Special Attacks: Fear, stench
Special Qualities: Fearless, undead, alcohol weakness, damage reduction 5/special
Saves: Fort +0, Ref +0, Will +2
Abilities: Str 13, Dex 10, Con –, Int 7, Wis 8, Cha 6
Skills: Climb +4, Hide +4, Listen +3, Move Silently +4, Spot +3, Swim +5
Feats: Power Attack
Climate/Terrain: Aquatic
Challenge Rating: 4
Alignment: Always chaotic evil
Advancement: By character class

The corpse is grossly swollen and distended. Its flesh is of a consistency similar to soap-sludge and has a glistening, pale white sheen. The eyes appear as tiny black marbles in its bloated face.

A cowpoke isn't even safe from the walkin' dead out on the water. Bloats are waterlogged walkin' dead, perfect for menacing heroes with a nautical bent.

To become a bloat, a zombie has to have been submerged at the time it was reanimated and remained submerged for at least a few months. As a result, these abominations are usually only encountered near large bodies of water, such as the Great Maze or a major river.

Over time, the water reacts with the corpse's tissues, turning most of it into a waxy substance that has a nearly overpowering stench to it. The flesh becomes pale and distended, hence the name 'bloat'.

Combat

A bloat's fingers are usually too swollen to manipulate a trigger, but they may have other simpler weapons if available, such as clubs, knives and other hand-to-hand weapons.

Fear (Su): Anyone catching sight of a bloat must make a Will saving throw against DC 19.

Stench (Ex): Any human within 10 feet of a bloat must make an Fortitude saving throw against DC 13 to avoid being sickened by the odor. Those who fail lose 1d4 hit points and are at –2 to all rolls for the encounter. Characters only have to make this roll once per combat.

Damage reduction (Su): Bludgeoning, slashing and shotgun damage are unaffected by a bloat's damage reduction.

Undead (Su): Focus–head. Immune to mind-influencing effects, poison, sleep, paralysis, stunning, and disease. Not subject to critical hits, subdual damage, ability damage, energy drain, or death from massive damage.

Alcohol Weakness (Su): Contact with alcohol does 1d10 damage to bloats. The damage continues at the beginning of each round, but is reduced by a die type each time. Once the damage is reduced to less than 1d4, it ends.

Desiccated Dead

Medium-Size Undead
Hit Dice: 2d12 (13 hp)
Initiative: +1 (Dex)
Speed: 35 ft.
AC: 11 (+1 Dex)
Attacks: 2 claws +1 melee, bite -4 melee; or by ranged weapon type +2; or by melee weapon type +1
Damage: Claw 1d4, bite 1d3, by weapon type
Face/Reach: 5 ft. by 5 ft./5 ft.
Special Qualities: Fearless, undead, fire weakness
Saves: Fort +0, Ref +1, Will +3
Abilities: Str 10, Dex 13, Con –, Int 7, Wis 9, Cha 6
Skills: Climb +5, Hide +5, Listen +5, Move Silently +5, Spot +5
Feats: Dodge
Climate/Terrain: Any Temperate or Warm land
Challenge Rating: 2
Alignment: Always chaotic evil
Advancement: By character class

The skin of these zombies is dried and brown, stretched tightly over their skeletons. Tiny, blackened eyes sit loosely in their sockets and their lips have drawn back revealing a mouth often bereft of teeth.

Usually manitous try to pick corpses that are fairly fresh. They pack a better punch and tend to hold up a little better in a fight. However, evil spirits from another dimension can't always be choosers, so sometimes they have to make due with bodies that have been out in the sun a while.

Desiccated dead are created from bodies that have dried up and decomposed to the point there is little left to them but a leathery skin over a skeleton. Cowpokes who've been bleaching in the desert and bodies from Indian above ground burial sites all fall into this category when reanimated by a manitou.

Feel free to use this type of walkin' dead for mummies from Southwestern or Mexican Indian tombs. The desiccated dead are also representative of lesser mummies from Egyptian tombs—servants buried with the head honcho. If you've found a way to use those in an adventure, desiccated dead can be handy. See page 67 for more-powerful forms of mummies to throw at your heroes.

Combat

The skin-and-bones bodies of the desiccated dead are quicker and more nimble than the usual dead, a fact they use to give zombie hunters a nasty surprise. Some desiccated dead may carry weapons, either those they were buried with or those taken from their victims. Although their original owners may not have been familiar with modern weaponry, the new residents of the corpses are quite capable of using firearms, and do so.

Undead (Su): Focus-head. Immune to mind-influencing effects, poison, sleep, paralysis, stunning, and disease. Not subject to critical hits, subdual damage, ability damage, energy drain, or death from massive damage.

Fire Weakness (Su): Desiccated dead are flammable; any fire-attack that does even one hit point to them causes them to catch fire and burn for an additional 1d4 damage each round thereafter. However, the firebug hero now has to fight a *flaming* zombie, at least until it crumbles to ashes; the creature does an additional 1d4 damage on successful hand-to-hand attacks—which may set the victim on fire as well!

Feral Walkin' Dead

Medium-Size Undead
Hit Dice: 2d12 (13 hp)
Initiative: +0 melee
Speed: 50 ft.
AC: 10
Attacks: 2 claws +2 melee, bite +0 melee
Damage: Claw 1d4+1, bite 1d3
Face/Reach: 5 ft. by 5 ft./5 ft.
Special Qualities: Undead, fearless, hunger
Saves: Fort +0, Ref +0, Will +3
Abilities: Str 13, Dex 11, Con –, Int 6, Wis 9, Cha 6
Skills: Climb +5, Hide +5*, Listen +5, Move Silently +5*, Spot +5, Swim +5
Feats: Multiattack
Climate/Terrain: Any land
Challenge Rating: 2
Alignment: Always chaotic evil
Advancement: By character class

Feral walkin' dead appear much the same as the more garden-variety walkin' dead. Their bodies may exhibit more decomposition or damage than those of their more intelligent cousins.

These zombies are created by a weak or watered-down version of Baron LaCroix's reanimation fluid. These are similar to the abominations spawned in Nacogdoches, Texas, after one of LaCroix's trains derailed nearby.

Combat

Feral dead are faster than the more commonly encountered walkin' dead. Their hunger for human brains is nearly all-consuming and, once aroused, becomes the zombies' sole concern. Although not as intelligent as other forms of undead, feral dead are frightfully cunning in laying ambushes. These zombies are cunning, hiding in places where they're least expected—like a barrel full of rainwater. However, unlike regular zombies, feral dead are unable to use firearms or other weapons, relying instead on their bite and claw attacks.

Undead (Su): Focus-head. Immune to mind-influencing effects, poison, sleep, paralysis, stunning, and disease. Not subject to critical hits, subdual damage, ability damage, energy drain, or death from massive damage.

Hunger (Ex): Once one of these zombies downs a victim, it must make a Will save DC (17) to keep from stopping whatever else it was doing and chawing down on the unfortunate sap.

Skills: Regardless of their victims' preparations, feral dead receive a +4 bonus to their Hide and Move Silently skill check rolls when attempting to surprise their prey.

Frozen Dead

Medium-Size Undead
Hit Dice: 2d12 (13 hp)
Initiative: +0
Speed: 20 ft.
AC: 14 (+4 natural)
Attacks: 2 claws +3 melee, bite +1 melee; or by ranged weapon type +1, or by melee weapon type +3
Damage: Claw 1d6+2, bite 1d3+1, by ranged weapon type, by melee weapon type +2
Face/Reach: 5 ft. by 5 ft./5 ft.
Special Qualities: Fearless, undead, resistance to energy 10
Saves: Fort +0, Ref +0, Will +3
Abilities: Str 14, Dex 9, Con –, Int 7, Wis 9, Cha 6
Skills: Climb +3, Hide +4, Intimidate +4, Listen +4, Move Silently +4, Spot +4
Feats: Multiattack
Climate/Terrain: Any Cold land
Challenge Rating: 2
Alignment: Always chaotic evil
Advancement: By character class

Frozen dead have a pale or even bluish cast to their flesh. Although their eyes move freely, the zombie's faces are locked into a single expression—that of their death mask. A palpable air of cold follows the frozen dead, and icicles, sometimes "bloodcicles," may hang from their bodies.

Sometimes the temperature in the northern plains or high mountain passes drops low enough to freeze a body solid. When a manitou decides to wreak a little havoc with a corpse that's been out in freezing weather like that, the end result is a walkin' dead with ice in its veins—literally.

The frozen dead are reanimated corpsicles—bodies frozen solid by incredible cold. They're only created when the air temperature is below -30° Fahrenheit. While their chilled bodies are a little slower and clumsier than those of room-temperature zombies, they make up for that in other ways.

Note that it's not necessary for the original body to have actually frozen to death to make one of these icy revenants. *Any* sort of corpse can become a frozen dead under the right circumstances. That's enough to make a fellow think twice about storing departed loved ones in the tool shed until spring!

Combat

The high water content of the frozen dead keeps them from sinking more than a few inches below the surface of water. A common tactic for these abominations is to float along a half-frozen river like so many undead icebergs and snatch unsuspecting victims from the banks. Like regular walkin' dead, frozen dead may carry weapons they've taken from their victims: firearms, axes, and so forth.

Undead (Su): Focus—head. Immune to mind-influencing effects, poison, sleep, paralysis, stunning, and disease. Not subject to critical hits, subdual damage, ability damage, energy drain, or death from massive damage.

Resistance to energy (Su): Fire and heat

Glom

Large Undead
Hit Dice: 4d12 (26 hp)
Initiative: +0
Speed: 20 ft.
AC: 9 (-1 size)
Attacks: 3 claws +1 melee, 2 bites -1 melee; or by melee weapon type +1; or by ranged weapon type +1
Damage: Claw 1d4, bite 1d3, by weapon type
Face/Reach: 5 ft. by 10 ft./5 ft.
Special Attacks: Fear
Special Qualities: Fearless, undead, corpse graft
Saves: Fort +1, Ref +1, Will +4
Abilities: Str 9*, Dex 10, Con —, Int 7, Wis 11, Cha 7
Skills: Intimidate +7, Listen +7, Move Silently +3, Spot +7
Feats: Multiattack
Climate/Terrain: Any land
Challenge Rating: 4
Alignment: Always chaotic evil
Advancement: 5 HD (Large), 6-8 HD (Huge), 9-12 HD (Gargantuan), 13-16 HD (Colossal)

A 'glom (short for conglomerate) is a group of corpses joined together into a horrifying mass and animated by an especially strong manitou. The parts of the component bodies can be seen clearly, although they are merged inseparably into a single abomination. Limbs protrude in all directions, and a variety of heads and faces can be seen all over the mass. Often the various heads giggle or gibber incoherently as the monster moves.

Most manitous are strong enough to animate only a single corpse, creating a Harrowed or walkin' dead. Some manitous, though, have grown strong enough to animate several bodies at once.

The creation of a 'glom requires a very high Fear Level, and vast quantities of corpses; at least two. One corpse, in which the manitou houses its primary essence, must be relatively intact, but the others need not be so tidy. Most 'gloms are formed from considerably more than two corpses, and are commonly found arisen from the piles of dead on battlefields.

Even more terrifying is the 'glom's ability to join other corpses to its seething mass, increasing its power proportionately. Earlier in The War, reports of monsters containing more than 15 bodies were not uncommon.

With the current stalemate in The War and fewer large-scale battles, these abominations are becoming fewer in number. Only in a few recent cases, such as the mass starvation in the City of Lost Angels, have there been circumstances favorable to the formation of this particular monster.

Combat

'Gloms use their limbs and whatever weapons are handy to kill any (usually terrified) person in sight. Whenever possible, 'gloms add corpses to their mass. 'Gloms can wield guns if available. In general, there is no more than one gun per two bodies in the 'glom.

Fear (Ex): Anyone catching sight of a 'glom with six or more component bodies must make a Will saving throw against a DC of 19. As 'gloms increase in mass they become even more frightening as well: add +1 to the save's DC for each component body in the 'glom above two.

Undead (Su): Foci—The head of the first corpse the manitou reanimates. Immune to mind-influencing effects, poison, sleep, paralysis, stunning, and disease. Not subject to critical hits, subdual damage, ability damage, energy drain, or death from massive damage.

Corpse Graft (Su): A 'glom can graft additional recently dead bodies to itself. These corpses must have been dead for longer than 10 minutes. It takes one round for a 'glom to add another corpse to its mass. During that round, the 'glom can do nothing else because grafting requires concentration. For every body in the 'glom above the original two, the mass gains +12 hit points as well as +2 to Str (to a maximum of 23). A 'glom can make one additional attack each round (without penalty) for every two bodies in its mass.

Glom, Colony

Large Undead
Hit Dice: 4d12 (26 hp)
Initiative: +0
Speed: 20 ft.
AC: 9 (-1 size)
Attacks: 3 claws +1 melee, 2 bites -1 melee; or by melee weapon type +1; or by ranged weapon type +1
Damage: Claw 1d4, bite 1d3, by weapon type
Face/Reach: 5 ft. by 10 ft./5 ft.
Special Attacks: Fear
Special Qualities: Fearless, undead, corpse graft
Saves: Fort +1, Ref +1, Will +4
Abilities: Str 11*, Dex 10, Con –, Int 6, Wis 9, Cha 5
Skills: Intimidate +7, Listen +5, Move Silently +2, Spot +6
Feats: Multiattack
Climate/Terrain: Any land
Challenge Rating: 4
Alignment: Always chaotic evil
Advancement: 5 HD (Large), 6-8 HD (Huge), 9-12 HD (Gargantuan), 13-16 HD (Colossal)

A colony 'glom looks much like a regular glom: a mass of bodies (some horribly disfigured) melded together. Arms, legs and other parts protrude from the mass at random. Colony 'gloms share many characteristics with normal 'gloms. They are a mass of corpses joined into a single entity and can add other dead bodies to their mass to grow more powerful. These bodies must have been dead for at least 10 minutes to undergo the grafting process, but 'gloms are patient when it comes to "recruitment."

While regular 'gloms are inhabited by a single, very powerful manitou, colony 'gloms are host to a horde of lesser, but closely allied, manitous—a group sometimes called a "Legion." This allows the colony 'glom to separate into individual zombies and rejoin later into a large mass, or to simply sprout off a walkin' dead scout to enter places the larger abomination can't squeeze into. This dual nature can send the most experienced trackers into fits of apoplexy!

Note that a colony 'glom cannot reproduce itself—a spawned zombie cannot start a new colony unless the original core is completely destroyed. Mercifully for the heroes of the Weird West, the cohesiveness of the manitou Legion usually prevents that from occurring.

Like regular 'gloms, colony 'gloms are usually only found in areas where a large number of fresh corpses are available and the Fear Level is fairly high. A bad train wreck could spawn one if it occurred in an area with a Fear Level 5 or greater.

Fortunately, these monsters are very rare indeed in the Weird West. The conditions necessary for their creation just aren't that common.

Combat

Colony 'gloms employ similar tactics to their more unified cousins, but also take advantage of their unique powers by dividing and combining as it becomes more or less advantageous to do so. 'Gloms can wield guns or other weapons if available.

Fear (Ex): Anyone catching sight of a colony 'glom with six or more component bodies must make a Will saving throw against DC 19. As 'gloms increase in mass they become more frightening as well: add +1 to the DC for each component body in the 'glom above two.

Undead (Su): Foci—Each component body's head. Immune to mind-influencing effects, poison, sleep, paralysis, stunning, and disease. Not subject to critical hits, subdual damage, ability damage, energy drain, or death from massive damage.

Corpse Graft (Su): A 'glom can graft additional recently dead bodies to itself. These corpses must have been dead for longer than 10 minutes. It takes one round for a 'glom to add another corpse to its mass. During that round, the 'glom can do nothing else because grafting requires concentration. For every body in the 'glom above the original two, the mass gains +12 hit points as well as +2 to Str (to a maximum of 23). A 'glom can make one additional attack each round (without penalty) for every two bodies in its mass. Component bodies of a colony 'glom can slough off and function as normal walkin' dead in all respect. However, while the body is detached, the 'glom's Str, hit points and number of attacks are reduced appropriately.

Orphaned Head

Tiny Undead
Hit Dice: 3d12 (19 hp)
Initiative: +0
Speed: 20 ft.
AC: 12 (+2 size)
Attacks: Bite +4 melee
Damage: Bite 1d3+1
Face/Reach: 2 1/2 ft. by 2 1/2 ft./0 ft.
Special Attacks: Improved grab, constrict 1d3+1
Special Qualities: Fearless, undead
Saves: Fort +1, Ref +1, Will +4
Abilities: Str 13, Dex 10, Con –, Int 10, Wis 12, Cha 13
Skills: Climb +6, Hide +8, Intimidate +7, Listen +6, Move Silently +6, Ridicule +6, Spot +6
Feats: Power Attack
Climate/Terrain: Any land
Challenge Rating: 4
Alignment: Always chaotic evil
Advancement: By character class

This monster is a severed head that has the bad manners to still be moving around. Once grafted, the head looks much like any walkin' dead, although its own skin and that of its new body may be mismatched. While an orphaned head can and does graft to a body of the opposite sex, it usually only does so for long enough to gain control of it.

Occasionally, a manitou gets a stubborn streak and refuses to let go of a ruined walkin' dead. As long as the original head remains intact, the spirit continues to keep house in it—even when it's nothing but a severed head. Usually, the noggin was removed by an edged weapon, but a rare few are chewed loose by the head itself.

Manitous can tap a great deal of energy from the Hunting Grounds—more than enough, in fact, to graft a head to another body. All the spirit needs is a corpse, preferably one without a head, but the manitou is more than willing to make exceptions—and headless corpses.

When attached to a body, an orphaned head has a profile identical to that of a regular walkin' dead (see the *Deadlands: The Weird West D20 Rulebook*), but substitute the new head's Int, Wis and Cha. Simultaneously, it also can animate and control any corpse to which it has previously been grafted. If you hadn't guessed, Marshal, these other corpses are now headless, but that doesn't seem to cause them too much difficulty in getting around the Weird West.

Orphaned heads concentrate their efforts on obtaining more corpses to which to graft themselves—thus also increasing the number of headless corpses under their control. A community plagued by an orphaned head usually finds a number of severed heads left over from the abomination's activities. A head that's had a good deal of time to operate can amass a large number of headless "drones" and become a rather formidable opponent for a posse.

Orphaned heads don't have the easiest time of it when it comes to getting around. Most of the time, the head is forced to roll along the ground—a dizzying experience for anything other than the undead. However, this rough and tumble method of travel doesn't cause the head any harm and they can build up a good deal of speed on a downhill slope.

The abominations do have *extraordinarily* long tongues, though—3' long or more! They can use these to open door knobs, drag themselves stealthily along the floor, or even strangle a victim. This tongue is what gives the orphaned head a Dex ability, by the way.

Combat

An orphaned head with no body is in dire straits. It's relatively easy pickings for any cowpoke that happens upon it in the open. Strangulation is the head's best method for obtaining its first body. It creeps up on a sleeping or unconscious victim, strangles them, and then begins the gory process of gnawing through the neck to make room for itself.

Improved grab (Ex): An orphaned head is capable of grabbing up to Medium-Size targets, and may employ this ability to strangle (constrict) victims without a weapon.

Undead (Su): Focus—head. Immune to mind-influencing effects, poison, sleep, paralysis, stunning, and disease. Not subject to critical hits, subdual damage, ability damage, energy drain, or death from massive damage.

Headless Dead

Medium-Size Undead
Hit Dice: 3d12 (19 hp)
Initiative: +0
Speed: 30 ft.
AC: 10
Attacks: 2 claws +2 melee; or by melee weapon type +2; or by ranged weapon type +1
Damage: Claw 1d4+1, by melee weapon type +1, by ranged weapon type
Face/Reach: 5 ft. by 5 ft./5 ft.
Special Attacks: Fear
Special Qualities: Blindsight, fearless, undead
Saves: Fort +1, Ref +1, Will +4
Abilities: Str 12, Dex 11, Con –, Int 10, Wis 13, Cha 11
Skills: Climb +5, Hide +5, Intimidate +6, Move Silently +5, Ride +5, Spot +6, Swim +5
Feats: Blind-Fight
Climate/Terrain: Any land
Challenge Rating: 4
Alignment: Always chaotic evil
Advancement: By character class

Combat

Headless dead carry weapons they've scrounged from their victims or own homes. Firearms are common, but due to the head's lust for more bodies, each one also carries an axe, knife, or other bladed weapon—for reasons that should be obvious.

Fear (Ex): Anyone catching sight of a headless dead must make a Will saving throw against DC 19.

Undead (Su): Focus—the orphaned head. Immune to mind-influencing effects, poison, sleep, paralysis, stunning, and disease. Not subject to critical hits, subdual damage, ability damage, energy drain, or death from massive damage.

Severed Hand

Diminutive Undead
Hit Dice: 1d12 (6 hp)
Initiative: +2 (Dex)
Speed: 35 ft.
AC: 16 (+4 size, +2 Dex)
Attacks: By melee weapon type +6; by ranged weapon type +6
Damage: By melee weapon type +2, by ranged weapon type
Face/Reach: 1 ft. by 1 ft./0 ft.
Special Attacks: Improved grab, constrict 1d3+2
Special Qualities: Regeneration 10, fearless, undead, blindsight
Saves: Fort +0, Ref +2, Will +2
Abilities: Str 14, Dex 14, Con –, Int 11, Wis 11, Cha 10
Skills: Balance +4, Climb +4, Demolitions +4, Hide +12, Jump +4, Move Silently +4 Open Lock +4, Pick Pocket +4, Ridicule +3, Search +4, Sleight of Hand +4, Spot +4, Tumble +4, Use Rope +4
Feats: Dodge
Climate/Terrain: Any land
Challenge Rating: 4
Alignment: Always chaotic evil
Advancement: 2-3 HD (Diminutive)

This abomination comes into existence after a hand has been severed by some means, preferably one that makes it worthwhile for the hand to seek vengeance. The Reckoners then provide it a disgusting life of its own.

The thing skitters along using its fingers and thumbs, and it can sit up on its stump to manipulate other objects. If it can find something to lean against so it can balance the weight, it might even use a pistol. However, if it does use a weapon, it's more likely to try a knife or something else small—and sharp.

The hand always has a specific target, but it doesn't mind harassing and terrorizing anyone that gets in its way. Eventually, though, after making folks fearful for a while, it gets around to the business at hand (so to speak) of getting real revenge on the person it blames for its early separation from its home arm.

The thing is pretty adept at avoiding damage, and it's resistant to a lot of things that might annoy other abominations. This can make a hand a very persistent and extremely irritating opponent.

The hand might have some identifying characteristic, like a ring or tattoo. Identifying it doesn't really do anyone much good but it might make a revenge victim a little more fearful to know exactly what's after him.

Combat

It loves to ridicule and tease its victims before closing in for the kill. It might knock and knock, always stopping to hide before its enemies can locate the sound, or it might slam doors, set trip-wires, shove things off shelves or even find a match and light some dynamite (if it feels like pulling a really explosive prank). As mentioned above, when the severed hand finally decides to strike it has a predilection for edged weapons.

Improved grab (Ex): A severed hand is capable of grabbing up to Medium-Size targets, and may employ this ability to strangle (constrict) victims without a weapon.

Regeneration (Su): Fire or acid deal normal damage to a severed hand.

Undead (Su): Focus—hand. Immune to mind-influencing effects, poison, sleep, paralysis, stunning, and disease. Not subject to critical hits, subdual damage, ability damage, energy drain, or death from massive damage.

Skeleton

Medium-Size Undead
Hit Dice: 3d12 (19 hp)
Initiative: +0
Speed: 30 ft.
AC: 10
Attacks: 2 claws +1 melee, bite -1 melee; or by melee weapon type +1
Damage: Claw 1d4, bite 1d3, by weapon type
Face/Reach: 5 ft. by 5 ft./5 ft.
Special Qualities: Damage reduction 10/All bludgeon, undead, fearless
Saves: Fort +1, Ref +1, Will +2
Abilities: Str 10, Dex 11, Con —, Int 8, Wis 7, Cha 6

Skills: Climb +5, Hide +5, Intimidate +5, Listen +2, Move Silently +5, Spot +3
Feats: Multiattack
Climate/Terrain: Any land
Challenge Rating: 3
Alignment: Always chaotic evil
Advancement: By character class

Skeletons are, well, skeletons. Their eye sockets are unnaturally dark, but beyond that—and the fact that they're walking around—there's little to distinguish them from normal skeletons. Occasionally, they may have tatters of ancient clothing still clinging to their bones.

On very rare occasions, manitous may choose to reanimate bodies so old that nothing remains of them except bones. Evil black magicians also sometimes create these abominations as special servants.

Skeletons are a little less "aware" of their surroundings than other undead. The life has been gone from the bodies for so long, it hinders the animating force to a degree. On the other hand, skeletons are remarkably resistant to modern firearms—bullets pass harmlessly through their framework most of the time.

Combat

Like other reanimated dead, skeletons can with their natural claw and bite attacks, but prefer to use melee weapons whenever possible. For some reason, skeletons don't use firearms.

Undead (Su) Focus—head. Immune to mind-influencing effects, poison, sleep, paralysis, stunning, and disease. Not subject to critical hits, subdual damage, ability damage, energy drain, or death from massive damage.

Undead Animals

Variable Size Undead
Hit Dice: As original animal
Initiative: As original animal (+ modified Dex)
Speed: As original animal
AC: As original animal (+ modified Dex)
Attacks: As original animal, plus bite (if animal does not possess this attack)
Damage: As original animal, bite 1d3 (+ modified Str; if animal does not possess this attack)
Face/Reach: As original animal
Special Attacks: As original animal
Special Qualities: As original animal, plus fearless, undead
Saves: As original animal (+/- modified Abilities)
Abilities: Str +2, Dex +1, Con –, Int -2*, Wis -1*, Cha -3* (*May not be reduced below 1.)
Skills: As original animal
Feats: As original animal
Climate/Terrain: As original animal
Challenge Rating: As original animal plus 1
Alignment: Always chaotic evil
Advancement: As original animal

Undead animals look like dead critters that don't have the good sense to lay down. They display characteristic signs of death and decay.

As undead go, reanimated animals are fairly rare in the Weird West. On the surface, this may seem odd, but bringing unlife to a dead body represents something of an investment on the part of a manitou and there are several reasons why an animal corpse just isn't the best choice.

First, there are plenty of human bodies just waiting to rent out some space. With the War Between the States still grinding on, there's seldom a shortage of prime walkin' dead candidates. Why settle for a poodle—granted, a creepy, decomposing poodle, but a poodle nonetheless—when you can get a perfectly good dead man?

Second, the main reason manitous inhabit walkin' dead in the first place is to increase fear in the populace. An undead mountain lion is frightening for certain, but not *that* much more frightening than a live one. A visit from a dear relative who lacks the common decency to stay in their grave is another matter altogether.

Finally, human zombies are able to perform a wide variety of tasks. An undead wolf might be unsettling, but you really don't need any special protection from it. A doorknob is pretty much proof against it.

Sure, a simple walkin' dead isn't the same kind of commitment that a Harrowed represents; a manitou's immortality isn't at risk with a regular zombie. But when all's said and done, it's really just not worth a manitou's time to reanimate an animal.

But...

Okay, now that we've gone to all the trouble to tell you why animal zombies *don't* happen that often, we do have to grudgingly admit there are times when they *do*. In these instances, the corpse is almost never spontaneously animated; nearly always an outside influence does so.

What kind of twisted creature brings good old Spot back from the pet cemetery to hound his beloved master? Some abominations may reanimate animal corpse, particularly ones closely associated with the wilderness or nature. Occasionally a human cultist may do so as well, just to unnerve an interloper. This sort of tactic is perfect for Appalachian witches (see page 115).

Increase or reduce the animal's abilities by the amounts shown above. The critter's abilities cannot drop below 1, regardless of any modifications made for being undead.

Certain abilities the animal had in life, like poison, are lost, but others, like burrowing or swimming, aren't. Marshal, it's pretty much your call.

Combat

As per animal type.

Undead (Su): Focus—head. Immune to mind-influencing effects, poison, sleep, paralysis, stunning, and disease. Not subject to critical hits, subdual damage, ability damage, energy drain, or death from massive damage.

More Weird Western Weirdness!

Look for other exciting **Deadlands** products in your local game store, or online at WWW.PEGINC.COM. There are over 50 sourcebooks, adventures, and Dime Novels already written for the original Deadlands, and we're adding conversion rules for D20 players every week!

You'll also find a passel of miniatures, the official Deadlands soundtrack, fiction, and more! So make that Search roll, amigo, and join us out here in the Deadlands. We'll be waitin' for you.

Weird War Mayhem!

If you like Deadlands and the D20 system, check out our newest game of historical horror, Weird Wars!

The first book, *Blood on the Rhine,* introduces the Western Front of "Weird War Two." Inside are military character classes, the weapons of the war, vehicles and how to use them, and even a full-length adventure, the *Dogs of War.*

Future books cover the air war and the other theatres, including Africa, the Pacific, and the Russian Front!

WWW.PEGINC.COM